C000005834

MARRED: KYLE AND VIOLET

CLIFFSIDE BAY SERIES, BOOK 4

TESS THOMPSON

4kids5cats
EDITIONS

All rights reserved.

This work is licensed under a Creative Commons Attribution–Noncommercial–No Derivative Works 3.0 Unported License.

Attribution — You must attribute the work in the manner specified by the author or licensor (but not in any way that suggests that they endorse you or your use of the work).

Noncommercial — You may not use this work for commercial purposes.

No Derivative Works — You may not alter, transform, or build upon this work.

This is a work of fiction. Names, characters, places, brands, media, and incidents are either the product of the author's imagination or are used fictitiously. Any resemblance to similarly named places or to persons living or deceased is unintentional.

For Violet Estrin.
Best friend, second mother to my children,
and future roommate in the old lady home.
I hope they have wine.

CHAPTER ONE

Kyle

KYLE HICKS HADN'T had an episode for two years. Until now. He stood under the shower with the water as hot as he could stand it and scoured his body with a rough kitchen sponge. Steam as thick as morning fog obscured his vision. His skin stung. He would not stop. Not until the stench was gone.

The child outside of the food bank with the ravenous eyes. That's what did it. The memories like a riptide snatched him from the present and swallowed him whole. Sucked him into the vortex of memory. He couldn't fight them off. They just kept coming.

Pig. Pig stinks.

The taunts and jeers of his childhood rose around him, ghost-like in the steam.

Please, just leave me alone.

Recollections of fists and steel-toed boots blotted out the past twelve years with an invading darkness like black ink spilled on his expensive stationary. The memories devoured his accomplishments. They crushed his friendships. The stunning properties he'd created tumbled under their weight.

1

He crossed over to that other time when he was a scrawny, hungry, shell of a boy. The bullying and poverty and shame. The stench of it all.

The children called him *Pig*.

The telephone rang from the other room. A lifeline to the present.

I am Kyle Hicks. I helped build this resort. I'm a partial owner. I am no longer afraid. No one can hurt me.

He tore out of the bathroom with only a towel wrapped around his waist. Steam followed him as he stumbled to the phone. "This is Kyle Hicks." His voice was normal. *I am the boss.*

"Yes, sir, Mr. Hicks. This is Robert from the front desk. There's a lady in the lobby asking for you."

"Does this lady have a name?"

"No, sir. I mean, yes, I'm sure she does, but she wouldn't give it to me. She has a baby with her. She says it's your baby."

"*My* baby?"

"That's what she said."

"I'm sorry? Could you repeat that one more time?"

"Yes, sir. She said you're the father of the baby. She wants you to come downstairs, so she can give it to you."

"I'll be right there."

"Please hurry, sir. She's creating quite a scene."

"The woman?"

"No, the baby."

He knew what this was—one of the Dogs playing a trick on him. Of his four best friends, which of them would do this? Probably Lance. He had a wicked sense of humor and had recently been chiding him for his lack of support regarding Zane and Honor's adoption of a six-year-old orphan named Jubie. This was the type of joke Lance would find hilarious. A joke wrapped up in a morality lesson.

He would have his revenge. This was *not* funny. They should know better than to mess with him in front of the staff. But still, he had to give it to them. This was good. They knew he was not a family man. If they knew why, they would have more sympathy. But he would never tell his secrets. Not even to the Dogs.

He went to the window, breathing deeply, purging the darkness. The child outside of the food bank had looked like him. That's all this was. It had been years since he'd had an episode. He examined his arms. They were pink but not bleeding. He was fine.

His reflection in the window stared back at him. His muscular frame, expensive haircut, and capped teeth told the story of the new Kyle. When he dressed it would be in the finest clothes money could buy.

Outside the windows, rain fell in dogged stripes. This October was particularly dreary, even in quaint Cliffside Bay. That's right. He lived here. The Dogs were his family. He had everything. Wealth, cars, land. Most of all, friends. The Dogs had his back. He didn't have to be afraid ever again.

Minutes later, he exited the elevator into the lobby. The sound of a screaming infant reverberated against the marble floors and cathedral ceiling. Even the crystal chandelier seemed to shake. Kyle looked in the direction of the racket. A young woman with a stroller stood by the glass windows. He quickened his pace. His staff shot him worried glances as he passed by the desk. Several patrons wrinkled their foreheads in irritation, clearly annoyed their peaceful afternoons sipping cucumber water had been interrupted by reality.

The Dogs had gone to a lot of trouble. How had they convinced a woman and a baby to go along with the act? This was the work of Zane and Lance. Jackson and Brody were too mature to think of something like this. Plus, as the town doctor, Jackson had sick people to care for. Brody was currently halfway through the football season. The highest paid quarterback in the AFL did not have time for pranks.

Having arrived at the source of the racket, he peered into the stroller. He took inventory: pink blanket, and a baby no bigger than the span of his two hands. A girl baby, probably a week or two old. He vaguely recalled holding his baby sister when she first arrived. This baby clenched her fists and kicked at her blanket, her complexion a disconcerting shade of purple. Perhaps she was hungry? Or needed a diaper change? He had no idea. Kyle knew nothing of babies.

He did, however, know about angry females, and this was one of them, albeit a tiny one. He looked away from the baby to study her companion. Dingy blond hair in need of washing hung in her eyes. Her right tennis shoe had a hole near the big toe area, and her leggings were thin from wear. She smelled of grease and the inside of city bus. Who was she? No one he knew. He never forgot a face or a name. Real Estate development was about people. The secret to people was to be generally interested in them. He could tell you a person's life story after one afternoon of golf.

"May I help you?" he asked.

"You can say that again." She glared at him with hostility mixed with triumph. Her features were flat and her complexion gray, like a rock honed by years of rushing water. She reached into the stroller and picked up the baby, who immediately stopped the terrible howling. Why hadn't she done this earlier? This was a mystery he couldn't explore now because the woman's next words eviscerated all coherent thought. "This is Mollie Blue Hicks. Your baby. I have the paperwork to prove it."

The gazes of every person in the lobby bored a hole into the back of his head. "Perhaps we could talk in the office?"

"Whatever." She thrust the baby toward him. "Take her."

He couldn't think of what else to do but accept the parcel. Kyle Hicks took Mollie Blue into his arms, cradling her close to his chest, then indicated for the sullen young woman to follow him with a nod toward the office. The manager was out this afternoon, so it would be free.

Zane and Lance were going to pay for this.

He shut the door of the office with his foot. Still holding the surprisingly warm baby in his arms, he asked the woman if she'd like to sit.

She plopped into a chair and rolled her eyes like she was disgusted by his suggestion that she sit.

"Good joke. How did the Dogs convince you to go along with it?" Man, this girl could act. Contempt practically dripped from her.

"Who are the Dogs?" she asked.

"My best friends. Apparently, they think they're comedians."

"I'll cut to the chase. My name's Paulina Shore. Do you remember Katy Theisen? You had a one-night stand with her about nine months ago."

Any moisture in his mouth evaporated. "Sure, yeah. I mean, of course I remember her." Katy Theisen was a bartender in the town up north where he had spent several months working on a shopping mall deal. *About nine months ago.*

"Katy was my best friend. She died last week from complications of childbirth." For the first time, Pauline's expression wavered from livid to that of extreme sadness. Her body seemed to sag under the weight of grief as she sank into the armchair.

"Died? From childbirth?" Kyle perched on the edge of his desk. Mollie Blue shuddered.

"Yep. That's what happens when you're poor."

"In America?" He knew poverty. It ran through his veins, like the blood of his family, unseen but there, waiting to remind him of the past he'd escaped from. Generations of poverty was his family legacy. Still, no one he knew had ever died from having a baby.

"Impoverished women are more likely to die in childbirth. It's on the rise in rural areas. Look it up. I did when Katy died."

He gazed at the baby in his arms. She'd fallen asleep. *She's sweet when she's not howling.* "I'm sorry to hear about Katy, but this isn't my baby."

"Katy wasn't the type to sleep around. She knew Mollie was yours. Broken condom, dude." She reached into the stroller and pulled out an envelope. "It's all in here. The DNA test proves it."

"But how?" How would she have had his DNA?

Pauline answered his silent question with a roll of her eyes. "Think about it. Stained sheets."

"Don't you need permission for that kind of thing?" he asked.

"Not when they sell DNA tests at Walmart."

"Jesus, they do?"

"A guy like you should probably buy them in bulk," she said. "Or maybe double up on condoms."

The broken condom. He was always careful. Condoms were his friend. Until, like the night with Katy, one of the damn things broke. *Water.* He needed a glass of water.

A DNA test was undeniable.

This was his baby. His daughter.

He put Mollie back into the stroller. His arms felt light without her.

Paulina crossed her arms over her chest. "Don't you dare judge Katy. You're the one who couldn't keep it in your pants."

He flinched. "I wasn't. I'm just in shock here. You could give me a chance to catch up."

"Sorry."

"What happened—I mean during the birth?"

"An infection they should've caught." Paulina's voice wavered again. "Look, it's obvious you're rich, so there's no reason you can't take care of your kid unless you're a jerk. If that's the case, then I suggest we put her into the system, so a nice couple can have her." She scowled and blew her dirty bangs out of her eyes. "But I know Katy, and she would've preferred you take her. There's nothing like flesh and blood."

He laced his hands together behind his back. Sweat rolled down his spinal column. What was he supposed to do with a daughter? He could barely take care of himself. Should he give her up? Let someone else raise her? Surely anyone in the world would be better than him. He wasn't father material. All anyone had to do was look at his past to see that truth.

He sucked in a deep breath. The air thinned like he'd reached a mountain peak. He tugged at the collar of his shirt, breathing hard.

An image of his mother pierced his consciousness. Skinny with those dull eyes, she stood by the front door with the tattered blue suitcase in her hand. *I'm leaving. You look after your brother and sister.*

His heart pounded harder. He staggered over to the desk and perched on the edge. The room tilted. Black dots danced before his eyes. His recently scrubbed skin burned. *I can't do it. Not this. Anything but this.*

The day his mother left roared to life and played out in front of him.

Where are you going? Are you coming back?

He ran after her. The trailer door slammed behind him. Rain dumped from a stormy Oregon sky. *Wait. Don't go. Please, Mama.* She pulled the hood of her faded raincoat over her head. A man stood waiting by the car. He grabbed her suitcase and tossed it into the back seat. Kyle slipped in the mud and fell. By the time he rose to his feet, they were gone, tire tracks on the muddy driveway their only legacy.

Now, he rubbed his eyes and looked over at Paulina. "I have money, but nothing else to offer her." *I'm a single, selfish womanizer with secret panic attacks.*

"That's better than most."

Was it? Money would hire staff to help raise her. Yet, a daughter needed an emotionally healthy father, one who knew how to give and receive love. Not him. Anyone but him.

"I'm sorry about Katy. Truly. She was a sweet girl."

"She was." Paulina picked at the skin around a fingernail. Her nails were short—not trimmed neatly with clippers, but ragged and uneven, like those of a nail biter.

"Does Katy have any family?" he asked.

"No one. And I can't keep her if that's what you want to know."

He didn't say anything. No one would expect her to. She was young and probably broke. A baby was the last thing she needed, especially one that wasn't hers.

"It hurts too much to look at her," she said as if he'd asked a follow up question.

"Why?"

"Katy was my best friend. I thought this baby would ruin her life. I had no idea how right I was. I'll just leave it at that."

I can't be like my mother. I must to do the right thing. This is my child.

Kyle crossed back to the stroller and stared down at the sleeping infant. She was so small and helpless. He was her only family. It had to be him. He picked her up and cradled her close, catching a whiff of her head. "Her head smells good."

"Yeah."

With the baby in his arms, he went around the desk to sit in the chair before his legs collapsed under him.

"I know Katy wasn't the type to go home with some loser she met at the bar," he said.

"But she did."

"I was having a rough night. She took pity on me." He stroked the peach fuzz on Mollie's head. Should she be wearing a hat? He touched the tips of her ears. They were cold. Should they be?

"That sounds like her."

"It wasn't my finest hour," he said.

Paulina stood. "I'd love to stay for a gabfest, but I've got to go. There's some formula and a few diapers in the stroller. You'll need more. Get ready for some sticker shock." This last part was muttered under her breath.

"I don't know anything about how to take care of a baby."

"There's this thing called the internet," she said.

Mollie squirmed in his arms and opened her eyes and looked directly into his. A strange feeling spread through his stomach, like warm soup sliding down the back of his throat and into his stomach on a cold day. He gritted his teeth, almost willing himself to remain distant. Mollie was having none of that. She pursed her mouth and blew a bubble before closing her eyes again.

At the door, Paulina turned back to him. "Good luck."

"Wait, before you leave. Why didn't she have an abortion?"

Paulina shrugged. "She wasn't the type—not a brain in her head when it came to that stuff. She thought it was meant to be—that God wanted her to have this baby. I guess she was wrong."

"One more thing." He reached into his pants pocket and pulled out several hundred dollars from a money clip. "Take this."

Her eyebrows lifted. She stared at him like a feral animal, evaluating whether he wanted something in exchange.

"Please, take it," he said. "Diapers and formula and everything probably set you back."

"It did." She took the money from the desk. "Katy said you were a good guy. Sad but nice. You'll do fine with Mollie." With that, Paulina disappeared.

* * *

Dazed, Kyle pushed the stroller out of the elevator and into the hallway, then used his keycard to enter the penthouse suite. Mollie woke with a whimper that within seconds turned into a howl. Hunger perhaps? Or a wet diaper? He recalled these ailments from movies. There might be a bottle of formula somewhere in the contraption, which now that he took a closer look, seemed like it had been rescued from the town dump. A stroller shouldn't have rusted parts. He didn't know much, but that seemed obvious.

What was the plan? Should he call one of his staff to come up and help him? Surely one of them would know what to do to make the baby stop crying. But no, he had to do this himself. If he let one of the staff see him this out of control, they'd lose all respect for him. He'd have to reason through this without help. The most important thing was to stop this poor mite from hurting herself with all this shrieking and flailing of limbs. He rolled the stroller inside and closed the door.

Seriously, how can something this little make such a commotion?

He lifted the squirming, screaming baby into his arms. She arched her back and kicked her arms and legs with surprising ferocity. The blanket fell to the floor. She wore an outfit that looked like a t-shirt with buttons. What was that heinous scent? The offensive odor came from the red-faced Mollie's bottom. He almost gagged.

No question. First things first. He would change her diaper. Sure, no problem. He bought and developed real estate up and down the state of California. He could surely change one diaper.

He held her at arm's length and made a shushing sound. She howled even louder. Great, he'd made her angrier. He carried her over to the sofa. Should he place her on there or would she fall off? What, with all the kicking and fussing, she might launch herself onto the floor.

The rug was safer. When he had her settled there, he sprinted back to the stroller. A bag hung from the back. He hadn't noticed that until now. *A diaper bag? Has to be.* He unzipped it and found diapers and, hallelujah, a full bottle of what must be formula. There was also a box of cleaning wipes. No doubt these were for wiping the offensive bottom. Sweating, he brought all three items back to the baby.

You can do this. The little bug can't sit around in a dirty diaper.

His hands shook as he unbuttoned the romper. *Romper?* Where had that word come from? He had no idea what a romper was, let alone if this was one. Whatever it was called, the outfit was cute, with little ducks scattered across the soft material. Mollie's legs parted like they were attached to springs. Three snaps were in the center of the crotch area. *Crotch area?* Was that what it was called when referring to a baby? That didn't seem right, especially for a baby girl. *Never mind that. I must focus on the task.*

He tugged at the snaps. Voilà. They loosened with no problem. This was genius, now that he looked at it more carefully. One could change the diaper without taking the entire outfit…or romper…off the baby. He lifted it up and over the diaper, despite her flaying limbs, then gasped. There was a horrific stump where her belly button should be. Pink and painful looking and covered with dried blood, it stared up at him like the head of a snake. "Does it hurt Mollie Blue?"

She kicked her legs in response.

He'd take that as a no.

Next, he lifted the sticky flaps that held the diaper on the baby. The smell was bad. He held his breath as he lifted her legs to slide the diaper from her puckered bottom. That's when he saw it. A gooey substance the color of burned butternut squash soup stuck to every crevice of the little one's private area.

The wipes? Surely this is what they were for. They'd better be superpowered if he was going to coax the goo from this bottom. *Breathe through my mouth.* He went in, holding her legs in one hand and swiping with the other. This was totally fine. He could do this.

A few swipes later, she looked clean. Should he use one more to make sure? Yes, he would. He'd heard of diaper rash. Given that goo, it would make sense that a rash could develop if not cleaned properly.

He reached behind him for another wipe. When he returned, a yellow puddle had stained the brand-new rug of his brand-new penthouse suite. He cursed under his breath and reached frantically for another diaper. His hands shook so badly and were so slick with sweat that it took several attempts to open the stupid plastic potential rug-saver. By the time he'd accomplished that task, Mollie was done urinating all over his rug. For heaven's sake, what now?

But wait? What was this? Silence. She'd stopped howling. It must feel better to have the disgusting diaper away from her skin. And, taking a leak when one really had to go was always a happy relief.

He lifted her from the soaked area of the carpet to a fresh spot. This time he put the unfolded diaper under her bottom before he wiped her. "I'm a quick learner. Always put a diaper under you before turning away. And you're much more pleasant when you're not screaming."

How many of these wipes would a parent use in one day? He'd already used a dozen. Sticker shock indeed.

Assured he had her nice and clean now, he fastened the diaper. Was that right? It looked a little crooked. One side had more of a gap—from which nasty fluids could leak. He repositioned the diaper and fastened it tighter and straighter. *That should do it.*

She whimpered. Was she cold? Maybe she needed a romper with legs. Was there such a thing? Never mind, he would feed her the bottle first. Then, he would call for backup.

He grabbed the bottle and settled with her on the couch. The moment he placed the bottle in her mouth, Mollie sucked with ravenous intent. Was there anything in her face that looked like him? She was a particularly pretty baby with dimples on either side of her mouth and ears close to her head. Not his ears, thankfully. He'd had ears that stuck out when he was a kid. Finally, around fifteen, his ugly mug grew into them.

Katy Theisen. He knew at the time it was wrong to sleep with her. She was an innocent, sweet and guileless. No match for his wicked charm. He knew it then and he knew it now. Like the broken condom, she was out of his normal mode of operation. His women, and yes, there were a lot of them, were female versions of himself. Sex was a game of fun. Physical connection only. No emotional intimacy allowed behind closed doors or anywhere else. Occasionally he made a mistake and misread a woman's capacity for casual sex. Those were the times he got himself into trouble.

But that wasn't the situation with Katy. It was the damn anniversary of the car accident that had made him vulnerable.

The day came around once a year, like a dark holiday. He anticipated the date for weeks beforehand, dreading his inevitable collapse into despair. Over thirteen years had passed since that day, but the memories were as easily refreshed as a drink in Zane's bar. That night, nine months ago, they'd been brisk and relentless. To escape them, he'd taken a long run. Not even exercise or loud country music through his headphones could chase them from his mind. After his run, instead of collapsing into bed like he usually did after a day of work and punishing exercise, he got into the shower and scrubbed his skin raw. No relief. Without a plan other than to find a numbing mechanism, he wandered out of the hotel and into a little rundown, depressing bar that matched his mood and his memories.

Katy had been behind the bar. He hadn't noticed her, too troubled to engage in his usual flirtatious antics with any attractive woman within the vicinity. She'd poured him a tumbler of the best scotch she had. After a few drinks, she'd started asking him questions. What was he doing in town? Why was he out alone? He'd started answering. Somehow, he couldn't say precisely how, Katy had gotten him to talk about his sister. With lovely blue eyes and a sympathetic mouth and a way of cocking her head to the side when she listened, she dragged the past out of him like a magician pulled a never-ending scarf from his sleeve. Each time she tugged, a new aspect of the story slipped out of him.

He'd told her the whole sordid tale. That had surprised him most of all. Not even the Dogs knew the story of the one event that molded every single aspect of his adult personality. No one in his current life even knew he had siblings.

No one knew the story of *Pig and the Miller Brothers* either. He'd never shared it with another human being after he drove away from the little Oregon town where it had all unfolded. Until Katy. He cringed now, remembering how he'd cried. Too many drinks and a sympathetic woman had unhinged him. *And guilt. Don't forget guilt.*

Katy had reminded him of Sheri from back home. Sheri Swanson with her kind heart and beautiful face. *Gone too soon.* That had been the title of the newspaper article when she'd died at fifteen. If he'd written the article he would have described her kindness, her utter intolerance to cruelty of any kind. Even to Pig. She'd been the only one who had been kind to him. Everyone hated Pig. They tortured him and taunted him. Not Sheri.

Katy didn't know *that* Kyle. She had seen him as he was now—

muscular, charming, rich. She'd seen him around town, she'd said. *There's something about a man in a suit.*

They'd had sex. No doubt about that. Even as drunk as he'd been, he remembered her little apartment and the water stain on the ceiling above her bed. She'd told him this wasn't the type of thing she did—bringing home a man she didn't know. He would have liked to have said the same, but he didn't lie to women. Yes, he slept with a lot of them, but he never lied, and he never promised anything he couldn't deliver.

The sex had been sweet. Shy and inexperienced, she'd evoked a strangely protective feeling in him. When he realized the condom had broken, he'd hoped like hell she was on the pill. She fell asleep afterward, curled up like a child. He'd slipped out, hungover and ashamed. He'd taken advantage of a nice girl who was way too young for him and way too accommodating.

What the hell was he going to do now? He needed one of the women in his circle to come over and help him figure out what to do. Three of the Dogs were in steady relationships with women. His first thought was Brody's wife, Kara. She was a nurse. No question she'd know what to do with a baby. That said, he wasn't sure how he felt about sharing all this with her just yet. He didn't know her well and she would probably be horrified that he had a baby from a one-night stand. It couldn't be Maggie, Jackson's wife, even though she was more compassionate than anyone in the world. She was on her way home from the city after an interview on a local television station. That left Zane's fiancée, Honor. She was clearly the best choice. He needed someone who could help him sort out what to do and no one could figure a way out of a pickle better than Honor. Plus, she wouldn't judge him. Or would she? It didn't matter, really, because eventually he was going to have to tell everyone that instant fatherhood had been thrust upon him.

How did one use the phone while feeding a baby? He was stuck on the couch with baby pee soaking deeper into the carpet. There was nothing to do but let her finish and then he'd call

Honor. No, first he'd call someone to clean up the pee and get rid of that heinous smelling diaper.

When Mollie Blue was done, she stared up at him with glazed blue eyes. Was he supposed to burp her? How was that done exactly? He'd seen women do it before. He lifted the baby up to his shoulder and patted her back. Not long after the fourth tap, a large burp erupted from her tiny body. Afterward, she snuggled into his shoulder and stopped squirming. She'd fallen asleep. Thank the good lord. He breathed in the scent of her head and closed his eyes. He'd never smelled anything better in his entire life.

Smells. The bane of his existence.

Pig. The taunts of his childhood echoed through his mind.

Take care of Mollie. Don't think of the past. Not now.

He gingerly positioned her back in the stroller, figuring that was the closest thing he had to a crib. His hands shook when he punched in Honor's number. She answered on the second ring. "Hey dummy. What's up?"

"I have a little situation."

"What you'd do, get someone pregnant?"

His mouth dropped open.

"Kyle? Are you there?"

"Yes. I'm here. I need you to come over to the resort. I'm staying in the penthouse this week." He cleared his throat. "It's urgent."

"Are you all right?"

"I'll explain when you get here."

"I'm at Brody's finishing up some work, but I can be there in ten minutes." Honor was Brody's manager and often worked from the office at his home. Brody was away in San Francisco for the football season and only came home occasionally.

After they hung up, he moved over to the bank of windows that looked out to the small town of Cliffside Bay. By design, the top floor of his resort looked out to the ocean. Today it reflected the ash-colored sky. Fall had come suddenly at the end of September. Now, just days into October, shades of gray replaced nuanced hues of blue. The landscape here reminded him of an independent woman. An expensive view was of no consequence to her. She approached and retreated as she wished, regardless of where you ranked in the human order of things. Rich or poor, young or old— no title or status were of any use to her. If she wanted to hide beneath a sheath of fog, she would. If she wanted to drown you in the powerful forces of her riptides, there was nothing to be done but succumb.

The main street of town was quiet today. Tourist season ended after Labor Day, leaving the sleepy town to doze. His new resort had opened several weeks ago. So far, the weekends were full, but during the week most rooms remained vacant. He wasn't worried. The winter would be sluggish, but by spring every room would be booked. For the first time in the history of Cliffside Bay, there would be a place for tourists to stay. Someday he would build a house on the piece of property outside of town that he shared with Jackson. For now, he'd been content to make hotels or his friends' homes his home. No need to commit to one place given his travel schedule. Up until now, that is. A baby changed everything.

What was he supposed to do with Mollie? He had multiple projects going, including a new shopping mall in a suburb up north. His calendar was packed with travel and meetings. A baby. He wasn't a family guy. Nothing about him, neither his past nor his present, would give him a chance in hell of being a good father.

A knock on the door startled him. It was one of the house-keepers to clean the soiled rug. After he pointed it out, she dropped to the floor with a spray and a rag without comment. The staff knew better than to ask what in the name of God a baby was doing in his room. The boss was the boss.

No sooner had the maid left than Honor arrived. He put his finger to his lips before he allowed her inside the room. "I have a little situation."

"So you said. What's up?"

He gestured toward the stroller. "This."

Her eyes widened as she covered her mouth with her hands. "What the what?" she asked through her fingers.

As quickly as he could, he told her of Mollie's arrival. Then, he handed her the DNA test and the birth certificate. "So, there's no question she's mine."

"Holy crap, this *is* a situation. A major situation."

"I don't know what to do."

She placed her hands together under her chin. "Tell me what you've done so far."

"I changed her diaper and fed her. By the way, no one should have to see what I just saw. She sucked down the only bottle of formula and I don't know what to feed her if she wakes up."

"Formula. You have to get more formula."

"Okay. Where does one get that?"

"The store will have it. It comes in a powder. You just mix it up with water."

"How do you know that?"

"Everyone knows that."

"I most definitely do not know that," he said.

"It's fine. That's not the problem here."

"No kidding."

"How did this happen?" she asked.

"The condom broke."

"Oh, Kyle. This is bad. Very bad."

"I know." He covered his face with his hands and sank onto the couch. "Jesus, what am I going to do?"

Honor sat across from him on the coffee table and placed her hands in the long strands of her blond hair. He'd never known what the term intelligent eyes had meant until he met Honor. "We need a plan."

"Yes, a plan. A plan's always good," he said.

"First things first. We'll send one of your staff out for supplies to get us through the next few days, but bottom line—you have to hire a nanny."

"A nanny. Right. And where do we find one of those?" Not the same place as the formula. He knew that much.

"We'll ask Nora to help us."

"Great idea," he said. Nora ran a small placement agency out of her home. She had the resumes of most residents of Cliffside Bay in her database. In fact, she'd helped his manager staff the entire resort. "Yes, Nora will know someone."

"Until then, we need to get Violet over here," Honor said.

"Violet Ellis?" His mouth twisted like it did when he bit into a grapefruit. "I hate that woman."

"I know. However, you're going to have to put that aside for now. She's the only one who knows how to take care of a baby."

Violet Ellis was his arch enemy. With her chocolate brown eyes and silky caramel skin and her rock-hard yoga body, she looked like an angel. However, she worked like the devil to make his life miserable, including picketing the building of this very resort during its construction. He hated to admit it, but Honor was right. Violet would know how to take care of a baby because she was a single mother to three-year-old Dakota.

"She's not going to help me. Violet despises me." Just saying her name made him want to spit.

"She won't be able to say no to a baby." Honor moved to the stroller and peered down at Mollie. "What a doll." The tremor in Honor's voice betrayed her. A full hysterectomy at eighteen meant she would never have a baby of her own. Although she and Zane had adopted six-year-old Jubie, he suspected she wanted a baby of her own. Shame and self-hatred coursed through him. Why should he get a baby when poor Honor and Zane pined for one? *I suck. Pig.*

"I know what you're thinking," Honor said, looking over at him. "Don't feel bad. I've accepted that I can't have one of my own. We'll figure out a way to have a baby. You don't have to apologize for having one."

"But I don't deserve her and we both know I'm not qualified to take care of her."

"Do you want to put her up for adoption?"

A tunnel of blackness blighted his vision. Images floated through the tunnel of his own lonely childhood. His father passed out on the couch with his arm slung over his eyes. The red dress his mother wore the day she left them. His sister's mangled body on the highway. "I can't. I won't. I'm keeping her. When I look at her I get this feeling in my stomach."

"It feels like nothing you've ever felt before, right?" Honor asked.

"Something warm and soothing but that stings at the same time."

"That's parental love. I felt it with Jubie right away, even though she was six when she came to us. Once you feel that, it's all over."

"I had such a bad childhood." He paused, swallowing the tremor that had crept into his voice. "What if I can't do this?"

"You can do it," Honor said. "It'll be the hardest and easiest thing you've ever done. Trust me."

He sighed, resigned to his fate. Violet Ellis would have to come to his temporary home and help him with his very permanent daughter. "Call Violet."

"I'll call Violet."

"Just until Nora can find someone else," he said.

"It's good timing, actually. Violet's parents are coming back from South America and want their house back. She doesn't have a new place, so she'd planned to stay with Kara and Brody. She could stay here with you instead."

"Why can't she stay with her parents until she finds a house?"

"Her dad didn't know she and Dakota were living there. Apparently, he doesn't approve of her having a baby out of wedlock."

"Does he think it's 1952?"

"I guess so." She dismissed the topic with a jerk of her hand. "Anyway, she'll have to bring Dakota with her."

"That's fine."

"I'll make the call."

CHAPTER TWO

VIOLET

VOILET ELLIS'S BLOUSE stuck to her hot, damp skin. She couldn't find her car keys. Her son's church preschool closed in exactly four minutes. The teachers chastised parents if they were even thirty seconds late. For Christians, they were not especially forgiving of human failures. Last time she was late, the elderly Mrs. Knight had shaken her knobby finger right in Violet's face and given a terse lecture about teaching children responsibility through one's own example.

She never used to be late for anything. Her life used to be in perfect order: five minutes early to appointments, bills paid on time, house neat and orderly, clothes folded into perfect squares. She was a yoga teacher, for heaven's sake. Sweating on a cool autumn day while madly searching for lost keys did not suit her. But the past few months of failure and humiliation had ripped through the fabric of her very existence. Her calm demeanor had eroded into a hot mess.

She yanked open drawers. This was an exercise in futility if there ever was one. The keys couldn't have magically jumped into one of them. Even in her current state of dishevelment, she wouldn't put keys into a drawer in which they didn't belong. Then, where were they? She dumped the contents of her purse onto the counter. A pack of gum, hairbrush, cell phone, wallet, hair tie, and lipstick tumbled onto the bare counter. Nothing unusual, other than the fact her keys were not in there.

Fighting tears of frustration, she circled the kitchen. A shiny object glistened on the windowsill by the breakfast nook. The keys. How in the name of God had they gotten there? There were no pets to blame and Dakota had been at preschool all morning. She grabbed the keys and ran out the door. Exactly two minutes to get down the hill and to the church by five o'clock. It was a physical impossibility.

Violet's hands dampened the steering wheel as she turned out of her parents' driveway and onto the narrow road that headed down the hill. A drop of sweat dribbled between her breasts. She hated this quality about herself—this apologetic and nervous attitude when confronted with authority figures. Who cared if cranky Mrs. Knight was annoyed at her? Violet certainly did enough volunteer work for the preschool and the church to be given a late pass occasionally.

This character flaw explained every single bad decision she'd ever made. When given a choice, she always succumbed to authority. Her father's hypercritical parenting had made her desperate to please. Not that it mattered. Whatever she did wasn't good enough for him.

The parking lot of the church was empty. Fantastic, that meant she was the only late parent. How were the other mothers so perfect?

A drizzle dampened her overheated face as she sprinted into the building. Mrs. Knight and Dakota sat outside the classroom on the *naughty bench*. The children were sent there to think about how to make *better choices*. Violet thought that was such a stupid expression. *Choices*. They were preschoolers, not taxpaying adults.

"Hi, Mama." Dakota grinned and scooted from the bench to run toward her. "I'm in trouble because you're late."

"I'm sorry, Mrs. Knight. I couldn't find my keys," Violet said.

Dakota wrapped his arms around her legs and looked up at her.

"Wasn't that the excuse last week?" Mrs. Knight folded her arms over her abundant chest and pinched her eyelids into narrow slits. *Shame. Well played, Mrs. Knight.* She would not cry in front of this mean woman. No one could be expected to remain strong under the disappointing gaze of Mrs. Knight, but that didn't mean she couldn't fake it until she got out to the car.

"I'm sorry," Violet said again. "Between closing my shop and moving, I've been scattered."

"Miss Ellis, life will always present challenges. The important thing is to rise to said challenges."

"Yes, I know. I'm trying." Violet inwardly cringed at the conciliatory tone of her voice. Allowing this battle-axe to bully her over being a few minutes late was silly. She was so tired. Her defense mechanisms had evaporated under the pressure of the last few weeks. She bit the inside of her lip, trying not to cry.

Dakota, however, didn't crumble under the hot beams of Mrs. Knights eyes. His protective instincts seemed to kick in when he heard the tremble in his mother's voice. He crossed his arms over his chest in a perfect mimic of his teacher. "Mama said sorry."

"Sorry isn't always enough," Mrs. Knight said.

"*You* say sorry to Mama now," Dakota said. "You were mean."

"Young man, you will spend the first five minutes of tomorrow on this very bench," Mrs. Knight said.

"I don't care," Dakota said.

Violet almost laughed despite the tears that stung her eyes. She must keep it together or he'd have ten minutes on the naughty bench before they were out of here. "Dakota, we should always be respectful to adults," Violet said. "Please apologize to Mrs. Knight."

He looked up at her like she'd just suggested they join the circus. "I won't. Not until she says sorry to you."

"Despite his above average intelligence, this is just the kind of rebellious behavior that will keep him from a good college," Mrs. Knight said.

College? That was a stretch.

"I've seen it a hundred times. Brats in preschool turn to drugs and a life of crime." Mrs. Knight stood, her impressive girth now only inches from them.

Violet stared at her new nemesis, so stunned she couldn't think of what to say next.

"Tell me you're sorry." Mrs. Knight glowered down at Dakota.

He stepped closer to her and stared right back at her. "I will not."

"Da-Dakota…" Violet stammered.

"That's it. You'll spend all day on this bench tomorrow." Mrs. Knight's face had turned the color of a cooked beet. Faint white whiskers on her upper lip glistened with perspiration.

"I don't care," Dakota said. "I hate it here anyway."

"You do?" He did? She thought he loved school. When she picked him up, he smiled and bounced like a brightly colored beach ball.

Dakota stepped closer to his mother and took her hand. "Let's go, Mama. I'll cheer you up at home."

"He apologizes to me or he cannot come back to school," Mrs. Knight said. "This is what happens when a child doesn't have a father. Born in sin becomes sin."

"How dare you," Violet said. "You don't know anything about our life."

"I know you have no husband and a very rude little boy," Mrs. Knight said.

Dakota tugged on her hand. "Let's go, Mama."

"Let me tell you something, Mrs. Knight. I'm doing the best I can to raise a person who is kind and generous, like Jesus asks of us. *You* are not the kind of example I want for my son. He will not be back. Not tomorrow. Not ever. And you can bet your ass I'm going to tell anyone who will listen how utterly terrible you are with children. I'm not sure why someone like you would become a teacher in the first place." Violet turned away and let her little son lead them down the hallway of the church basement and up the stairs to the main floor.

Rain fell harder now. She tilted her face to the sky and let the drops cool her overheated skin. Dakota continued to squeeze her hand. At the car, he climbed obediently into his car seat and raised his arms so she could buckle him in.

Once settled into the driver's seat, she turned on her windshield wipers. This was the first earnest rain of the year and these wipers were no match for it. They barely scraped the water from the glass. Her old car might not make it through the winter. Two hundred thousand miles might be its limit. Old Zelda was as tired as she. The only difference was that Violet was twenty-eight and shouldn't feel two hundred.

She pulled out of the church parking lot and onto the main street. "Mama, you said ass."

"Dakota Ellis, that's a bad word."

She looked at him in the rearview mirror. He nodded, looking earnest and serious. "I know, Mama. That's why you shouldn't say it."

"Okay, but you don't say it just because I did. You could have just said that I said a bad word and not said the word itself."

His big blue eyes blinked as he stared back at her. "Okay, Mama. I'm sorry."

How complex her little guy was. He could quickly apologize to her but not that old battle-axe.

"Do you really hate school?"

"I don't know."

"Well, you don't have to go now." How was she going to get a job if he had no preschool to go to?

She turned the wipers on high speed, which did nothing to influence their competency.

The plan was to live with Kara and Brody Mullen until she could find a place of her own. When you're the best quarterback in the AFL, houses with several wings come with the territory. Fortunately for her, the Mullens were generous people. Thank God, she could use their home as a temporary residence. There were no places to rent in Cliffside Bay. Not that it mattered if there were any. She didn't have a job. Plus, there was a mountain of debt from her small business loan. Landlords didn't rush to rent to people like her.

They passed the empty building where her shop had been. Since she walked into a store back in Boston that sold items made from recyclable or refurbished material, she'd dreamt of opening one of her own. She'd felt sure it would be a hit in Cliffside Bay. She'd been wrong. A purse made from old tires or jewelry twisted from chicken wire—who wouldn't love that? Apparently, most of the people who walked into her shop. Nothing to do now. It was over, done, finished. Inventory had been returned to vendors. The accounting books were closed. She was officially a failure.

She'd rented her side of the building from the owners of the town's bookstore. The owners were retiring and had sold the bookstore business and the building to Lance Mullen, Brody's younger brother. Fortunately, Lance had graciously let her out of her lease with no penalties. Soon, the walls between her shop and the bookstore would be torn down to make way for a bigger space. Lance planned to merge an old-fashioned soda fountain, coffee shop, and bookstore into one space. Mary Hansen, a former librarian, would run the bookstore portion of the business. Lance had offered Violet a job as a clerk when they were ready to open, but that was months away. She needed a job now.

A job for a person with no skills in a small town with few opportunities? It was a tall order. As she often did when thinking about how exactly her life had gone so epically into the dumpster, she blamed her father. If he'd allowed her to attend UC Berkeley instead of demanding she attend a conservative Christian college back east she might have a career in the environmental studies.

You go where I want, or I won't pay. Off she went with her suitcase and her bible.

Violet was about to turn onto her street when the phone rang. It was Honor. She'd called every morning and afternoon for weeks to check up on her.

"Hey, Honor. I'm fine."

"Hey girl. So, we have a little situation."'

"A situation? Is Jubie okay?" Sometimes she asked for parenting advice. *Like I know what I'm doing.*

"Yeah, she's great. It's…Kyle."

"Kyle? What does that have to do with me?" She despised Kyle Hicks. Loathed. Abhorred. He was nothing but a greedy planet-imploder with no respect for the past or the future. His irresponsible resort had opened just as she closed her shop. If that wasn't a sick irony, she didn't know what was.

"Well, there's a baby here. Kyle's baby. We don't know how to take care of her."

"A *baby*?"

"He didn't know about her until today. She was kind of left on the doorstep, so to speak."

"Could the guy be any more of a cliché? What did he do, just get some girl pregnant and take off?"

"Not exactly like that. Yes, on the pregnant part. But he didn't know she was pregnant. It was more of a one-night type of thing."

Reckless, careless, immature Kyle Hicks.

"Where's the baby's mother?" Violet asked.

"She died from complications of childbirth."

"That's awful," Violet said.

"The baby—Mollie Blue—she's only a week old and there was only one bottle of formula and she already ate that and now we don't know what to do. We need you."

Mollie Blue. What a sweet name. A little girl. In Kyle Hicks' hands? The poor child didn't have a chance.

"I'll come, but only for the baby. Make sure you tell Kyle that it's not for him."

"Trust me, he knows that already."

"Where are you guys?" Violet asked, turning the car in the other direction.

"The penthouse suite at the resort," Honor said.

"*Of course* he's in the penthouse suite." *He disgusts me.* "I'll be right there, but I have Dakota with me."

"Totally fine. And thanks. I realize he isn't your first choice of someone to help."

"He's not even my last choice," Violet said.

* * *

Violet hadn't stepped inside of the Cliffside Bay Resort and Spa until today. She'd spent plenty of time on the outside while they were building this blight on the land. With a picket sign in her hand. Little good it did. Kyle Hicks just went right on with his plans to clear acres of trees and meadows. For what? To build a resort in what should have remained an isolated and pristine area of the world. His sole purpose was money.

She had to admit the lobby was beautiful. Breathtaking, even. The room seemed like something from the past, a more elegant and sophisticated time where women wore gowns to dinner and men still opened doors. White marble floors, a fountain, and a sweeping stairway that led to a glittering restaurant on the second floor reminded her of something out of *The Great Gatsby*. She half expected Daisy to come down the stairs with a long cigarette hanging from her mouth.

She instructed Dakota to hold onto her hand. "No running or shouting in here. You got it?"

"Yes, Mama."

They crossed the lobby. As they passed the fountain, Dakota's gait slowed. She knew he wanted to put his grubby fingers in the spray. This could not happen. There would not be a second accusation of poor mothering skills today. Once was quite enough.

"Dakota, no touching."

"I know, Mama."

She spotted the concierge desk near the glass doors that opened to a terrace. Was that Joan Adams at the desk? It was. What was she doing working for the enemy? Joan Adams had lived in Cliffside Bay all her life and had once worked at the feed store, which was currently being torn down to make way for Zane Shaw's new brewery. Sadly, no one needed farm and garden supplies. Beer, however, was popular with both tourists and townspeople. Yet another business morphing their secret town into a tourist destination.

Mrs. Adams looked up from her computer screen. "Good afternoon, Miss Ellis. Welcome to Cliffside Bay Resort and Spa." She slid a keycard across the shiny surface of the desk. "Mr. Hicks is expecting you. You'll need the keycard to access the top floor."

"How have you been, Mrs. Adams? I didn't know you were working here."

"Yes, Miss Ellis. I was one of the first employees. It's a pleasure to serve you." Mrs. Adams sounded like a polite robot. What had Kyle done to her?

"Why are you talking so weird?" Violet whispered.

She lowered her voice. "Our manager likes us to speak formally, even if we know the guests. Stellar customer service begins and ends with precision and attention to detail."

"You used to sneak me a candy every time my dad took me to the feed store. Formality is a little ridiculous."

"Please let me know if I can be of further assistance." Mrs. Adams' mouth stretched into a smile, but her eyes were pleading with Violet to let it go.

Letting go wasn't Violet's strongest attribute.

"How could you sell out like this?" Violet asked.

"Sell out?"

"This place is like the devil moving into town."

"That's a bit of an overstatement," Mrs. Adams said.

"You've lived here all your life. How could you agree to work for a business that...that poor excuse for a man Kyle Hicks tore down the forest for?"

"Kyle Hicks is a *wonderful* man. Smart and fair." She lowered her voice again. "And he's quite handsome. If I was a young woman, I wouldn't hesitate to flirt my way into his heart."

Violet stared at her, horrified. What was wrong with this world? "He's a money-grubbing pig."

There was a brief pause as Mrs. Adams looked at her hands. When she looked up, her voice had dropped to just above a whisper. "This resort—Kyle Hicks—brought over a hundred jobs to this town. I don't know if you've noticed from your parents' enormous home where you live for free and dabble in your little store, but we need these jobs. *I* need this job. My husband's not well enough. I'm an old lady. No one wants to hire me. But Kyle Hicks did. He and Mr. Kauffman, our manager, said no training was necessary. They would teach me everything I needed to know. I won't hear one bad word out of your mouth about him, young lady."

Violet flooded with heat, embarrassed and angry all at once. Why did everyone in this town feel it necessary to lecture her today? "I didn't know Mr. Adams was sick."

"He has rheumatoid arthritis," Mrs. Adams said.

"I'm sorry," Violet said. "My dad has that too."

"You didn't know. Still, sometimes you need to think about people over causes."

"I *am* thinking about people. I'm thinking about the health of our planet. We only have one, you know. I'd like it to still be here for my son."

"We all saw you down here with your picket sign, and frankly, it was embarrassing. I thought you had better manners than that."

"Manners? What is everyone's obsession with manners? Sometimes manners are exactly opposite of what we need. Nothing ever changes without protest. Women who make a difference in the world are rarely polite."

"It must be nice to have time and money to think of such high ideals. I'm too busy paying for my husband's medicines to concern myself with such things."

"I'll have you know I closed my store last week. It's all over. Finished. I have no place to live either now that my parents—who were so dedicated to manners—are coming back to town. I'm pretty worried about feeding my son, so I don't appreciate the lecture." Violet stopped. If she started crying in front of Mrs. Adams in the middle of this glossy lobby, she would die right there on the spot.

Dakota tugged on her hand. "Mama, I see Honor."

Honor. Thank God. A way to escape.

Violet picked up the keycard from Mrs. Adam's desk and sniffed. "Have a great day, Mrs. Adams."

"You as well, Miss Ellis."

Dakota broke from her grip and sprinted across the lobby toward Honor. Violet cringed when he shouted Honor's name and leapt into her arms. So much for quiet. She glanced at the front desk. Thankfully, busy with guests, Mrs. Adams and the rest of the staff weren't paying any attention. An older woman sitting on a lounge chair looked up from her magazine to smile at Violet. "What a darling boy."

Violet thanked her and quickened her pace. Honor and Dakota were by the elevators. Apparently, her son had managed to tell Honor the entire story of their altercation at school.

"So now I can't go to school," Dakota said.

"Are you sad about that?" Honor asked.

"No. I don't like that old battle-axe."

"Dakota! Where did you hear that word?" Violet asked.

"You said it today." Dakota wrinkled his forehead as if she were the most perplexing woman on the planet. Maybe she was.

"Never mind that. Honor, what can we do to help with the baby?"

"Baby 101, that's what," Honor said as they followed her into the elevator. "We had one of the staff go out and get formula and diapers." She put a keycard into a slot and punched the top floor button.

The elevator moved. Dakota squealed. "Elevator, Mama."

Violet's stomach lurched as they came to a stop. They all exited into a hallway. A plush, sage-green carpet felt wonderful under her feet, like walking on a firm mattress. She would love to take off her shoes and let it soothe her tired feet. The scent of lilies from a vase on a rectangular table tickled her nose. Where did he get lilies this time of year? Probably flown in from some third world country for exorbitant amounts of money. None of which trickled down to the poor farmers who grew them.

"Dakota, this is a very special floor," Honor said. "Kyle's a part owner so he stays in the very nicest suite in the whole resort."

"Wow," Dakota said.

"He's not Superman," Violet said under her breath.

Honor shot her a look. "Be nice. You have the power right now."

"I'll try not to let it go to my head," Violet said.

"Stop being so grumpy," Honor said. "Wait until you see this baby. She's precious. Seriously, you'll want to eat her up."

"Eat a baby?" Dakota asked.

"Not really," Honor said. "It just means she's yummy. I mean, she's pretty and I just want to kiss her all over."

"Oh," Dakota said. "That's weird."

"I have a thing for babies," Honor said. "What can I say?"

Violet flushed with shame. Honor couldn't have a baby of her own. Seeing a newborn must hurt. And here was cavalier Kyle Hicks with one just dropped into his lap like everything else in the man's life.

They reached the door of the suite. Honor didn't bother to knock; she simply pressed the keycard against the door and entered, gesturing for Violet and Dakota to follow.

"Don't be loud," Violet said to Dakota. "The baby might be sleeping."

Dakota mimicked her finger to her lips and made a shushing sound.

When they entered the suite, Violet had to physically restrain herself from gasping out loud. The suite was magnificent. The same white marble floors as the lobby shone under the light of a chandelier made of sparkling glass. Posh, richly hued furniture in greens and purples, fluffy rugs, and glass tabletops with silver trim were arranged in geometric perfection. Paintings of various bright and vibrant flowers decorated the creamy sage walls. The bank of windows looked out on the entire town of Cliffside Bay, surrounding country roads, forests, and meadows. If it weren't foggy today, you would be able to see the endless waters of the Pacific.

She quickly forgot all of that at the sight of Kyle Hicks with a baby in his arms. A spot of sunshine had broken through the gray sky and washed the room and the man in a warm glow. She drew closer, mesmerized. He cradled the baby against his chest and softly sang "You Are My Sunshine." Kyle Hicks knew a lullaby. Go figure.

He looked up from the baby and smiled at her. Triumph glittered in his deep blue eyes. "I got her to sleep," he whispered before his gaze turned back to Mollie. Those thick, black lashes didn't belong on a man. *Whatever*. That was of no consequence. Pretty is as pretty does.

She glanced around the room. A dilapidated stroller was parked over by the couch. "It's like 1972 is looking for its stroller."

Honor laughed from across the room where she had Dakota on her lap.

"No, seriously," Violet said. "You must never use that again. It's not safe."

An empty bottle and a used diaper sat on the coffee table. Apparently neither Honor nor Kyle knew how to roll a dirty diaper because it was wide open with the baby's last deposit displayed for all the world to see. Violet rushed to the table and arranged the diaper into a tight ball.

They needed a diaper pail or things were going to get stinky very fast.

"What do we do first?" Honor asked.

"Kyle, put the baby on the ottoman here." Violet pointed to the large ottoman adjacent to the armchair near a gas fireplace. "She'll be nice and warm there." She instructed Dakota to switch on the fire. He leapt from Honor's lap and gleefully pushed the switch.

"What if she rolls off?" Kyle asked.

"She can't roll yet," Violet said. "We've got weeks and weeks before she can do anything close to rolling."

Violet grabbed the pink blanket from the couch. "Before you put her down, we need to swaddle her."

"Swaddle?" he asked.

"I'll show you how," she said.

Surprisingly, Kyle followed her directions and put the baby in the center of the blanket.

"Does she seem healthy?" Kyle pointed to her head. "What's that dent there?"

"There's nothing to worry about," Violet said. "All babies have that when they're first born." She gently caressed the soft dent in Mollie's head, remembering when Dakota had been that age. "I didn't know that when Dakota was born. I freaked out." The plates of the head had to fully grow together. Her nurse at the hospital had kindly explained it to her. She now explained this to Kyle.

"What about her eyes? Do you think she can see out of them?" Kyle asked.

"You mean because they look kind of glassy?" she asked.

Kyle nodded.

"Totally normal. All white babies are born with blue eyes that look like this. They turn their real color later."

Kyle nodded again. *His* eyes looked like a startled animal's. Arrogant Kyle Hicks, all shook up.

She deposited the blanket on the ottoman and instructed him to put the baby in the middle. "Now you wrap her up like a burrito, as tight as you can get it."

"Won't it hurt her?" Kyle asked.

"No. They like it. Mimics the womb," Violet said, amazed how fast all this came back to her. She hadn't had the luxury of anyone advising her. Not that she needed anyone. Books had everything a new parent needed to know. *If* you had a chance to read them before the baby appeared on your doorstep.

"We need a plan." Honor glanced at her wristwatch. "I've got to pick up Jubie in thirty minutes."

"You need supplies," Violet said. She explained the need for a crib, pacifier, car seat, stroller, and changing table.

"Can you rent that stuff?" Kyle asked.

Violet shook her head. "No, but you can buy them online and have them rush delivered."

"Right." Kyle let out a deep breath. "I'm not thinking clearly."

Honor patted his arm and drew him over to sit on the couch. "You look a little pasty. I think we need to get some food in you."

"We can call for room service," Kyle said. "Whatever you guys want."

From over by the window where Dakota had decided a knick-knack of a seashell was better as a truck, replete with engine noises, he looked up, suddenly interested. "Can I have a cheeseburger?"

"Absolutely. If it's okay with your mom. Do you let him eat meat?" Kyle asked.

"Yes. Why wouldn't I?" Violet asked. What was it with this guy? Did he have to make a case about everything?

"Can I have a milkshake?" Dakota asked.

"If your mom says yes, then I say yes," Kyle said. "Your mom's saving me right now."

"You can have one for dessert. Burger first," Violet said.

"Yes, Mama."

"After we order dinner, let's get on the internet and order what we need," Violet said.

"How much is this going to cost me?" Kyle asked.

"Why are *you* worried about money?" Violet asked.

"I'm not worried. Old habits die hard, that's all," Kyle said.

Was he referring to an impoverished childhood? Despite herself, curiosity poked through her annoyance. No one knew much about his past, other than he'd come to USC as an emancipated adult.

"It's a little late to worry about money now," she said in a tone sharper than she meant. "You made a baby and now you have to pay to take care of her."

"I get it. Back off with the judgey tone," he said.

"I'm not judging you."

"Yes, you are, but it's fine," Kyle said. "I don't care what you or anyone else think about me. I haven't for a long time. Regarding furniture, I want the best. Top of the line."

"*Of course*, you do," Violet said.

"Didn't you just lecture me that I need to take care of my daughter?" Kyle's eyes darkened when he was annoyed. She'd noticed that before. They darkened every time she was anywhere within his vision.

* * *

After Honor left, they ordered dinner and went to work. In less than forty-five minutes, they'd ordered furniture and the other supplies. Shopping was speedy when you simply ordered the most expensive item in every category. Violet kept her opinions to herself. Who cared if this guy wanted to waste his money on designer names? It wasn't her concern.

Mollie Blue woke up and began to cry the moment they all sat down to eat.

"It's a baby thing," Violet said. "They have some kind of radar to ensure you never eat an entire meal or get an entire night's sleep."

Kyle's shoulders slumped. "I'm starving."

Despite her intentions to the contrary, she softened. "You eat. I'll feed her this time."

"She probably needs to be changed first," Kyle said.

She looked over at him, surprised. "You catch on quick."

"That's what it was last time anyway," Kyle said.

While the boys ate, Violet changed Mollie's diaper and fixed a bottle from the powdered formula, careful to read the directions. She'd breastfed Dakota exclusively.

"Is it supposed to be warm or cold?" Kyle asked.

"Room temperature is fine, but they prefer if it's the temperature of breast milk."

"What the heck temperature is that?"

"Body temperature. See here?" Violet sprayed a small amount of formula on her forearm. "If you can't feel either hot or cold then it's the exact temperature of a person's body. Whatever you do, don't heat a bottle in the microwave. Hot spots."

"Hot spots? What is that?"

"Hot spots in the water that could burn her. Microwaves don't heat liquids evenly."

"Jesus. I had no idea."

"It's all right. You know now."

Violet sat in the armchair and placed the bottle in Mollie's mouth. The baby sucked with no fussing, which meant she probably had not been breastfed. How sad to think the child would never know her true mother. The poor woman. To leave before they could know each other was incomprehensible and so unfair. She wondered, too often, how God let a tragedy like this happen. What had an innocent little baby ever done to deserve this fate? Her father would say that it was not our place to ask, but Violet had a few questions she planned on asking God when she arrived in heaven. Mollie would be on the top of the list of questions, right after how did a man like Cole Lund thrive despite his hypocrisy?

Cole Lund. America's Pastor. Dakota's father. Someone else's husband. She'd been naive to believe he loved her.

She'd gone to work for him after leaving college. His strategic seduction had taken time. It started with lunches, then dinners out, all under the pretense of a working meal. As one of the administrators to the pastor staff, her job was to take notes while he brainstormed sermon ideas or plans for church growth. After a few months, he started dropping by her apartment in the evenings to ask her opinion on a sermon or a staff decision. Flattered and beguiled, she'd let him kiss her one night after he confessed to his feelings. *I can think of nothing but you.*

America's Pastor, as it turned out, *could* think of other things besides Violet Ellis—his status in the church, his family, his Mercedes where he'd first placed his hand on her knee. When she told him she was pregnant, he dropped her so fast she could almost hear the thump of her head hitting the proverbial curb. That night, a man showed up on her doorstep with a check and a threat. *Tell anyone and you won't live long enough to give birth. Don't come back to work. Don't contact him ever again.*

A sliver of loneliness crept of her spine. She was alone with her questions, alone with her mistakes.

Violet stroked the peach fuzz on Mollie's head. "What a pretty one you are," she said under her breath.

Mollie was a concentrated eater with an occasional appreciative grunt. Although, they should have Jackson or Kara give her an exam right away. She said as much to Kyle.

"Doctors? But she isn't sick, is she?"

She almost laughed at his worried expression. *Welcome to parenthood.*

"No, it's just standard for newborns to have frequent visits for checkups. They weigh and measure them and make sure they're thriving. They call them 'well-baby visits'."

Kyle ran both hands through his hair as he crossed the room and sat on the coffee table across from her. "I don't know what I'm doing. This is a disaster."

"You'll be fine." She smiled, remembering her first few weeks as a mother. "I thought they were insane when the hospital sent me home with Dakota after less than twenty-four hours. I told the nurses I had no idea what I was doing, and I had no one to help me. They assured me I would be fine and to trust my instincts. I wanted to say, but I have no instincts. I'm too young for this. And my mother wasn't speaking to me—I didn't tell them that part, but seriously, I had no one. That said, the nurses were right. It all fell into place. Although, Dakota was an easy baby. For one thing, he was giant. He weighed nine pounds when he was born."

"How did nine pounds come out of you?" He gestured toward her narrow hips.

"It wasn't pretty. At all." He'd ripped her in several places. She wasn't sure everything was good down there, even now. It would require having sex with someone to find out, which seemed unlikely to happen anytime soon.

"Are bigger babies better?" he asked. "Because she doesn't seem very big."

"I'd guess she's just over six pounds. I've heard the smaller they are, the longer it takes them to sleep through the night. They have to eat more frequently than a big fat baby like Dakota."

"Sleep. How am I going to work and take care of her by myself?" His eyes had darkened to the color of the night sky just after twilight when the first of the stars appear.

"You'll hire a nanny for during the day and a nanny for the nights. Once she starts to sleep through the night, you'll be fine with just a day nanny."

"There's such a thing as a night nanny?"

"Yes, all rich people have them."

"They do?" he asked.

"*A lot* of rich people have them."

"Did you have one?" he asked.

A bitter taste at the back of her throat prevented her from a sarcastic laugh. "I couldn't afford one. My parents had disowned me. I was solo. Fortunately, Dakota slept through the night at six weeks."

"Six weeks? That seems like forever." The corners of his mouth turned downward. "This cannot really be happening."

It was almost endearing how bewildered and frightened he was. Almost, but not quite. This was Kyle Hicks. Rich and self-satisfied with little regard for anyone but his smug, attractive self. "It'll be fine. Looking back, those weeks were just a blip on the radar. Honestly, cherish every moment. Before you know it, she'll be three."

He sighed and rubbed his eyes. "I don't know if I can do this. Truly."

"Do you have younger siblings?" Violet asked.

He looked away, scratching behind his ear. "Yeah. A brother and a sister."

"Do you remember helping with them at all?" She couldn't recall ever hearing that he had siblings. Not that she exactly asked around about Kyle Hicks.

"No. They were two and four years younger than me. I don't remember anything under the age of six."

"I was an only child, so I had the same problem. No memories to recall—like my mom did this, so I'll do this. I couldn't ask her either, since she wasn't speaking to me."

"Were they that uptight for real?"

"My parents are very religious." She glanced at Dakota. He was dipping a french fry into his vanilla shake without a thought to what the adults were doing or saying. She lowered her voice anyway. "They were mortified I was pregnant without a husband."

"Kind of antiquated, isn't it?"

"You don't know the half of it. My dad's a real charmer." She rolled her eyes to hide the pain behind those words.

"I'd choose supporting my daughter over any belief system I'd read in stories written a long time ago."

Not religious. Duly noted.

"Don't look like that," he said, matching her subdued volume. "I'm not a total heathen. All I'm saying is that if I had a daughter like you and a grandson like Dakota, I'd be proud, whether you had a husband or not. The fact that Dakota's father bailed tells me everything I need to know. Good riddance. Take it from me. No dad is better than one who doesn't want to be there."

She stared at him, shocked. A dozen questions floated across her mind. Had he given her a compliment? What was his father like? Instead, she surprised herself by sharing something of her own father.

"My dad hasn't spoken to me in almost four years. We've been staying at their house without his knowledge. My mom kept it from him. Their house burned down in South America, so they have to come home. If it weren't for Brody and Kara, I'd be majorly screwed right now."

He ran his hands through his hair once more. "Hey, listen, I'm sorry about your shop. Lance said he offered you a few months free rent, but you turned him down."

"Yeah." She shrugged as Mollie took one last suck and then shook the nipple from her mouth. Violet gathered her to her shoulder and patted her back until a nice loud burp erupted. "Good girl."

"Here, I'll take her," Kyle said.

Violet placed her in his arms. He kissed Mollie's head. "She smells so good," he said.

"They always do."

"Why didn't you take Lance up on it?" Kyle asked.

"Have you ever heard the term 'bleeding cash'?"

Kyle grimaced as he cradled Mollie closer to his chest. "I'm familiar, yes."

"It was more than just rent. The whole shop was a failure." She looked away, embarrassed by the tremor in her voice. "I'm not cut out for business, I guess."

"A lot of successful people had early failures. *Most* successful people."

"It doesn't matter. I have no place to live and a son without daycare."

"What happened to daycare?"

"We had an incident today. I was late, and I got into it with Mrs. Knight. He's no longer welcome."

"You have a bit of a temper, don't you?" He raised his eyebrows, teasing her. It wasn't funny.

"I *do not* have a temper, but I won't be pushed around. Not anymore."

"Anymore?"

"Never mind that. Anyway, I need to focus on paying down my debt and finding a job." *Stop talking. He doesn't need to know all this. Keep your guard up. This is the enemy.*

He narrowed his eyes and pressed his lips into a thin line. "This is going to sound crazy…given our past, but we both need something the other could provide. I need a nanny. You need a place to live and a job where you can bring your son to work. What if you moved in here with us for a while? There are two bedrooms and two bathrooms. You and Dakota could have one and I'll take the other with Mollie. You can have the day shift, and I'll pay you twice the going rate for a full-time nanny, plus free room and board. You can get back on track financially, and I can rest easy that Mollie will be taken care of by someone I trust."

You trust me?

"I'd ask only that you stop picketing my building." He smiled, but it stung just the same.

"It's done now. There's nothing to picket. You've already ruined the land and the town."

"Ruined? Really? Do you actually believe that?"

"You don't get it and you never will," Violet said.

He sighed and kissed Mollie's head again. "That's probably true. But we can agree to disagree, right? Just say yes. I promise to play nice from now on."

"What about the night nanny?"

"I don't want one. If I have you during the day and someone else at night, it means nothing's left for me. She's my baby and I should be the one up with her at night. I should be the one who feeds her and comforts her. *You* did it."

You say that now.

"I know you don't believe I can do it," Kyle said. "For all I know, you might be right. But I should try. I have to try. I can't bail on my kid like my parents did. I have to be present."

"So, you're really doing this?"

"I have to." He stood and rocked the baby in his arms, gazing down at Mollie. His expression softened. Had he fallen in love with his baby already? "I mean, look at her. She's perfection. I can't let her down. I won't."

Two sudden thoughts flooded her resolve to remain strong. *I wish a man would look at Dakota that way. I wish a man would look at me that way.*

The first step was to recover financially. If she had to work for the enemy, then so be it. Plus, she'd get to hold sweet Mollie every day. A job where she could be with her son every day was the best she could do.

"What do you say?" he asked.

"Let's try it for a month. Trial period only."

"Fine, that's reasonable."

He bent over the baby again. His black hair shone in the lamplight. Was it as silky as it looked? *No, no, no. This is the man you hate.*

He represented everything in this world she loathed.

Or, did he?

She would never have predicted his reaction to the sudden appearance of a baby. Additionally, there were the references to his childhood. Had he grown up in poverty? Were his parents cold like her own? Were these the reasons he was so driven to succeed? Honor had suggested as much before, but Violet had dismissed it, assuming their friend was overstating to persuade her that he wasn't so bad.

"Mollie looks like you."

"Do you really think so?"

The hopeful, vulnerable tone in his voice gave her pause. Kyle Hicks was full of surprises today.

She pointed to Mollie's mouth. "That's your mouth. See the fullness of her bottom lip?"

He touched his fingertips to his own bottom lip. "Yeah?"

"She has your dark coloring too," she said.

"Supposedly we have some Italian in us," he said.

"I bet she'll have your eyes too. If she's lucky." His were an unusual blue that turned from light to dark like the fickle Pacific. Not that she'd noticed...much.

"Her mother was pretty," he said. "Blond and tall."

Violet didn't say anything for a moment, thinking about how tricky it would be for him, like it was for her, when his child grew old enough to ask about her mother.

"Dakota asks about his dad sometimes," she said as if they'd already broached the subject. He seemed to follow her line of thinking without having to ask.

"What do you tell him?" Kyle asked.

She glanced over at her son to make sure he wasn't listening. He was intently removing the seeds from his pickle wedge and singing the words to "The Wheels On the Bus" under his breath. "I tell him not everyone has one, but that I love him enough for two parents."

"Does he buy it?"

She grimaced. "For now. Later, I'll have to tell him the truth."

"What is the truth? Are you in the one-night-stand club with me?"

"Not exactly."

"Don't judge me. I can't take it." His eyelids drooped as if he were suddenly exhausted.

"I'm not. Truly." She touched his forearm, wanting to reassure him. "I'm not in much of a position to judge, even if I wanted to. Which I don't. I've been judged enough today for both of us."

He gazed into her eyes for a moment before looking back at the baby. "It was when I was up north working on a project. It was a hard night for me and I drank too much at this dive bar where she worked. We talked. She had this way about her—one of those women who gets you talking about things you wouldn't normally. Like Kara."

"Yes, sure. I know exactly." Kara Mullen was a witch that way. Two minutes into their first a conversation and she had cut through all the pleasantries.

"One thing led to another and I followed her home like an injured dog. She was a sweet girl. Way too young for me." Kyle sighed. "Believe it or not, I felt bad afterward. I let my own weakness get the better of me. It's not my thing, despite what you've heard, to seduce innocents. My women are usually of the savvy and sassy variety." He paused and gazed down at the baby in his arms. "I don't know if I can be enough for two parents. I look at you and I don't know how you do it. Dakota's a great kid."

Her chest swelled with pride. "Not everyone's a fan of my parenting."

"That meanie at the day care? Screw her."

"Everything I do seems to turn to sand in my hands." Why was his kindness undoing her, making words tumble from her mouth?

"Don't let anyone tell you that you're a bad mother. It's simply not true. As much as you and I disagree over certain things, I've always noticed how good you are with Dakota. Why do you think you were the first person we called?"

She flashed him a rueful smile. "I'm the only one of us who has raised an infant."

He laughed for the first time since she'd arrived. "It's not just that. And listen, I'm grateful you're willing to help. I know it's for Mollie, not me, but I'll take it."

"There's no better reason for calling a truce than a baby." *A motherless baby.*

He kissed Mollie's forehead. "I couldn't agree more."

"It's so sad about her mother."

"Yeah. Now she's stuck with me. Katy's friend told me mortality rates for mothers in poor rural areas is on the rise. In America. There's a cause in need of Violet Ellis."

"Are you mocking me?"

He met her gaze. "Not one bit. I'm completely serious. We need to figure out what's happening and do something about it. Isn't that what you're all about?"

"Kind of." She looked down at her hands. "I don't seem to have influence on much of anything, despite my efforts."

"You don't know if you are or not. These things aren't measurable. Not all the way, at least. I know you prompted a few of my decisions on this place."

"I did?"

"Have you noticed how green it is?" He pointed to the ceiling. "Solar panels on the roof? The sustainable kitchen in the restaurants. Ten percent of our profits will go to environmental groups."

"You're lying to me."

"I'm not."

"Why didn't you tell me?"

"You never asked," he said.

"Oh."

Dakota called out from over at the table. "Can I be excused now, Mama?"

"*May* I be excused," she said.

"May I be excused, Mama?"

"You may. Come on over here, I have something exciting to tell you."

Her little boy, her heart, ran from the table on his chubby legs. Why walk when you could run?

She pulled him onto her lap. "How would you like to move in here with Kyle for a little while? Baby Mollie needs our help. I'm going to take care of Mollie while he goes to work."

His eyes widened. "Live in a hotel?"

"Sure. It'll be an adventure. And no, you can't have a milkshake every day."

"What do you say?" Kyle asked. "I need another guy around here."

Dakota's gaze moved from her to Kyle. "My friend Jacob has a mom and dad and sister."

"He does?" Kyle asked.

Dakota nodded. "But I just have my mom."

"You're lucky to have such an awesome mom. And we're just borrowing her for a bit," Kyle said. "She'll still be your mom and your mom only."

Kyle didn't understand. Dakota wasn't expressing angst over sharing his mother. He wanted a family like his friend Jacob had.

Maybe this wasn't such a great idea. All she needed was to break her son's heart when they had to leave.

No, she had to do this. None of it mattered if she couldn't provide the essentials. Shelter and food for her son had to be her priority. A job and a place to live had fallen in her lap. Kyle was right. They needed each other. She would just have to hope for the best regarding her own baby. Providing a place to live and food to eat was about as good as she could do now. Later there would be therapy bills, no question. Yet another reason to escape the mountain of debt. For now, however, one grown man, a little boy, and an infant girl needed her to do what she did best—take care of them.

"We have work to do, gentlemen," she said. "*Operation Take Care of Mollie* starts now. Can you both accept the mission?"

"Yes, Mama."

"Bring it," Kyle said.

CHAPTER THREE

Kyle

KYLE FOLLOWED VIOLET into his bedroom. As his temporary home, the suite had been more than satisfactory. He loved the bed and the sheets' ridiculous thread count. Up until a few hours ago, this bedroom had everything he needed. Now, he needed a nursery. A house that could be a home. *Put it aside to figure out later and follow Violet's lead.*

Violet stood with her hands on her hips surveying the room. "Changing table over there." She pointed to the armchair. "Dakota, go into the bathroom and bring back three towels."

The little guy ran off to do his mother's bidding. He ran most places. Kyle liked that in a person.

Mollie wriggled in her burrito blanket. One hand and then a full arm escaped. She opened her eyes and made a face almost like a smile. "Is she smiling at me?" he asked.

"No. Usually babies don't smile until around seven weeks. She probably has gas."

"Gas. Does it hurt?"

"You'll know if it hurts. She'll start screaming."

47

"What do I do if that happens?" Kyle's shirt stuck to his damp skin. Thus far, parenting involved a lot of bodily fluids, including his sweat.

"If she starts crying and she's not wet or hungry, assume it's gas," Violet said.

"*Again*, what do I do?" He couldn't keep the irritation from his voice, but she didn't seem to notice.

"Tummy rubs, pumping their legs like they're riding a bicycle, warm baths, burping. Also, I ordered some slow sip bottles. They'll help."

He sank onto the end of the bed. "All those at once? Slow sip bottles?"

"Sometimes one after the other." She pulled a drawer from the dresser and placed it next to him on the bed. "It all depends."

Depends? On what?

"Can I dump this out?" she asked. The drawer was lined with his socks, all folded into balls and placed in neat rows.

"Dump them? Like on the bed?" he asked.

She squinted her eyes, as if deciphering whether he'd spoken to her in a foreign language or if he was simply slow.

"I need this drawer for her temporary crib. We need to put the socks somewhere else."

"Right, yes, put them here. Sorry, I wasn't following."

Her expression softened. "Just sit there with the baby and I'll put everything together."

He nodded in agreement and watched as she covered the seat of the armchair with a towel and placed a stack of diapers and wipes on the arm. She rolled two more towels and lined the dresser drawer with them. "That reminds me, we should order a pack-and-play, in addition to the crib. You'll need that for when you travel or visit friends." She stepped back, seemingly satisfied with the makeshift bed. "Honestly, this is the safest place for her until the crib comes. It's like a cradle."

Dakota climbed up onto the bed and sat next to him, his plump hand resting on Kyle's knee. He instinctively put his arm around the little boy and pulled him close. Mollie only needed one of his arms. Perhaps this was the reason a man had two?

"You smell like ketchup," Kyle whispered.

"I do?" Dakota yawned and wriggled closer to him.

"And milkshake."

A memory jolted him like a jab of a sharp fork. His little sister, when tiny like Mollie, had slept in a drawer. "My sister slept in a drawer. I'd forgotten that."

Violet stopped what she was doing and straightened to look at him. "It's clever, really. People spend money on cradles for no reason."

"A baby shouldn't have to sleep in a drawer."

"It's safe and that's all we care about for now."

"One night. That's it. Never again after this." He crossed his arms over his chest.

"You'll have that designer crib by this time tomorrow."

Had she rolled her eyes or was it just her tone that told him what she thought of his purchases? "I don't care if you think it's ridiculous that I spent so much money. She's going to have the best."

"It's sweet," she said. "If unnecessary."

This woman was insufferable with her judgments and disdain. Just when he'd started to like her a little, she went back into her pontificating ways.

"Sleeping in a drawer could stunt a baby's growth," he said, like he knew anything about the subject.

Violet flicked her hair behind her shoulders. "That's ridiculous. Did your sister grow up to be short?"

Kyle shrugged and looked back to Mollie. Violet's scrutiny felt like a bandage being torn from the hairiest part of his arm. "I don't know."

"What do you mean you don't know?" Violet asked.

"I don't know how tall she is. I haven't seen her since she was fourteen."

That shut her up. *For once.* She went back to the drawer, fussing for a moment before declaring it ready. Seconds later, as if what she wanted to say had suddenly come to her she said, "I was dead broke when I had Dakota and he slept in a drawer for the first six months of his life. Does he look like he suffered any?"

On cue, Dakota grinned up at Kyle. He *was* adorable with those big blue eyes and chubby cheeks.

"He looks big and strong to me," Kyle said.

Dakota beamed.

"There you go. Being poor doesn't make you a bad parent," she said.

"This isn't about you," Kyle said.

"I know that."

"You're acting like it is," he said. "I wasn't criticizing you."

"I get that you're trying to guarantee she has everything she needs, but I can tell you with assurance that what she needs most from you is love. In the long term, anyway. What she needs now is a routine and a schedule."

"I *had* a routine." He tucked Mollie's arm back under the blanket. "But I have a feeling it's about to get blown to pieces."

She placed her hands back on her hips, causing her skirt to ride up over her knees. Man, she had pretty legs, even if she did nothing to show them off in those flat canvas tennis shoes. "Kyle Hicks, you're about to embark on the best routine of your life. This little bundle of pink is about to become the most phenomenal thing that ever happened to you."

What was this strange lump in his throat that made it hard to swallow and the prickling sensation at the corners of his eyes? Did becoming the father of a little girl reduce a man to a sentimental pile of sniffles?

Will she call me Daddy or Dad?

Dakota tugged on the sleeve of Kyle's shirt. "What's the difference between a crib and a pack-and-play, Kale?" *Kyle* sounded like *Kale* when Dakota said his name. Kyle tousled Dakota's hair.

"I have no idea," Kyle said. "Ask your mother."

He repeated the question.

Violet frowned. "A crib is for home. A pack-and-play is for taking places, like on a vacation or to a hotel."

"*This* is a hotel." Dakota said.

Kyle laughed. Mollie's eyes fluttered open for a brief second. He held his breath. Would she wake and start up with the awful howling? *Note to self—no loud laughing while holding the baby.*

Dakota wrinkled his nose. "Can the baby *play* in a pack-and-play but not a crib?"

Violet took in a deep breath. "For goodness sake, Dakota, it's just named that. Beds are for sleeping. So are cribs and pack-and-plays."

"Maybe it shouldn't contain the word *play* then?" Kyle asked, winking at Dakota, who agreed with a solemn nod of his head.

"Here's what's going to happen now." Violet pointed at Dakota. "You, young man, are going to have a treat and watch a show on television while I run home and get our suitcases." They were all packed and waiting in the hallway for their temporary move to the Mullens'. The rest of their things were in storage. "Kyle, you need to put Mollie in her drawer, I mean, bed, and go back to finish your dinner. I'm going to eat something in the car on my way to the house. My stomach's growling and I've got the hangries."

"Oh no." Dakota's blue eyes widened.

"Is your mom grumpy when she's hungry?" Kyle asked.

Dakota nodded.

"We don't want that," Kyle said."

"We'll establish a routine tomorrow," Violet said.

Again, with that word routine.

* * *

Kyle fixed himself a three-finger scotch in celebration of surviving the forty-five minutes it took for Violet to return from her old house. He was about to take a glorious first sip when she walked into the main room from putting Dakota to bed. "I'm sorry to bug you, but Dakota wondered if you could come say goodnight."

"Sure thing." He pointed to the table where her cold turkey burger remained untouched. "I ordered you another meal. It should be here within minutes."

"This would have been fine."

"The least I owe you is a warm meal."

He walked away before she could protest.

Dakota was tucked into a twin rollaway bed. Violet had said she didn't want him sleeping with her because it was a bad habit to get into and had asked for the bed to be arranged in the large walk-in closet. Kyle wasn't in love with the idea of the boy sleeping in a closet. Now that he was here, however, he realized the closet was bigger than the room he'd shared with his two siblings when they were kids. Their trailer had been about fourth of the size of this suite, now that he thought about it. He scowled, chiding himself. *You don't think about the past. Ever.*

"Hi Kale." Round blue eyes looked up at him.

"Did you have a good bath?" Kyle asked.

"That tub has jets. They tickled."

"Did you like it?"

Dakota nodded and grinned. His teeth looked like miniature Chiclet gum. "I have Spider-Man jammies." He lifted the covers to expose the super hero emblem.

"Those are cool," Kyle said.

"Mama could get you some."

"I might just ask her to."

"Kale, will you marry my mom?"

"What? Um, no, no. We're just friends."

"Honor and Zane are best friends. She told me."

"Oh, well, your mom and I aren't *best* friends like Honor and Zane. That's the difference." *Up to a few hours ago, we were arch enemies.*

"I wanted to marry Honor," Dakota said.

"Zane beat you to it, huh?" Kyle asked.

Dakota nodded solemnly.

Zane, that lucky bastard.

"You're a little young to get married anyway, don't you think?" Kyle asked.

"Honor said I'll be a heart squeezer like you when I get big."

"You mean a heart breaker?"

"I guess so," Dakota said.

Kyle rubbed the stubble on his chin. "Don't be like me, Dakota. Be like Zane." *Or Brody or Jackson or Lance. Anyone but me.*

"I'll be like you. I've decided." Dakota tugged the blanket up to his chin. "Now you kiss me on the forehead and say goodnight."

"All righty then." He leaned down and did as asked. Dakota's head smelled good too. This must be a kid thing.

Dakota closed his eyes. "Night, Kale."

"Night, Dakota."

Violet's food had arrived by the time he got back to the living room. She stood at the picture windows, eating her turkey burger. The sky had darkened completely. Night came early this time of year.

"You shouldn't eat standing up," he said.

She remained at the window with her back to him. "Why?"

"Meals are supposed to be enjoyed at a table."

"There's always more to do at the end of the day. No time to sit around sipping champagne and eating caviar." As she turned to look at him, she popped the last of her burger into her mouth.

"Is that what you think my life's like?" he asked.

"Maybe."

"Can I get you a glass of wine?"

"A small one."

He chose a mini bottle of white wine from the bar and poured it into a glass, then joined her by the window to deliver her drink. The cloud cover made it impossible to see stars or the moon, but the lights of town and the hillside homes twinkled in the distance.

"I love this view," he said. "Doesn't matter what time of day or year, there's always something pretty to see."

"Cliffside Bay's a special place."

Sensing the tension in her voice, he feared they were headed into dangerous territory. He didn't have the energy to fight with her about the preservation of the town.

She crossed the room to sit on the couch. "This was the longest day in the history of man. I think I'll take your advice and sit."

"I agree." He grabbed his scotch and turned some music on. A country ballad blared through the speakers. He turned it down. Only a few hours ago he'd been rocking out with the volume blaring. Would he ever be able to do that again? He plopped onto the other end of couch.

"Thanks for saying goodnight to Dakota. He's smitten with you," Violet said.

"What's up with the way he talks? Is that normal for a three-year-old?"

"He's been tested." She blushed. "It sounds pretentious, but apparently he's gifted."

"I'll say," Kyle said. He'd been tested as a child. They'd said the same about him when he was a child. *Not smart enough to keep from getting a girl pregnant.*

"I'm afraid he's going to get attached to you," Violet said.

Kyle shook his head. "I'm not the type of man a child gets attached to. The rest of the Dogs, but not me."

"You're the type of man Dakota's drawn to. Powerful, successful, athletic. You're like a superhero."

"I'm the opposite of that."

"What makes you think so?" she asked.

"Never mind. Too long a story to go into." That was a lie. It wasn't a long story. His recklessness had ruined his sister's life. Period, end of story.

"Don't feel like you have to talk to me," Violet said. "I know we're both used to living alone."

"Feel free to spend evenings in your room."

"I will. Thanks." She pulled her legs under her and drank from her glass. "I'll just give Dakota a chance to fall into a sound sleep before I go in there. What is this music? Hillbilly hour?"

"No. It's modern country. What's wrong with you?"

"It sounds like caterwauling," she said.

"No way. This is Eric Church. He's awesome."

"Twangy, at best."

"You're so wrong. What do you listen to? Classical? Everything has to be old with you?"

"I like pop music just fine."

"Country is pop music these days. Anyway, I love the old stuff too. Waylon. Willie. George Strait."

She looked at him blankly.

"Do not tell me you don't know who they are?" he asked.

"I've heard of them, yes." She rubbed her temples like the music was giving her a headache.

He shut off the music and tossed her the television remote. "You want to watch something?"

She slid it back to him. "You choose. I haven't finished a show in years. I'm always so tired by the end of the day I fall asleep on the couch. Next thing I know, I wake up at two a.m. totally disoriented."

Kyle flicked on the television. The channel was set on ESPN where commentators were analyzing the upcoming Sunday games, including Brody's San Francisco Sharks.

"Brody Mullen's in top form," one of them said. "Never better. In an interview last week, he shut down the rumors of his retirement."

Football. Would he be able to watch the games over at Brody's with the rest of the Dogs? Was his life over as he knew it?

The enormity of the day's events washed over him. Who was he kidding? He couldn't do this. It didn't matter how many nannies he employed. Raising Mollie was his job and his alone. Therein lay the exact problem. Alone was no good. A little girl needed a mother. He needed a wife and a house and a desire and skills to become a family man. He *wasn't* a family man. He couldn't be like Zane and immediately jump into fatherhood without a moment's hesitation. How was he supposed to have any kind of life? No dating, no women. He couldn't bring some random woman home when he had a little baby. Not that he could even go out anyway. He had a baby.

I have a baby.

Kyle changed the channel to CNN and muted the volume. He rose from the sofa and went to the windows. What he wanted was to talk to his Dogs. Whenever one of them was in crisis, they called an emergency meeting. Tonight, it was impossible. No one had time for him or his problems. Brody was in the middle of the football season and rarely home. Lance was in San Francisco for a few days with Brody and Kara. Zane was busy building the brewery and planning his wedding with Honor, not to mention being a father to six-year-old Jubie. Honor, an honorary Dog, had done what she could for him, but she needed to be home with her own child. That left Jackson. He was the best guy in the world to talk to when you were in trouble, but he was with Maggie doing whatever married people did. They were all where they belonged. Together with their families. As much as he'd like to pretend otherwise, he was alone.

Kyle looked at the clock. Only nine. Another hour before it was time to feed Mollie.

"You want to talk about it?" Violet's voice made him jump. He'd been so deep in thought he'd almost forgotten she was there.

He turned to look at her. Earlier she'd changed into sweats and a t-shirt and wrapped her hair into a bun, which highlighted her long neck. The woman was a beauty with her silky caramel skin, light brown hair kissed with streaks of blond, yoga-hard body, and delicate facial features. Her brown eyes, when not focused with laser beams of hatred on him, exuded warmth. That perky little mouth had caught his eye the moment he'd met her—until said perky little mouth had opened and started talking.

Kyle sat back on the couch. "The truth is, I'm a pack-and-play type of guy."

"You've *been* a pack-and-play type of guy. Unless you've changed your mind and want to give her up?"

The idea of giving Mollie away left him gutted. He couldn't let her go to strangers. She belonged with him. He was her father. God help her, he was her father. "I can't give her up. Even though it would probably be better for her."

"It wouldn't be." She paused and drank from her glass. "My dad's an awful person, but he once told me if I was worried about something to come up with a plan of attack."

"I suppose I need a house." He ran his fingertip around the rim of the glass as words floated through his mind. *House. Home. Family.*

"Just take it day by day for a few months. She's little and won't remember anything of this time. You can find a permanent home later. This parenting gig is hard enough without beating yourself up. Believe me, if I had a nickel for every time I felt like I'd failed Dakota I wouldn't have money problems. Which I do. I most definitely do."

"That bad?" His heart softened. He knew what it was like to be desperate. Nothing could remedy the stress of money problems.

"Pretty much," she said.

They drank in silence for a few minutes.

"Is Dakota why you're still single?" he asked.

"You mean because having a kid means you have no life?" she asked, clearly amused.

"That, yeah."

"You're right to be worried, honestly. I'd love to tell you differently, but I'd be lying. Although, you have money, so you can hire people to help you. It's just been me with an occasional sitter since day one."

He groaned and pressed the ridge of his nose between his thumb and finger. "Oh, God."

She laughed. "It's going to be okay. I promise. You'll get used to it."

"I'd appreciate if you refrained from a lecture on my shallowness, but I was thinking about football."

"Football?" she asked.

"Will I ever be able to watch another game? And what about poker night?"

"Your life's not over. You'll get babysitters lined up or you can bring Mollie with you places. Honor or Kara will look after her from time to time. Everyone's going to fall in love with Mollie Blue in an instant."

"She's cute, right? Like extra cute?" he asked.

"Yes, Papa, she is. You have a village. That village is about to become super important. Days of being a lone wolf are over."

"Am I a lone wolf?" he asked.

"About as lone wolf as a man can get, yes." She drank more of her wine. "Anyway, everyone but me is about to start having babies. I'll lay money on it that Kara and Brody are pregnant by spring. I know Maggie and Jackson want one. They're waiting until her career gets going, but we both know that's only a matter of time."

"Honor and Zane want to adopt if they can," Kyle said.

"Or use a surrogate. Zane's sperm and a borrowed egg."

"Borrowed? Is that the right word?"

She giggled. "No, I mean donated."

"That's not right either. Donor. It's a donor egg."

They both laughed, veering toward the hysterical. Long days and secret babies did that to guy.

"To answer your previous question, yes, I'm probably single because of Dakota. It's not that easy to find a man who wants a woman with a kid."

"Tons of single mothers get married." Did they? If he were honest, he wouldn't have considered getting serious with any woman with a child. That said, he didn't want to be serious with any woman. He'd vowed never to get married or have a family. He'd already ruined his sister's life. The one girl who'd needed him more than anyone else, he'd hurt in the worst way. *Don't think about that.*

"Living here's part of the problem. It's a small pool of eligible men under the age of seventy," she said.

"Have you thought about leaving?" he asked.

"I probably will."

"Really?" He looked over at her, surprised.

"I *should* anyway. Someplace bigger. With more opportunities. I need a career. One that will support my son."

Kyle didn't say anything, thinking that through. He understood—probably more than most people—how important it was to have a career that made money.

She stretched her legs in front of her and flexed her feet. The muscles of her calves were certainly well-developed. Seriously, such pretty skin too. *Hello, focus here. She's the enemy.* Suddenly, she didn't feel like the enemy. She felt like a friend. An ally. Someone who understood his life better than anyone else.

"I need a house," he repeated.

"I thought you were building a house up by Jackson and Maggie?"

He and Jackson had bought a two-acre piece of land outside of town. His plan was to build a house on his half once he was ready. "I hired an architectural firm last month. They showed me preliminary plans last week. I wasn't sure it was time. It's a big expense."

"A home of your own, though. I mean, think about that."

"It's what everyone seems to want."

"Except you?" she asked.

"I've been on the fence, to be honest. I like my pack-and-play life."

"Mollie needs a home with a yard and playdates. Cookouts and birthday parties. Daddy and daughter dances. A chance to grow up with the other Dogs' kids."

The sadness in her voice caused a strange aching sensation in his chest. These were all parts of life she wanted for Dakota but didn't think she'd ever have.

"The difference between you and me is—you can give it to your child." She peered into her glass. "That was the idea for my shop. I naively thought it would do so well I could buy a house for us. My friends here would be our new family. I'd give him a real home. My dad was right about me."

"What was he right about?" he asked.

"He told me I'm in love with failure, that I choose it on purpose." Violet flushed and looked away. "I don't know if it's true that I choose it on purpose, but it's undeniable I'm a failure. A big old flop in the game of life."

"You're not a failure. Your shop didn't work, yeah, okay, fine. You tried your hardest and it didn't work. There's no shame in that."

Violet had turned away from him, obviously distracted by the television. Her faced drained of color. She leaned forward slightly as if she couldn't quite believe what was before her. He looked at the screen. A panel of people debated a subject. He wasn't a fan of the talking heads that gave their opinions on everything and anything just to fill news channels for hours upon hours.

"Can you turn it up, please?" Violet asked without looking over at him.

He turned up the volume. The guy in the middle of the panel was Cole Lund, a conservative pastor of a mega church back east. He wasn't sure who the other men were, but they were having a heated debate over abortion.

They listened for a moment. Lund was a windbag who looked like a movie star.

"Turn it off," Violet said.

She'd just asked him to turn it up and now she wanted it off all together?

He didn't argue. When it was off, he turned to look at her. "Everything okay?"

"I'm tired, that's all."

"Did I do something to upset you?" he asked.

"You? No." She looked at him with a blank look in her eyes. "No, not you. I hate Cole Lund."

"Not surprising," Kyle said. "Given your leanings."

"My lefty leanings?"

"Well, yeah."

"His conservative viewpoint is *not* why I hate him," she said.

He waited for her to continue, unable to read her expression but certain she wanted to say more.

"I hate him because he's a hypocrite," she said.

"How do you know?"

"I used to work for him," she said.

"Was he one of those bosses that yells and screams at his staff but acts nice on television?" Kyle asked. "I can't stand people like that."

"No, he's very charming. Too charming."

A shiver ran down the back of his spine. The truth struck him. Violet had had an affair with this guy. Was Lund Dakota's father? Before he could stop himself, the question was out of his mouth. "Is he Dakota's dad?"

She looked at him for a moment then up to the ceiling. A muscle in her cheek clenched as she seemed to wrestle with whether or not to tell him what he already knew. "We had an affair. It was a mistake. But Dakota came from it."

"Did he disappear when you got pregnant?"

"He offered money, but I refused."

"Wow. I don't know what to say," he said.

"Nothing *to* say. I'm not sure why I told you. I never tell anyone."

"Your parents don't know?"

A bitter explosion burst from her chest that might have been laughter, but just as easily could have been a sob. "God no. He's their hero. My dad's the one who got me the job there."

"But shouldn't they know who and what he really is?" Why should Violet have to carry the burden alone? At the very least, her parents should know the man for who he truly was—a hypocritical adulterer who abandoned a young woman bearing his child. An urge to wrap her in his arms rushed through him. She seemed to have shrunk. The woman who usually annoyed him with her assured elitism was no longer evident in the slight, sad woman in front of him.

"I'm afraid of what my father would do if he knew. He'd lose his mind over this—probably march into a service shouting the truth. It has to remain a secret."

"In my experience, secrets never turn out well," Kyle said.

Again, she looked at him for a drawn-out moment before speaking. "I'm sure that's correct, but my family's built on secrets, lies, and deception. There's no other way to appear perfect from the outside looking in."

"One of those?"

Violet nodded. "Everyone here in town thought we were the ideal family. We were wealthy and churchgoing. My mom headed up every committee and volunteered at school. My dad was an attorney. Pillars of the community and all that. But at home they were cold and rigid, hypercritical."

The pieces that made up Violet were starting to fall into place. Were her causes a way to prove her worth? He could relate. He could say the same about his own work.

She walked over to the bar and washed her glass out in the sink before turning to him. "I should get to bed. Dakota's an early riser."

He wished she would stay. Facing the baby by himself seemed too much for him to handle. What if he dropped her? How many ounces had she said? Four or six?

"Good luck tonight with Mollie. She's small, so don't be surprised if she wakes up every two to three hours. Remember, four ounces of formula. Water no warmer than body temperature.

"Four ounces. I've got it."

"You'll be fine. After tonight you can decide if you want a night nanny. I won't hold it against you, I promise. You have a company to run, which you can't do without sleep. Tap on my door if you need me. I'm a light sleeper."

He stood as she crossed the room and reached for her arm. "Thank you. For real."

"You're welcome. For real."

He held out his hand. "Peace?"

"Peace." She placed her hand in his. Her skin was like the softest he'd ever felt. She smelled great too. For a fleeting moment he wondered what the rest of her felt like. *None of that.* They were no longer at war, but if he read her right and he usually did when it came to women, Violet Ellis didn't like him any better than she had earlier in the day. The woman was merely performing a job.

Good. He needed a nanny, not a girlfriend.

After she left the room, he went to stand at the window for the second time that night. Without Violet next to him, the lights of town seemed dimmer than earlier. *I am alone. As I've always been. No reason to cry about it now.*

* * *

Kyle woke at 1 in the morning to the sound of a kitten's mew. He rolled to his side, his head thick with sleep. The previous day's events rushed over him. The sound was no kitten. This was the cry of a baby. His baby daughter. He sat up and looked over to the makeshift cradle. He'd changed her and given her a bottle at ten, as instructed. The timing was just as Violet had predicted.

Violet had said babies had different cries for different needs. Soon he would be able to tell them apart. Right now, they all sounded the same. They all had a similar effect, which was to break him into a cold sweat.

Shivering, he threw off the blankets and rushed over to Mollie. He waded through flailing arms and legs—she'd escaped the burrito—and carried her over to the armchair to change her. *Change first. Feed next.*

How was he supposed to fix a bottle with her screaming like

63

this? His hands shook as he loosened her diaper. *Only wet, thank God.*

He held her legs in the air like Violet had shown him and swiped at her little bottom with a wipe. Amazingly, he managed to secure the new diaper on despite the howling and kicking. He cradled Mollie in his arms as he walked into the bathroom. Earlier he'd measured the powder and poured it in the bottle. All he had to do was get the water in there and shake. *I can do this.*

"You'll have to lie on this nice rug for a moment," he said.

Mollie's face turned purple as she continued to scream. Could a baby hurt themselves this way?

His hands continued to shake as he filled the bottle with water. Once he had it ready, he sank into the chair and put the bottle in her mouth. She immediately quieted and commenced with the same violent sucking she'd done earlier.

He gazed at her as she ate. How could anyone be this tiny or cute?

When she finished her bottle, Kyle wrapped her in the burrito and put her back into her drawer. He watched her sleep. Everything about her was perfect, from her fingernails to her toes. Tears stung his tired eyes as he gazed down at the person he'd helped bring into this world. His carelessness and selfishness had aided in the creation of this beautiful baby girl. In some perverse turn of events, he was alive and her mother was dead. Katy was the one who should be here, raising this precious infant into an adult. Not him. Anyone but him.

He spoke silently to his little girl. *I'm not worthy. I know that. You'd be better off with just about anyone else. But I'll do my best to take care of you. I won't leave you. I'll try and be a better man for you.*

But could he? Really? Autumn. He'd wrecked his sister's life with his carelessness. He saw her as she'd been that day, mangled and bloody in a hospital bed. Would he do it again? Was he fated to destroy those he loved the most?

Pig Boy.

Pig for short.

He stumbled back to bed and turned off the lamp. As tired as he was, sleep didn't come. Instead, he tumbled backward through the years.

He was born Daniel Kyle Hickman.

His family's trailer, with its sunken roof and boarded up windows, resided next to the Keller's pig farm. His father worked for the Kellers, shoveling pig excrement and hay and trash from one place to another. *That's all it is, kid. Shoveling nasty shit from one end of the property to the other.*

The odor of pig dung permeated every aspect of Kyle's life. The scent had worked its way into the fabric of his clothes, the strands of his hair, even the lining of his nostrils. Every breath reminded him of who he was. *Pig.*

He was six years old when the Miller boys gave him the nickname that haunted him from that day forward.

That first day of school, the sun baked and cracked the dirt playground. Insidious dust covered his holey tennis shoes. His jeans were three inches too short and dirty; the material of his t-shirt so thin that his ribs showed through. He was even more embarrassed by his greasy hair, unwashed skin, and grime under his fingernails. Their utilities at home had been shut off for weeks. His mother had washed clothes in the creek until it dried up under the late summer heat. He smelled bad. He knew it from the moment he'd taken a seat next to a girl on the bus that morning. She'd held her breath and moved as far from him as she could.

At recess, cruelty thrived like the weeds under the leaky drinking fountain. The other children ran and played, despite the heat, in their new shoes and first day of school clothes. He made himself as small as he could, shrinking into the shadow of the awning by the back doors, avoiding eye contact. The Miller brothers had already spotted him. It was too late. Tim and Jason Miller. A year apart in age, they were in the same grade and bigger than the other kids with flat, mean faces and eyes made for detecting the weak and vulnerable. They'd found Kyle without trouble. He'd seen them staring at him as he gobbled his free school lunch.

The Miller family had lived in that part of Oregon for longer than anyone could remember. They were rough, uncultured men who hunted bear and deer with a ruthless desire to kill as many live animals as they could in one lifetime. One day, Kyle and his dad had been behind their truck as his father drove into town. A tarp covered the back of their truck. Every time they hit a bump in the road, the tarp would flutter open. At least a dozen deer carcasses lay mangled and lifeless. One seemed to stare at Kyle from eyes frozen in the moment before death.

Their father worked in the woods, like so many other men in town. The old man had served jail time for logging on protected land. He'd come out of prison meaner than when he'd gone in and took his frustrations out on his boys. Bullies beget bullies.

On the playground that afternoon, they drew close and pinched their noses with their finger and thumb.

"You smell like shit," Jason said.

"He lives on a pig farm, dummy," Tim said.

Kyle shook his head, but no sound came from his mouth. *No, we don't own the pig farm. We don't own anything.*

He crossed his skinny arms across his sunken chest that matched the roof of his parents' trailer.

"Let's call him Pig Boy."

"Just Pig."

"Pig Hickman. Has a nice ring to it."

So it began. As these things do, the name stuck and soon most of the children called him Pig whenever they were out of the earshot of adults. There were many who tortured him throughout his school years, but no one more than the Miller brothers. Wherever Kyle went, it seemed the Miller boys were there to trip him, kick him, beat him, and threaten to kill him if he ever told anyone.

He didn't allow himself to think of the Miller brothers or of the little boy he once was, not in concrete blocks of memory anyway. The bullies were with him, just as Pig was, lingering in the shadows of his heart, reminding him to fight with everything he had.

There in the bed, with the thousand-thread-count sheets, he let the tears drip from his eyes. *I will not let them win. They will not ruin my relationship with Mollie like they did with my sister.* Autumn with her auburn hair and trusting green eyes.

For the first time since he left home, he spoke to her as if she were there beside him like when they were kids. *I tried, Autumn. But they were too strong, too fast, and I was too weak.*

They'd taken everything from him. His childhood. His sister. His brother, Stone.

I'm strong now. I'll protect Mollie like I couldn't protect you.

You can do it, Kyle. I believe in you.

And somewhere in the dark night, a peace washed over him. Tomorrow would come. He would meet whatever came head on with courage. He would be the man Mollie needed. He was Kyle Hicks now. Not Pig. Not Daniel Kyle Hickman.

I am Kyle Hicks, Mollie Blue's daddy.

CHAPTER FOUR

VIOLET WOKE TO a wet kiss on her cheek and the blue eyes of her son. Light snuck in under the drawn shades. Daylight. What time was it? She glanced at the clock. Just after seven. How had Kyle done? She must get up and take her shift.

"Hi Mama."

"Good morning. Did you just wake up?"

"No. I been awake." He pointed to the corner of the room where a stack of magazines lay scattered on the floor. "I looked at pictures so you could sleep."

"Where did you get those?"

"In there." He pointed to the living room. "Kale's on the couch with Mollie."

On the couch? He must have had a rough night.

She got out of bed and slipped on a pair of leggings and a t-shirt. "Come on, let's go check on them."

Dakota led the way. Kyle was indeed on the couch, as was Mollie. She was asleep on his chest without her burrito blanket and dressed only in a onesie. This wouldn't do. He must not get her accustomed to sleeping with him. She would convince him today to hire a night nanny. This was no job for a single man.

She put her finger to her lips to make sure Dakota knew to be quiet. They would let them sleep while they could. The baby had different ideas. Mollie fluttered her arms and started to cry. Kyle jerked awake, his eyes as wild as his hair.

"Good morning," Violet said. "Give me the baby. I'll take over. You go get some rest in your room."

He sat up and ran his hands through his hair. "I can't. I have a meeting."

"What time?" she asked.

"Eight. Crap, what time is it?"

"Language," Violet said.

"Sorry," he said.

"It's a bit after seven." She went to the sink and grabbed an empty bottle. One handed, with the baby cradled against her, she scooped formula into the bottle, added water, and shook. She sat in the armchair and stroked Mollie's fuzzy head. Mollie clamped onto the bottle, sucking with a slight sigh of contentment.

"Mama, I'm hungry." Dakota scowled at her. "Not just the baby."

"We can order something from room service. I'm starved too." Kyle sat on the edge of the couch with his head in his hands. "I've got to take a shower before my meeting. I smell like sour milk. Mollie was up at least three times last night. I feel like death."

He didn't look so great either. Dark circles and bags under his eyes, in addition to his scruffy face, made him look like he'd been on an all-night binger. "Babies will do that to you."

"I want pancakes," Dakota said.

"Yes. Pancakes and bacon and twelve cups of coffee," Kyle said.

"I want bacon too," Dakota said.

Kyle moved over to the small desk and picked up the phone. "I'll order extra bacon."

Mollie arched her back and jerked her mouth from the bottle.

Violet raised the baby to her shoulder and patted her back. While Kyle ordered, Mollie let out a rather large burp for such a small person.

"Good girl." Violet brought her back to her chest and placed the bottle in Mollie's mouth once again. Dakota had moved to a spot of sunshine near the window to play with his toy truck.

She listened to Kyle ordering a ridiculous amount of food for three people, including a vegetarian omelet. *Thoughtful.* She put that thought aside for now. No reason to soften toward the enemy.

After he hung up, he wandered across the room like a man after a battle.

"Uncle. I need a night nanny."

"There's no shame in it." One night and he'd already given in? Men *were* the weaker sex. Truthfully, she couldn't blame him. If she'd been able to afford help, she would have done it too. Plus, he had a company to run.

"Can you call Nora for me today?" he asked. "I'm going to be in this meeting all day."

"Consider it done," she said.

He sank onto the couch. "I have to find a house, don't I?"

"That would be best."

"I'll have my assistant put her feelers out in the community for a rental." He rubbed his eyes. "There's got to be a temporary situation for us while I get my house built."

For us? Did that include her and Dakota? "Will you start building from the plans?"

"I haven't got much choice," he said. "Mollie needs a nursery." His gaze darted to Dakota and back to her. "I'm going to lay all my cards on the table here. I need you. Is there any way you can commit to a year with us? I need stability and so does Mollie."

A year? It would give her enough time to get her life back on track.

"I'll find a big enough rental for all of us," he said.

"Why me? You could find anyone else."

"I trust you," he said. "This is my baby girl we're talking about. It can't just be anyone."

Welcome to parenthood.

"I can give you a year," she said. *God help me.*

* * *

After Kyle left for his meeting, Violet called Nora, the town's one-woman employment agency for Cliffside Bay. Mollie was down for her morning nap. Dakota sat cross-legged in front of the television in the living room, thrilled to be allowed to watch a show during the day. Usually he was allowed only a half hour after dinner, but these were desperate times.

She and Nora exchanged pleasantries, including confirmation of the demise of her shop. "I'm so sorry to hear it didn't work out," Nora said with a sympathetic cluck of her tongue. "But you know what they say. When one door closes, another opens."

Violet was glad they were on the phone. She could roll her eyes without fear of hurting the older woman's feelings. If Violet could choose a grandmother for Dakota it would be Nora. She was kind and plump with white hair and pink cheeks and smelled like cookies. Yet, her general optimism and assurance of a happy ending grated on Violet's nerves these days. Nothing like utter failure to turn a person into a hater of encouraging platitudes.

"What can I do for you, dear?" Nora asked.

Violet was about to launch right into the description of what they needed. However, she realized Nora would need context. "You know Kyle Hicks, right?"

"Do I ever. What a dashing young man he is. You know I do a little matchmaking on the side, and goodness knows he's exactly who I would choose for you. Please tell me you two have mended your disagreements and fallen madly in love."

"In love with Kyle Hicks? Never in a million years. Nora, you *know* what he did to this town with his monstrosity of a resort. How can you even suggest I have a relationship with him?"

Silence greeted her from the other end of the phone. She could practically feel the waves of disapproval coming through the cell phone tower and into her phone.

"Dear, I've known you a long time," Nora said.

"Yes." Great. Here comes the lecture on how she needed to find a nice young man and a father for Dakota.

"I know life hasn't been easy for you. Not just raising Dakota alone, but your parents…well, I believe I have some insight into the challenges of your childhood. You're a clever girl, and I admire your sense of conviction and your ability to stand up for what you believe in."

"Which is this town." Violet moved from the desk to pace in front of the window.

"Righto. However, convictions don't keep you warm at night."

"We won't need warmth at night if we keep destroying the planet. Global climate change will keep us darn warm at night."

"Yes dear, all true. But love is our only chance of saving the planet."

"All due respect, Nora, love has nothing to do with protecting our environment. Large, greedy countries of the world need to stop emitting dangerous fossil fuels into the environment." Violet glanced over at her son happily grinning back at Elmo. Her precious boy. What kind of world would they leave him?

"Your parents convictions made them unyielding and without compassion. They hurt you. Perhaps your own convictions are just as damaging. Don't be so sure of your beliefs that they blind you to something wonderful." Another silence. "Now, enough of the lecture. Let's get back to what Kyle needs."

She'd almost forgotten the whole reason for her call. How did she explain? Maybe she shouldn't. Perhaps the old busybody deserves to be in the dark, given the juiciness of *this* gossip. *Not nice. Nora means well. Don't be mean.* "Kyle has unexpectedly become a father." She explained about the mother's death and subsequent arrival of baby Mollie Blue.

"I'll be," Nora said.

"He's asked me to become her nanny for a year, which as you know, comes at a good time given my personal circumstance."

"It does appear to be perfect timing. Almost meant to be." Already Nora had recovered sufficiently to return to her previous theme of *Kyle and Violet sitting in a tree.*

Violet suppressed a sigh but went ahead with another giant eye roll. "After only one night with a week-old baby, he's decided he needs a night nurse."

"It makes perfect sense. He can't possibly work without decent sleep."

I did it.

Out loud, Violet murmured a polite agreement.

"As luck would have it, I might have the perfect candidate. Melissa Tipton is her name. She just moved to town from the city after working for a family there. Shall I send her over this evening for an interview?"

Without a doubt, Nora had the perfect candidate. Everything was just meant to be and fell right into place in *the world according to Nora.* It must be nice.

"That would be great," Violet said.

* * *

That evening, Violet and Kyle ushered Melissa Tipton into the living room of the suite. Since arriving home promptly at 5 p.m., Kyle hadn't abandoned the baby other than to gobble a quick dinner. If her mother were here, which thankfully she wasn't, she would have told Kyle that he was spoiling the baby. Mollie would expect to be held all the time if he didn't set her down for one blessed minute. Violet disagreed. A baby this young couldn't be spoiled. If anything, bonding with her father was just what she needed.

There was a further problem. Violet was falling in love with baby Mollie too. She must remember that she was the nanny, not the mother. Given the jealous way Dakota was acting, this fact seemed to be eluding them both. When Honor had called to offer to pick him up for dinner with her family, Violet gratefully accepted. He'd been clingy and whiney, neither of which were like him. Honor's arrival cheered him considerably. He took her hand and followed her out the door without a backward glance at his mother. Typical.

Now, as they gathered in the sitting area for the interview, Violet took a moment to observe Miss Tipton without drawing attention to herself, since the candidate seemed fixated on Kyle the moment she walked in the door. Melissa Tipton couldn't be over twenty-five but was probably closer to twenty. She had a sleek mane of black hair and exotic, almond shaped eyes that reminded Violet of a Siamese cat. Her interview outfit was a slim, fitted peach suit and four-inch black pumps that showed both her curvy body and shapely legs to utter perfection. Her full lips and wide mouth combined with high cheekbones bordered on the ridiculous. Who looked like this outside of Hollywood?

Violet hated her immediately.

As she leaned closer to peer at the baby in Kyle's arms, a velvety, almost lyrical sound rose from Melissa Tipton's ample and almost certainly cosmetically enhanced chest. "She's adorable. May I hold her?"

Kyle, without taking his eyes from the small-waisted Miss Tipton, handed the baby over like a man in a trance.

"What a doll," Melissa said. "Has there ever been a prettier baby?"

Kyle beamed. "Thank you, Melissa. I couldn't agree more."

"Call me Mel. All my friends do."

"Thanks, Mel. Will do." Kyle grinned. There he was. Wolfish Kyle. All thoughts of his baby forgotten the moment a sexy girl walked in the door.

"I'll take her back now, if you don't mind," Kyle said.

"Must I?" Melissa asked.

"You'll have plenty of time with her later if we agree on employment," Violet said drily.

"Yes, I suppose so," Melissa said as she placed Mollie back in Kyle's arms.

Mollie stiffened for a second but then settled back to sleep.

Violet slid back into her manager skin. Her business may have failed, but she knew how to interview and hire staff. "Melissa, your resume indicates you've been with two families as a night nurse."

"Please, call me Mel. Melissa reminds me of the nuns." She looked over at Kyle and smiled. "I went to Catholic school and suffer from PTSD."

Kyle raised an eyebrow and grimaced. "I'm sure." God, was he this much of a sucker for a pretty woman? *I wish he thought I was pretty.* Her stomach turned over the moment that thought slipped into her mind. *I can't stand this man, remember. I don't care if he thinks I'm the most beautiful woman in the world. What's it to me? This is a job. Nothing more, nothing less.*

Get your head in the game.

"Mel, what do you like about this kind of work?" Violet asked.

Melissa smiled and tucked her chin in an expression of reticence and self-effacement. She purred her answer in a tone worthy of a heroine in a classic film from the forties. "My story's simple, like me. I'm new to town. I'm an artist in need of a day job. Or, night, as the case may be." She smiled. The tips of her canine teeth were a smidge too sharp. "And, I'm *craving* time with a baby." She clutched her chest as she emphasized the word craving, like it was life-giving. "I adore newborns. Until I have my own children, this is the best work ever."

"Super cool," Kyle said. "The world needs more people like you."

If she were in a cartoon, Violet would have done one of those abrupt double takes. What had baby Mollie done to Kyle Hicks? *The world needs more people like you?* Was he really taken in by this Mel's act? Violet was not. She could see right through Mel, formerly known as Melissa. This woman was a fake, like a mean girl in high school with her shiny hair and gleaming eyes. She was the kind that acted nice around parents, but the moment they left the room, her panther claws whipped from her paws and slashed anything in her path.

Why had Nora sent this woman? It wasn't like her not to see through to the essence of a person. That said, Nora had Kyle pegged wrong too. This whole town had lost its bearings and any sense of heritage.

Kyle and Mel continued chatting. She told him of her travels to Europe and how she truly got in *touch* with her inner soul on the shores of Lake Como. All that clear air and pasta and wine had acted like a crystal ball. "I suddenly knew what to do. I needed to live in a beautiful place—my muse, if you will."

If you will?

Mel continued. "In art school, I'd lost part of myself because of the competition. Who had more talent? Who had the drive to carry one forward to the next level? These things ate away at me until I was an empty shell going through the motions. When I left my environment, it was as if everything were suddenly clear." Mel tossed her hair behind one shoulder and crossed her legs. "Now I know that to really connect with my art and the universe, I need to be in a quiet place." Mel was obviously the type of woman who enjoyed a man's attention. The type who focused only on the men in the room. She instinctually knew how to play to a man's weakness and how to exploit it.

Violet slid her gaze to Kyle. He was nodding like a fool, obviously taken with her. *I give it two weeks and he'll be sleeping with her.* Disgusted, she turned away and examined her nails. Why had she committed to a year with this ridiculous man?

Because you're a loser.

She pushed aside her father's voice and focused on the conversation at hand, asking several questions about Mel's ideas and experience with newborns. Despite looking like a debutante, she appeared to have a good sense about feedings, swaddling, and strategies for sleep training.

"The ultimate goal is for her to sleep through the night sooner rather than later, correct?" Violet asked.

"As much as it will pain me to leave her, yes." Mel flashed a dazzling smile.

"When can you start?" Kyle asked.

"Tonight, if you need me," Mel said. "I'm renting a room from an elderly lady just up the street from here. I can come at ten each evening and stay through until the morning, if that works for you guys." For the first time, Mel's gaze turned to Violet. "Look at the two of you. Wow, such a beautiful couple. Violet, you look amazing for just having a baby. Did you do the Kardashian cleanse?"

"What? No, we're not...I'm not Mollie's mother," Violet said.

Kyle, to her irritation, had the gall to look amused. "We're not together. She's my day nanny."

"Oh, my bad. I assumed you were married," Mel said.

Had she just sat up straighter and stuck her chest out another inch?

"Didn't Nora tell you about Mr. Hicks' situation?" Violet asked.

"Not really. She said you were a couple in need of a night nurse," Mel said.

Damn Nora and her meddling ways. Violet shifted in the chair. Why was it so hot in here? She played with the collar of her blouse to cool her overheated skin.

"I'm a single father," Kyle said.

His voice hitched, but he offered no further explanation. How was he supposed to explain it? *I had a one-night stand with a vulnerable young woman and she died.* A sliver of sympathy inched its way into Violet's consciousness. He was trying to do the right thing. Given the circumstances, he deserved a little grace, even though she hated to admit it.

"I'm sorry to have presumed," Mel said.

"We're friends," Kyle said. "Violet's doing me a favor."

"I have a little boy," Violet said. "Like you, I needed a job, so it's not really a favor."

Kyle smiled at her, his eyes like dark blue silk, and for a split second they were on the same team—the two of them in it together.

"How old is your little guy?" Mel asked.

"Dakota's three," Violet said.

"And you're all living here together?" Mel asked.

"For now. Until I find a house," Kyle said. "I'm a real estate developer, so it shouldn't take long. I have a piece of property I'm going to build on, but for now I need a rental. Something big enough for all of us." Kyle went on to explain that the crib would remain in the living room and that Violet and Dakota were in one room while he was in the other.

"Baby Mollie's arrival was a surprise, then?" The way Mel's eyes calculated and evaluated everything at once sent a shiver down Violet's spine. She could almost hear Mel's mind working. *Rich, gorgeous single father available for the catch.*

"You could say that, yes," Kyle said. Again, he didn't elaborate.

"May I ask about her mother?" Mel leaned forward slightly and widened her eyes as if so very sensitive and compassionate.

I can't stand her.

"She passed away. So, it's just Mollie and me." Kyle cleared his throat.

"How tragic," Mel said. "I'm sorry for your loss."

"Yes, it is." Kyle's tone and expression converted to an unemotional professionalism. "Let's talk details. I'll offer you the going rate for night nannies and will expect you every night of the week from ten p.m. until six a.m. We'll only need you until Mollie begins to sleep through the night."

"Excellent," Mel said.

"Now, I'll let you go home and do whatever you need to do. We'll see you around ten tonight." Kyle stood, still holding Mollie, who slumbered in obvious contentment. She was a good baby, despite last night's frequent feedings. If Violet guessed correctly, she would sleep through the night in just a few months. *Keep eating, baby girl, so we can get rid of Mel.*

Kyle looked down at the sleeping baby in his arms, then back up at Mel. "When you arrive tonight, I'll have a keycard waiting at the front desk. If you ladies will excuse me, I have some business to take care of." Kyle left the room with Mollie.

Violet stuffed her hands in the pockets of her jeans.

"I shouldn't have asked about his wife," Mel said. "But I like to understand the dynamics in a family. I have a holistic approach, if you will."

Again, with the *if you will.*

"I think he took it as merely curious," Violet said.

"I can see that now. It was insensitive of me. The poor man just lost his wife."

"She wasn't his wife."

"Girlfriend then?"

"Something like that. Anyway, your job is to take care of Mollie, not worry about her father." Even to her own ears she sounded like a scolding school teacher with her naughty pupil. Or a jealous girlfriend. She couldn't decide which was worse.

"Oh, I see." Mel elongated the vowels. "You poor thing. We've all been there."

"Excuse me?"

"How you feel about him. But he's put you in the friend zone even though you're the one who would do anything for him, even help raise the child he had with someone else."

"That's not it at all."

"Please, you don't have to pretend with me. I can assure you I'm no threat." There they were—claws fully extended while her voice dripped with honey.

"You've quite the imagination, but you have this wrong," Violet said. "Kyle and I are barely friends. We're certainly not involved."

Mel did the wide-eyed thing again and held out her hands in a sign of submission. "I'm sorry. Again, I've misinterpreted."

"Don't make a habit of it. I can assure you, I'm the one Kyle will listen to when it comes to his baby. You answer to me as much as you do him. This is a business arrangement. You're not family or even a friend and I expect you to remember that." Violet turned toward the door. "I'll walk you out."

"No need. I'm quite capable of figuring out how to get where I'm going."

I bet you can.

* * *

A few minutes later, Violet knocked on Kyle's bedroom. "Do you need anything?"

The door opened. Kyle appeared without Mollie in his arms. He'd changed from his work clothes into a pair of faded jeans and a t-shirt. His tousled hair and bare feet reminded her of an afternoon last August when they'd all hung out at Brody's pool. She'd stayed as far away from him as possible that day. Now she was close enough to smell his cologne. *The heady scent of Kyle.*

Behind him, Mollie was in the middle of the bed, swaddled in her pink blanket.

"She woke up, so I changed her," he said. "It's time for her evening bottle, right?"

She glanced at the clock. It was just after seven. "Yes, perfect timing. I think we're getting her on a routine already."

"You with your routines," he said.

"You'll thank me later."

"I'm thanking you now." He motioned for her to come inside the room. "Keep me company while I feed her?"

The request pleased her more than it should. "Sure."

She grabbed the already made bottle from the dresser as he gathered the baby into his arms.

"Let's go in the living room," he said. "Would you like a glass of wine? I imagine it was a long day."

"It was. I forgot how hard a newborn is." She led the way to the living room. "Plus, Dakota acted awful. I think he's jealous."

"He's used to having you all to himself."

"True."

She helped herself to wine while he settled into the easy chair with the baby. Without asking, she poured him a scotch. He thanked her when she left it on the end table.

Violet found her same spot on the couch from the night before and curled her legs under her. She stole glances at him as she sipped from her glass of wine. His sharp nose and angular features appeared softer in the dim light, making him seem younger and almost vulnerable. He *was* sexy. No question, unfortunately. His remarkably high cheekbones and chiseled jaw screamed of strength with a dose of danger. Not that he was her type. She liked blond men, surfers, like Zane and Jackson. Not this dangerous, wolfish man before her.

He surely didn't look wolfish now, not with the way he gazed down at his daughter with a look of pure love, his dark lashes splayed against his cheekbones. A slight dimple on the left side of his mouth twitched occasionally like an involuntary smile.

He glanced up, catching her staring. She flushed and looked away.

"Am I doing it wrong?"

Violet turned back to him. "Wrong? You mean the feeding?"

He nodded. "Is the angle of the bottle right?"

"No, you're just right."

"Are you sure? Because I feel like a giant oaf around her."

"You're anything but an oaf."

"She deserves the best. Sadly, I'm all she has."

"You're enough." The back of her throat ached.

"I'm hanging on to every word you're saying for dear life."

She looked toward the window, catching their reflection. They looked like a happy couple with their newborn. *Hardly.* "I remember what it was like those first few weeks. The utter terror."

"Terror. Yes." He smiled down at Mollie, who ate with her usual fervor. "The cutest terrorist in the world."

Tell me more.

Where had that come from? Twenty-four hours ago, she hated him. That was before she saw the human side of him.

She supposed when one sat across from an enemy and witnessed their vulnerabilities it wasn't so easy to marginalize them from your own experience. Without armor to deflect their innate humanity it became obvious how similar they were to you. Fear and love simultaneously steered the course of our lives. The study of history told the same tales repeatedly and yet we never learned. Wars continued over power and money, destroying lives and alienating cultures from one another. If only we could set aside our metal shields and bare our hearts. Perhaps then the world might solve its problems.

Had she taken the time to ask more questions of Kyle rather than to cast judgement, maybe they could have been friends and worked through a solution together. He'd brought jobs to their town. The town she cared so much about. Maybe she had been wrong.

Mollie had finished half the bottle. He hoisted her up to his shoulder and patted her back.

"Wait, here. You need this." She grabbed a burping cloth from the stack that she'd unpacked earlier and placed it on his shoulder. "This is to keep the spit-up from ruining every single one of your shirts."

"I wondered what those were. I thought they were cloth diapers."

She laughed. "They kind of look like them."

Mollie burped.

"You left kind of abruptly after the interview," she said.

"That girl." Kyle said placed the bottle back in Mollie's mouth. "She reminds me of a cat."

"A cat?"

"A smart cat about to catch a bird in midair and eat the entire thing, bones and all."

She smiled. "Would you believe I thought the same thing?"

He met her eyes. "I would."

"We can interview someone else."

"I could tell you didn't like her," he said.

"She's fake and pretentious. I can't stand people like that."

"She's like twelve years old, so that's part of it," he said. "Maybe trying too hard."

"I figured you liked that about her."

"What does that mean?" An edge crept into his voice.

She shrugged. "You know. Nubile and willing."

A faint pink flush spread over his neck. What would it feel like to press her lips against the muscle that connected to his shoulder? *Stop it.* What was happening to her? Loneliness, that's all it was. The last man to touch her in an intimate way had been Cole. She'd already made enough mistakes with one man for a lifetime. No reason to do so again just because her flesh was weak.

"I suppose I deserve that. Mollie's evidence of my ways."

Violet sipped from her glass, unsure what to say. "It's not as simple as that," she said at last.

"It might be." He spoke in hushed tones.

"She wasn't a child. You didn't coerce her."

The barest flicker of humor sparkled in his eyes. "I've never had to coerce anyone into my bed."

Desire shot through her. "I'm sure."

"Most women aren't cold to my charms."

"You mean like me?"

"I *could* be referring to you, yes."

"My convictions are stronger than my attractions," she said.

"So, you *were* attracted to me." His eyes twinkled at her, teasing. He lifted Mollie to his shoulder.

She flushed, remembering the first night they met. She'd been at The Oar with Honor for a much-needed break from motherhood and real life. He'd come in, all muscular and sexy with a gaze that combed her body and destroyed all reason. But then, he'd ruined it. "Until you opened your mouth."

"You were the one who attacked me," he said.

"Is that how you remember it?" she asked.

His voice lowered, seductive and husky. "As I recall, we were having a nice cozy dance and I was admiring your beautiful face and the feel of your silky skin against my fingertips."

She resisted the urge to lean closer.

"You shivered when I placed my hand on the small of your back," he said.

"And that told you what exactly?"

"I was quite certain I'd be taking you home with me later that night. That is, until we returned to the table and you learned of my connection to the lodge. Presto, you transformed into a raving lunatic."

"Could you be more arrogant? I wouldn't have gone to bed with you even if I hadn't discovered your nefarious plans for this town." She laughed, despite her best intention to the contrary.

"Nefarious?" He grinned. "I'm hardly nefarious."

"Seriously, stop talking." How could a man be so utterly charming and infuriating at the same time?

"You know I speak the truth. We had major sparks that first night." He tossed a throw pillow at her. "You felt it too. Admit it."

He *did* speak the truth. That dance had been imprinted on her consciousness. With his thighs pressed against her and one strong arm around her waist, she'd wanted to put her hands in his thick hair and pull his mouth to hers. Being in his arms had seemed like a revisit to a long-lost love, familiar and exciting. Truth is, had she not discovered his connection to the lodge that night, she might have gone to bed with him. She'd been drunk with desire. But that was then. Now she could barely stand to be in the same room with the guy. Right? Wasn't that her story? Was she sticking to it?

"It was different for me than you." She flicked a piece of lint from her jeans. "I was actually excited to meet someone smart and funny." *And gorgeous.*

"How is that different from me?" he asked.

"Because you take a different woman home every night. I don't get excited about someone easily." Why had she just admitted *that*?

Kyle Hicks was a player, a serial womanizer. She must not show weakness. God help her, right now he looked like a sexy dad.

"You *were* excited about me?" He kissed the top of Mollie's head. "I knew it, Mollie."

"Mollie couldn't care less," she said, laughing.

"So, do we hire Mel or not?" he asked.

"She has experience and good references." Now that she knew he wasn't fooled by Mel's act, she could rest easy.

"As long as you're sure." Kyle carried Mollie over to the crib. Violet watched as he swaddled her with surprising swiftness.

After he had Mollie settled in her crib, he wandered back to the couch and picked up his glass of scotch. "Would you like me to order dinner?"

"Not yet." She went to the window, pretending to be interested in the view, holding her breath as she heard his footsteps cross the room.

He stood behind her, his reflection a shadow in the window. "Regarding our earlier conversation, I've been with a lot of women." Dropping his head close to hers, he spoke softly into her ear. "But that doesn't mean I don't recognize a special one when I meet her." She caught the pleasant smell of scotch on his breath.

Her body was betraying her. Goosebumps spread up her arms. A throbbing warmth between her legs told her what her mind didn't want to accept. She wanted this man—all of him—his long fingers stroking her skin, his mouth on hers, his thighs pressing her into the window. If she merely leaned backward, their bodies would mesh into one form. *Two days, Violet Ellis. Two days and you've lost all reason.*

Without looking at him, she added a nonchalant shrug as if it all meant nothing to her. "You didn't think I was special. You were just doing your thing."

"Maybe. But that doesn't change the fact that you were…you are…beautiful."

She might burst into flames. Outside the window, the lights of town seemed to dance like fireflies before her eyes.

"Did you hear me?" he asked.

She tilted her face toward him, unable to resist the pull of his gaze.

"I heard you."

"You should show yourself more often."

"Show myself?"

"Show the softer side of you. The side I've gotten to see the past few days. Your huge heart. Your sense of humor..." He trailed off as if he wanted to say more but wasn't sure he should.

"I show that to people all the time," she said.

He turned so they faced each other and raised one eyebrow. "Just not to me."

"Maybe," she said, looking into her glass.

"Maybe I want you to like me just a little. I'm more than I appear."

"Are you?"

"I want to be."

She peeked up at him.

"What are you, Kyle Hicks, if not what you appear on the outside?" Impulsively, she touched the sleeve of his t-shirt for a split second. *Don't touch him or it's all over.*

His mouth stretched into a smile that made no difference to his mournful eyes. "I'm broken, Violet Ellis. Like millions of pieces of ice. Like Humpty Dumpty."

"What happened to you?"

Dark blue eyes watched her. The physical heat between them evaporated, replaced by an intangible familiarity. In those blue windows to his soul she recognized a sadness so deep, it chilled her bones.

"Life. That's all. Like everyone." He smoothed a section of her hair away from her face. "Sometimes I think the person we all started out to be gets chipped away and chipped away until we're left with nothing but the hard kernel—the place where we're merely surviving on the fumes of our former glorious selves. All that's left is the survivor who exists without redemption or grace.

We must get through, we think. Just one more day. One more deal. One more deposit into the bank account. One more conquest. I've lived like that for all my adult life. It's been a constant trudge up the hill to prove to myself that I'm not Sisyphus after all."

Her eyes filled. She nodded, unable to speak, knowing exactly what he meant. She imagined him as a little boy just then, hurt and scared. All her beliefs about the man in front of her crumbled. She saw him now for what he truly was: vulnerable, unsure, terribly alone. Like her.

"I don't want to live like that any longer," he said. "I want to be different. For Mollie. I want her to remain glorious. I don't want to be the one who chips away at her, who makes her nothing but a hard center. I'm afraid. I'm afraid I can't do it. Am I too broken? Is it too late for redemption?"

She placed her hand around his wrist and looked into his eyes as far she could. "It's never too late. Not when it's love you're fighting for."

* * *

After she left Kyle and went to bed, she lay awake for some time. Their discussion had stirred up memories of her parents and their reaction to her pregnancy.

She'd flown home that morning from Boston. Twelve weeks pregnant by then, she'd resigned from her position at the church, and like an injured dog wanted nothing more than to lick her wounds in the comfort of family. The problem? Her family wasn't comfortable.

The scene played before her eyes.

She folded her napkin in her lap and willed herself to get it over with. "I have something to tell you."

They looked at her expectantly. "What is it?"

"It might come as a shock," Violet said.

Her mother placed her fork carefully onto the plate and tugged on the diamond earring that hung on her left earlobe. She made this gesture often. Violet sometimes wondered if she realized how many times a day she played with that diamond. Her mother had gained weight over the years and her hair had turned white, but besides that, she remained virtually the same year after year. From her peach lipstick and Chanel No. 5 to her insistence that pantyhose never went out of style, her mother remained stubbornly in 1992.

"Does it have something to do with your abrupt decision to come for a visit?" Her father watched her from across the table, his eyebrows scrunched together like a pair of furry caterpillars. Terry Ellis was tall with thick white hair and stooped shoulders. *Slumped shoulders indicate a man who talks to God*, he often said.

Violet wished he'd take her advice and practice yoga. She figured a straight back could not affect his relationship with God.

"We barely hear from you for months and then you suddenly announce a visit home. I figured you'd screwed something up and needed money."

"It *was* rather abrupt." Like always, her mother piled onto his last statement with a fervor of agreement.

"Please don't tell me you've lost your work at the church." Her father's hands trembled as he reached for his water glass.

"I've taken out a small business loan to open a shop here in town."

"A shop? What qualifies you to run a shop?" Her father leaned back in his chair and folded his arms across his ample belly.

She ignored his question and told them about her idea for the shop and the small business loan she'd taken out. "I've rented the empty space next to the bookstore."

"You've never made any of your hippie schemes work in the past, why should this one?" Her father leaned back over his plate and proceeded with the detailed chopping of his steak.

"My hippie schemes?"

"He's referring to your change of major to environmental sciences," her mother said.

"Which I wasn't able to finish when you cut me off."

He stabbed piece of steak and waved his fork at her. A glob of fat flew across the table and landed in her mother's water glass. "Your choice. You always choose failure, that's what you do."

Violet breathed deeply, willing herself to stay calm. "I'm not asking for your permission."

"You never have." Her father took another sip of water. "Why start now?"

"Why here? Why would you come here to open a business?" Her mother's open mouth looked like one of those gaping fish at the fish market in Boston.

"Because I love it here. This is my home, my town. I love every inch of it. Every building, every grain of sand. Also, I'm going to have a baby. I want to raise him here—in a small town where community still matters."

She'd lost them at baby. They stared at her in shock.

"You're what?" The glass in her dad's hand shook even more violently until he positioned it next to his plate.

"I'm going to have a baby. I'm three months along already," Violet said, not nearly as calm as she sounded. Under the table-cloth, she twisted her cloth napkin into a rope.

"We didn't even know you had a boyfriend," her mother said.

"He wasn't a boyfriend. He was married and wants nothing to do with the baby or me." How had that just come out of her mouth? She hadn't planned to say that part.

"A married man? Violet?" Her mother's voice had risen a good octave and a half.

Violet lifted her chin and spoke silently to herself. *Don't back down. This is your life. You're almost twenty-five years old. You can do this. They do not define your worth. Not anymore.* "It was a terrible mistake. A foolish mistake. I fell in love with the wrong man. However, I have every intention of doing the right thing. I'll be having the baby and taking care of him without a partner."

Her father blew from his chair like a volcano. "What will our friends think?"

"Why does it matter?" Violet placed her hand on her belly.

From across the table, her mother wept into her napkin.

"A lot of women have babies on their own," Violet said.

"Whores. People from Hollyweird. Not decent women." He slammed his fist on the surface of the buffet. One of her mother's china cups fell from its hanger and smashed into pieces.

Violet's legs barely held her as she leapt to her feet. "You have no idea what it means to be decent. You're cold and rigid and overly critical of everyone, especially me. I've never felt loved by you. I'm just a trinket to parade around at church. Look at my pretty little girl with the bows in her hair. Be seen not heard because a woman can't possibly have anything worthwhile to say. Do you know how exhausting it was to be perfect all the time?"

He roared and slammed his fist on the wall this time. "You're hardly perfect. You never have been. You're in love with failure and boy howdy you sure love to embarrass me. Is it fun, little girl, to make a mockery of your father? Everything I believe in you've scoffed at and ridiculed—in love with the counter culture just to hurt me. Everything foreign and degenerate. Yoga like the Orientals. Environmental sciences like the tree huggers."

"Dad!"

"My own daughter's a whore, Rose. How do you like that?"

"I'm a grown woman, not a teenager. Get over it." Violet crossed her arms over her chest, mostly to stop shaking.

"You're not my daughter," he said.

Just like that, she filled with a calm assurance. She would no longer tolerate his presence in her life. Her voice, hoarse from rage, no longer shook. "You're an ignorant bigot. I should feel sorry for you but I'm too disgusted by you to have one ounce of pity left. All my life I've felt terrible about myself because of you. I'm done. Consider this the last time we will ever see each other."

"Good," he said.

"Great." Violet left the dining room and walked up to her childhood bedroom and grabbed her suitcase.

Like Kara did years later, Violet had rented a cold, depressing room in an old Victorian in the middle of town. When Dakota was just a week old, her mother had come for a visit. They were flying to South America in the morning. They might never come back, depending on her father's health. They would keep the house in Cliffside Bay for now, in case they wanted to move back. *Please, move into the house. Your father doesn't have to know. But you can't live here. Not with my grandson.*

She'd taken her up on the offer. In hindsight, perhaps she shouldn't have. Living in her father's home wasn't exactly being on her own two feet like she'd so brazenly sworn she would be.

She rolled over and pulled the covers up to her neck and gave herself a little lecture.

It doesn't matter now. I'm here. I have a job. Dakota is fine. I don't need their house and I don't need them. Kyle and Mollie need me. I'll focus on them and Dakota and all will be well.

CHAPTER FIVE

KYLE

FOR KYLE, THE days passed in a blur. Violet and her insistence on routine had proven to be just what Mollie needed. She was on a predictable schedule and only waking up twice during the night. Mel reported that she woke at one and four, drank her bottle, and then went right back to sleep. In the evenings after he returned home from work, he held Mollie or played with Dakota before the children were fed, bathed, and put to bed. When all had been accomplished, Kyle and Violet would order dinner and eat together at the table by the window. Was this what family life was like? If so, it wasn't so bad.

Not that it was real. They might seem to be happily playing house, but it was a business arrangement. One that his daughter needed desperately. He must keep that forefront in his thoughts. Violet was his nanny. She was also a friend. A good one, as it turned out. Alarmingly, neither of those facts deterred him from thinking about her in ways he shouldn't. After their exchange that second night, he knew he'd ventured into treacherous territory. After days of analysis spent in his car with country music blaring, he came to a disturbing conclusion. He was in trouble, plain and simple. Like in a country song, he wanted the girl he couldn't have.

Violet Ellis made him ache with desire. He longed to sweep her into his arms and take her to his bed and do things to her she'd never forget. Never in his adult life had he wanted a woman more. And yet, it was more than just lust. With her, his carefully built armor disappeared. There were no pretensions between them. They understood each other on a level he'd never experienced with a woman. Ever. Which made him more than a little nervous. For once, he needed to do the right thing and keep his hands to himself. For Mollie's sake. And, frankly, for Violet's sake. All she needed was for him to hurt her. After everything she'd gone through with her parents and that louse Lund, she didn't need him messing with her mind. Which he would, eventually. He wrecked lives. That was his deal. Violet needed a strong, whole man who would make her laugh and provide her the family she so deserved.

Not him. Not Pig.

Fortunately, his baby daughter was quite the distraction from his self-destructive ways. Mollie appeared to be thriving. She was chubby and energetic, and a keen eater. Still, Kyle worried. He spent many minutes staring at her, looking for any cracks in her seemingly perfect health. Once a week, he took her into see Doctor Jackson Waller, who reassured him the baby was not only healthy but thriving. The price for these visits? Major ribbing from Jackson and the other Dogs. They'd started calling him Helicopter, which was not as funny as he would have once thought.

One night in early November, Kyle put the baby down in her crib when his phone buzzed with a text from Mel.

I have food poisoning. Can't make it tonight.

The long night stretched before him. No Mel meant no sleep for him.

"What is it?" Violet asked as she came into the living room. She'd changed from jeans and a sweater into leggings and a t-shirt. He pulled his gaze from her thighs. *Get your mind out of the gutter.*

"Mel has food poisoning," he said.

An expression of irritation crossed her features. "Right. The old food poisoning excuse."

"It could be true," he said.

"She's twenty-two years old. I'll bet money someone sees her dancing at The Oar later."

"If that's true, I'll fire her."

"Anyway, we'll take shifts," she said. "Mollie's only waking up at one a.m. and four a.m. We can both take one feeding."

"How do you know that?" he asked.

"I wake up every time I hear Mollie cry. It's a mom thing."

"The mysterious world of women," he said.

They were interrupted by room service bringing their dinner.

Violet was quiet as they ate, obviously preoccupied.

"You all right?" he asked.

"Yeah. I heard my parents are back in town. They haven't called."

"Screw them."

She smiled and tossed her hair behind her shoulders. "I wish Dakota had family besides me. That's all."

"And the rejection hurts."

"That too."

He reached across the table and placed his fingers lightly on her forearm. "It's their loss."

"When I told them I was pregnant, he called me a whore and said that was the last time he ever wanted to see me."

"Would you say your life is better or worse without them in it?" he asked.

"Better, I suppose. Even though my dad's voice still echoes in my head."

"I'm not really in the position to give advice about anything emotional, but it seems to me that good riddance might be the way to describe it."

They were finished with their meals by then. He went to the

bar and pulled out a bottle of red wine. "If you're taking a night shift, then the least I can do is pour you a nice glass of wine."

She grinned. "I accept." Sighing with obvious pleasure, she folded into her usual position on the couch. She was like a pretzel the way she could bend those legs into every position. This morning he had caught her doing her morning yoga routine. Downward Dog would stick with him for a long while.

He opened the bottle and poured two glasses. When he turned back to look at her, Violet was twisting her hair into a bun on top of her head.

Don't put it up. He loved it when her hair cascaded around her shoulders. It was all he could do not to wrap his hands in the strands and kiss his way up her long neck until he reached her mouth.

"What?" she asked.

He jumped. "Nothing."

"You were staring at me."

"I was?"

"You were," she said.

Their gazes remained locked for a second too long.

"It's your hair," he said, finally. "I love when you wear it down. That's what I was thinking about."

She flushed and smoothed a stray strand of hair behind her ear. "Oh, well, thanks. I thought maybe I had kale in my teeth."

He crossed the room and handed her a glass of wine and fell into his end of the couch with his.

"No kale."

"Other than you," she said.

He laughed. "It's going to break my heart when he can say my name right," he said.

She didn't smile. *Strange.* She always smiled when they talked about Dakota.

He'd obviously made her feel uncomfortable. "I'm sorry. I didn't mean to make you feel weird." Why had he said it? *Just confirming what she already thinks about me.* She continued to watch him with a wary look in her eyes. "We're living so closely together. It's impossible not to notice every little thing about you."

"Like whether my hair is up or down?"

He nodded. "That and other things." He noticed it all. When she changed clothes; what she looked like in the morning with her face puffy from sleep; the way her honey hair shone in the patch of sun by the window yesterday when he came home from work; the expression on her face when she held Mollie. He cataloged it all, like a scrapbook in his mind.

"What else?" She gazed at him with her clear brown eyes.

He drank from his glass, biding time so he could think how to answer. A quip to make her laugh and deter from this line of questioning? But no, the truth came out of his stupid mouth. "You glow."

"Glow?"

"Your skin, hair, personality. You're the epitome of vitality. It must be all that yoga." He was almost dizzy. The wine had gone to his head. Or was it the woman sitting across from him?

"Thank you," she whispered. "I haven't had a compliment like that for a long time. Maybe ever."

"Even from a guy you can't stand?" He winked and grinned to lighten the mood. So much for a relaxing evening. *Good job, dummy.*

Still no smile. She moistened her lip with the tip of her tongue. "I can stand you."

"I'm tolerable," he said.

"More than tolerable. I've enjoyed these past few weeks a little too much."

He turned from her to look out at the view. Mist hovered outside the window, blocking the lights of town. "I look forward to coming home to you guys more than I should." Why had he said it? So stupid.

She downed the rest of her wine. Her eyes glittered in the dim room, somewhere between trapped and wild. "I get it now—why women fall at your feet."

"You do?"

"You're not as loathsome as I once thought."

He grinned and cocked his head to the side. "How nice of you to notice."

"But you're dangerous."

"Dangerous?"

"As in, I'm lonely."

He opened his mouth to speak but no sound came out. All he had to do was grab her into his arms and haul her into the bedroom. He could make her forget everything but the moment. No, he couldn't do it to her. Not to Violet.

"You can do so much better." He smiled to take the edge from his tone. His dry lips stretched painfully against his teeth. What did she see when she stared at him that way? Could she see through it all to the essence of his soul?

"Sometimes when I look at you, I can see the little boy you must have been." She held her wine glass with one hand wrapped around its foot. Precarious. It might fall from her grasp and smash into a thousand pieces on the marble floor.

"You wouldn't recognize me," he said.

"Your eyes. They'd be the same."

He studied his glass. "Pig." The word bounced to the tune of the country song playing softly in the background. *Pig. Pig. Pig.*

"What did you say?"

He thought about getting up and leaving the room. There was no need to hash out his pathetic past. Not even with Violet.

"That's what the kids in school called me. Pig."

Her mouth dropped open in obvious horror. "Kids can be so mean."

"Our trailer was on a little piece of land next to the Keller's pig farm. The stench from the animals could be smelled from the road. My bus stop was at the end of their driveway, so when I got on the bus the first day of school, everyone assumed I lived there."

"Because of that they called you Pig? That's awful." Violet's eyes snapped with anger.

"It wasn't because of that. I smelled." The words caught in the back of his throat. He ground his teeth together, waiting until he could gather himself enough to tell her the rest. "More often than not, our utilities were turned off because my dad hadn't paid the bills. No hot water. No washing machine. Dirty clothes and dirty bodies smell." The bitterness of those days filled his mouth with the stench that had once lived on his body. No amount of money could wash the shame of those times. "We wore our dirty clothes over and over. Baths were once a week, at best. We perpetually had lice."

"I'm so sorry."

He picked at a bit of rough skin on his thumb. "It was a long time ago."

"I had lice once. It happens to everyone. My mother was mortified."

"*My* mother left us when I was ten. Got into the car with some guy she'd met and took off."

"Just left? And never came back?"

"That's why…with Mollie…I have to do this right."

"You are." Her gentle tone should soothe him, but an image of the yard in front of their trailer flashed before his eyes. Several abandoned toilets, a decaying truck, and trash piled high and wide had made it look like the local dump.

"You've probably never known people like us." Kyle described his yard and their trailer. He almost flinched as he watched her expression change from concern to comprehension. *Like putting a puzzle together. The story of Kyle.* Would she be disgusted by his story? By him?

"After you left home, you focused on never being that boy again." Not a question, but a statement.

"That's right."

"You went to USC on a scholarship?" she asked. "And the rest was history, as they say."

"There was a counselor at the high school who encouraged me. She paid the fee to apply out of her own pocket. Between financial aid and scholarships, I had a full ride." He ran his hand through his hair and breathed in the scent of the wine. The scent of wealth. He had wealth now. No one could ever call him Pig again. Why then, did he still feel like that little boy who walked onto the bus that first day?

You stink.

"And you found the Dogs there," she said.

"That's right. We were in the same dorm suite and became tight friends almost immediately. Can you imagine a more mismatched pair?"

"Why do you say that?"

"I weighed a hundred and thirty pounds soaking wet. My clothes were hardly better than rags. I couldn't look a woman in the eye."

Her gaze swept over his large, muscular frame. "Really? That doesn't seem possible."

"The Dogs helped change all that. Brody took me to the gym with him. Taught me how to bulk up. He must have told his parents I didn't have much money for eating because suddenly he had twice as much money on his food card. Zane taught me manners and how to charm women. I watched Jackson to learn how to listen to people. That's been the number one secret to my business success, actually." His voice had thickened, remembering those first months of burgeoning friendship with Brody, Jackson, and Zane. "I never thought I'd have friends like them."

"You've left Pig behind." She gestured around the room. "Look at what you've done."

"Sure." He paused. "I have the Dogs to thank for it all. Their friendship changed my life. Did you know Brody gave me my first loan to start my business?"

Their first year of college had been tough for all of them but Brody. Jackson and Zane were grieving Maggie. He was trying to forget the entire first eighteen years of his life and start fresh.

"I used to hear Jackson sobbing in the middle of the night. We shared a wall. It's hard to ever see a man quite the same way when you hear them at their worst...especially when they don't know you're there." Kyle looked up at the ceiling. "I used to curl up in a ball and try to pretend I didn't feel the same way."

"Why *did* you feel the same way?"

He studied her for a moment. Why did he want to share all of his full story with her? It made no sense. No one knew the truth. If they did, would anyone love him? "I don't ever think about it now. I mean, I do, but just as quickly push it aside. I wanted to forget absolutely everything. Start over."

"Did it work?"

"It never does." He pressed into the callouses on the pads of his left hand with his thumb, remembering. Sheri Swanson. His sister, Autumn. He'd tried to save them both, but in the end, dark forces had proven too much. He was weak. Evil had won.

"What can't you forget?" Violet asked.

"I lost people that I loved very much. That's all. Please, I don't talk about it. Not even with you." *Don't go there.* The dark place could snatch him at any moment. He couldn't let himself remember or Pig would rear his head and dance around his memory like a demon danced above the flames of hell.

"Loss changes a person," she said. "Never for the better."

He looked up, meeting her eyes. "Yes."

She crossed over to sit next to him. "You don't have sole owner-ship of pain, you know."

"I know."

She traced the one-inch, skinny scar that ran down the side of his neck with her thumb. "What happened here? I've never noticed it before."

"Bar fight."

"Liar."

"A bully incident." *Don't ask me. Please just leave it be.*

"When you were young?"

"Yes." He covered her hand with his and drew it away from his scar and onto his thigh.

"But you don't want to talk about it," she said.

"Has there ever been a moment in your life when you've simply backed off from a subject? Like let a guy off the hook?"

"I'm not good at that." She smiled up at him. "Especially when it's something or someone I care about."

"You care about me now, huh?"

"Don't let it go to your head," she said.

"I won't."

He continued to hold her hand. If he yanked her onto his lap, would she bolt? With his free hand, he twirled a piece of her hair around his index finger.

She trembled, her gaze on their intertwined hands. "What's happening here? What're we doing?"

"You've put something in my drink that made me spill all my secrets."

She looked up at him. "I want to know *all* your secrets."

"You know about Pig. I think that's enough."

"You smell just fine now, by the way." She smiled shyly. "I've noticed."

He swallowed. *Get it together, man.* "You smell like a flower I can't put my finger on."

"It's my perfume. Hints of jasmine."

"Not Violets?"

"No. Not Violets. Such an embarrassing name. Who names their kids after a flower?"

"A lot of people." He didn't move, unable to escape from her gaze. "I love your name."

"My mother's name is Rose. If they'd had more children, they would have named them Daisy and Lily."

"I think those are nice names."

"I guess. I have trouble thinking anything my parents do is nice."

He let that go, not knowing what to say, other than, *yeah, I get it.*

"Did you ever have a nickname?" he asked.

"No, just Violet."

"Would you like one?"

"Depends." She paused, smiling. "On who's giving it to me."

"What if it's me?"

"Then I suppose I'd like it."

"Lettie. I'll call you Lettie. Beautiful Lettie." He touched the small of her back with his fingers. Her blouse fluttered as her breath caught.

"Do you know how badly I want to take you into my bed?" he asked.

Her eyes widened. He felt her shiver under his touch.

"I can't sleep with you," she whispered. "Even though I want to."

He didn't need her to explain why. The reasons were like Dakota's blocks in the corner of the room. There were blocks upon blocks of reasons why he was a bad idea. Stacked together they would eventually fall into a chaotic mess.

"It's nothing to do with you, actually. Or even that it would be terribly irresponsible when it comes to the children or even that I work for you," she said as if he'd named the blocks out loud. "It's me. I can't sleep with someone who doesn't love me. I won't ever do that. Not again. The next man I give myself to has to be willing to spend his life with me and take Dakota as part of the package."

The next man? She hadn't slept with anyone since Lund. How was that possible?

Her eyes glistened with unshed tears. "I understand it's a tall order and maybe I'm not even lovable, but I can't compromise again or fool myself into believing a man feels something for me that he's incapable of."

"It's not that you're unlovable. Don't ever say that about yourself again."

She stared at him, obviously taken aback.

"You're the most lovable woman in the world. Just because men are idiots...just because I'm broken...has nothing to do with you. Someday you're going to make a man's dreams come true. It's just not going to be me."

She leaned closer and kissed his cheek. "I better go to my own bed before I lose my resolve." Seconds later, she was gone.

He sat there for a long time with his hand pressed against the spot on his cheek where her soft mouth had been. For the first time in his adult life he wished he were not the broken man he was. What if he were like the other Dogs and deserved a woman like Violet Ellis? What would his life be like then? Would the slow burning fire in his gut be put out?

The question was irrelevant. He was incapable of intimacy. To be with someone like Violet he would have to tell her everything, all the puzzle pieces. She would have to know about Daniel Kyle Hickman.

No one could ever know.

CHAPTER SIX

<small>Violet</small>

TWO WEEKS BEFORE Thanksgiving, fog settled over the town like a cold, wet blanket. Violet shivered as she pulled into a parking space outside the grocery store. Dakota and Mollie were in their car seats in the back, bundled up in warm clothes. She turned off the engine, preparing herself mentally for the athleticism needed for the acrobatic maneuver of prying the children from their viselike car seats and into the store. She needed a bigger car than this compact hybrid. Last night, while watching television with Kyle, she'd seen an advertisement for a minivan with sliding doors and a built-in vacuum. She'd shocked herself when she found herself murmuring out loud how nice it would be to have one. Kyle hadn't said anything, just raised an eyebrow and smirked like he did when he wanted to tease her but restrained himself.

Now, peering out at the damp morning, she called out to Dakota. "You ready, little man, for grocery shopping?"

"Yes, Mama."

An elderly couple came out of the sliding doors of the grocery store. It took her a moment to realize the stooped man with the cane and the plump woman beside him were her parents. Her father, who had once been a tall man, now walked with a cane. Even from a considerable distance, she could see how his hands had gnarled from the arthritis that had taken them to South America in search of year-round warmth. When had that happened? Her mother looked the same, stout and sturdy.

Here were her parents, across a parking lot and yet no closer than when they'd been thousands of miles away. An ache some-where between homesickness and grief slammed into her chest. Almost four years had passed since she'd seen or spoken to her father. A lifetime, really, considering. Dakota had been a mere peanut in her tummy when they'd had their last and final battle. Her father had vowed that day he would never speak to her again. Obviously, he'd meant it. They'd been home for over a month and she hadn't heard from either of them.

She glanced at Dakota who sat in the back seat turning the pages of a picture book about trains. How could anyone resist knowing him? She would not cry. There was nothing to be done. Her parents had stated their position and there was no budging them from it. She could either waste time and energy mourning them or get on with her life. Her life. Not theirs to dictate. Hers alone. What did it matter if she had contact with them or not? If they were still in her life, it would be the same teetering act of walking the tightrope, knowing that one miniscule mistake would end in a painful plummet. There was no winning when it came to her father.

If she *were* to spend time with him, he would zero in on a weak-ness, big or small, almost immediately. As if it were his sole purpose in life, he'd pick at her until old scabs bled fresh or new wounds spilled blood or tears. Even now, from the safety and anonymity of her car, the words *prove your worth* seemed to hover above his head in a judgmental halo. In the presence of his daugh-ter, he turned the brightest of stage lights up to their highest level to ensure that she understood. *You're being watched.* She would not, could not, avoid his inquiry, his demand for evidence of her worth. But there was more—a tagline—just for Violet. *You there, Violet Ellis, what new failure do you have to share with me?*

She pressed her forehead onto the steering wheel, willing the cold plastic to numb her thoughts. *I don't care. I have Dakota. That's all I need.*

What had her father said to her that night?

You're in love with failure.

I'm in love with my son. Everything else, including you, can go straight to hell.

She waited until her parents drove out of the parking lot before getting the children out of the back. Once she had Mollie in her stroller and Dakota in his place by her side, she hesitated, disoriented for a split second about what day it was. Thursday. Their day for errands.

Routine. Stick with the routine. Peace was there in the simple arrangement of the hours and minutes of the day. Not only for the kids, but for her. The three of them had established a pattern to their weeks and days that were comforting to Violet: the park on Mondays, the library for story time on Tuesdays, gym time for Dakota at the local YMCA on Wednesdays, a playdate with Jubie and Honor on Friday afternoons. Thursdays were reserved for errands or appointments, or an occasional visit with a friend.

The days with the kids were busy and happy. Being with the them had given her a sense of purpose and belonging like she hadn't before experienced. Even more so than her studies at college or her attempt at running the shop. It was being with the children that brought her joy, gave her existence meaning. What did this mean exactly? How did this knowledge of herself fit with her studies of women's long history of fighting for equality, for their seat at the table, when all she wanted to do was spend her days here with her little boy and this chubby baby? Every milestone Mollie achieved was like watching the creation of the most beautiful piece of art ever made. And her son? This boy amazed her with his questions and his curiosity and his love of life. To be with him every day was indeed the greatest gift she'd ever been given. Did she have her failed shop to thank for it? Never ever would she have thought so. But now? She was happy. Despite everything, her days were filled with joy. If her shop hadn't failed, if her father hadn't rejected her, would she be here in this exact place? The answers were no.

And then there were the evenings. Kyle had adjusted his schedule so that he returned no later than six. From the moment he walked in the door, he spent time with Mollie, feeding and bathing her before putting her to bed.

Afterward, he always saved a few minutes to play trucks, card games, or roughhouse with Dakota. Her son loved Old Maid and Go Fish. She drew the line when he offered to teach Dakota how to play poker.

By seven thirty both the children were in bed. They would order dinner for themselves and open a bottle of wine and talk with music on in the background. She'd learned more about Kyle's business enterprises, both past and present. Sometimes he'd ask her opinion about how to make projects greener, which thrilled her. His country music was even starting to grow on her.

Since that night they'd confessed their mutual attraction, he'd been the perfect gentleman. No touching. He didn't even seem to look at her any longer. She should be relieved. Unfortunately, she wasn't. Like the fool she was, she couldn't help but wish he could and would fall in love with her.

Mel always arrived right at ten and they would say goodnight to her and each other and head in separate directions.

That didn't mean she didn't think about how she longed to cross the suite and crawl into his bed. But no. She would remain strong. Self-protection must be her primary goal. She would not allow her heart to be broken by a man ever again.

Right now, she must focus on their errands. Today, she'd made the decision that she had to get over her bitterness and go see what Lance had done with the bookstore.

She crossed the street to the building where her old shop had once resided. The entire front of the building had been given a facelift of new paint, large picture windows, and attractive blue awnings. New signage hung over the front of the building: Cliffside Bay Books and Sweets. Through the windows Violet spotted Lance putting books on shelves. She tapped on the glass to get his attention. Lance looked up and immediately broke into a smile, then crossed over to open the door. "Violet, it's great to see you." Lance pulled her into a quick embrace before leaning down to scoop Dakota into his arms and throw him over his shoulder. Dakota squealed, delighted.

Lance moved with a quiet grace, more like a dancer than his athletic brother. His light blue eyes, delicately carved nose, full bottom lip, and high cheekbones made him almost too pretty for a man. Combined with his warm, kind nature, he was could only be described as a *nice guy*. Violet suspected he had trouble with women for this very reason. The nice guy never got the girl.

"You put up awnings," she said.

"Do you like them?" Lance set Dakota on his feet.

"They're great," she said. "I love the signage too."

He invited her inside. "We reopen in a week. There's still a lot to do, but we're getting there."

Following Dakota, she wheeled the stroller into the store. Her hands flew to her mouth. "Oh my God, Lance. It's beautiful."

Lance had removed the wall that separated the two spaces. White walls with black trim and bookcases gave it a fresh, sophisticated atmosphere. Much of the space was filled with books, but on the far side of the room, where her shop had been, a modern version of the old-fashioned soda fountain shone under the lights. A shake maker, industrial espresso maker, and various bottles of sweetener resided behind the counter. Charming tables were arranged around the room. On one wall, a bank of cubbies for studying or reading had outlets for laptops or phone charging.

Dakota had his nose pressed against the glass freezer, looking at the ice cream. "Mama, can I have some?"

"Not today, sweetie. They're not ready for business. But when they open we'll come back."

Lance put his hand on top of Dakota's head. "You know what, though, I have some of Flora's cookies in Mary's office. You want one of those?"

"Can I, Mama?"

"I suppose," Violet said.

Lance and Dakota slipped out of sight, headed for the back office.

Violet wandered up the stairs to the loft. Cozy chairs and sofas and a soft rug invited people to read and linger. A chess game was positioned on a side table for players. When she returned to the main floor, Mary was there. Tall and slender, with long brown hair and fair skin, Violet had always thought she was exceptionally pretty in that intimidating way that women who looked like models but acted like intellectuals could be. With her hair in a ponytail and wearing loose jeans and a sweatshirt, she looked more like a girl than a grown-up librarian.

"Hi Violet. Lance said you were here," Mary said.

"The place looks great," Violet whispered as she gave her a hug. "I'm so happy for you guys."

The rest of the gang was undecided about Mary, but Violet liked her. She was quiet, yes. The others thought she was uptight, but Violet thought she was merely shy. She suspected there was more to Mary's story. Something had happened in her past to make her so cautious, so careful to keep people at a distance.

Mary looked straight into her eyes. "I know it must be hard and I'm sorry."

Violet squeezed her hands. "Don't be. Everything has a way of working out in the end."

Mary moved over to the stroller to look at the sleeping baby. "She's so pretty." She wrapped her arms around her waist, like she was cold.

"She is," Violet said.

Mary drew in a long, shuddering breath and straightened.

"Well, I should get back to it." Her skin had blanched of color, making the purple smudges under her eyes more evident. She staggered slightly. Violet put her hand out to steady her.

"Are you feeling all right?" Violet asked, knowing the answer was a definite no.

"Sure, yes. Just a little light-headed. I probably need some lunch."

"Come on, let's head up to The Oar and grab a bite."

Mary looked like she was going to say no, but she agreed. "It'll do me good to get out of here for a bit." She explained that she just needed to finish up one thing in the back and grab her purse. "Give me a couple minutes."

Violet agreed. Mollie needed a bottle anyway.

She had just finished changing her diaper when Lance came back with Dakota.

"I'm taking Mary to lunch," Violet said.

"Great," Lance said. "She needs to get out of here for a while."

"That's what she said."

"I'll keep Dakota here with me. Mary needs a little girl time." He lowered his voice. "Between me and you, she's been working way too hard. I'm worried she's going to burn out. Plus, she needs some friends in town."

"It seemed like something was bothering her."

Lance brushed away the lock of brown hair that constantly fell over his forehead. "She's got some ghosts." He tapped his temple. "In here. I don't know what they are, but she's sad. The kind of sadness that never goes away."

"I wonder why?"

"At first, we thought it was because Flora and Dax got married. She misses her dad, sure. But there's something else. I can't get a thing out of her. Maybe she needs a woman to talk to."

A few minutes later, Violet, Mary, and baby Mollie in her car seat were at a table by the window at The Oar. Business this time of year was notoriously slow and today was no exception. Zane's sister Sophie was on duty as manager this afternoon. She came over to say hello as soon as they sat down. "He's so busy with the brewery plans that I'm kind of solo these days." Sophie snatched a pencil from the bun on top of her head. "What can I get you ladies?"

Despite the dreary weather, Sophie and The Oar screamed perpetual summer. With her blond hair and tanned skin, Sophie looked like she just walked in from a day at the beach. Vintage surfboards decorated the walls and light flooded in through the tall windows, making the weather outside irrelevant.

After they ordered Brody Salads, the two women drank their iced teas and made small talk. Violet noticed that Mary seldom looked at the baby, almost like she was avoiding her on purpose.

When their salads came, Violet ate a few bites of chicken, watching her new friend pick at her food. "You sure you're feeling all right?" Violet asked.

Mary looked up from her salad. "Having a hard day today, I guess."

"Me too." She told her about seeing her parents coming out of the store. "It's a slap in the face, you know."

"I can imagine," Mary said, sympathy in her green eyes.

"If you ever want to talk about anything, I'm here. I know how hard it is to move to a place where you don't know anyone."

"I've met a lot of people since I've been here." Mary smiled. "The Mullen family comes with a lot of people."

She laughed. "That's true. I met everyone through Honor. She's my best friend, but I've gotten to know Kara and Maggie through her. They're the friends I always wanted. No drama or games like there are with some women. And they've been very supportive of me and all my failures."

"Kara doesn't like me. I don't blame her. I wasn't very nice when we first met. I can be kind of prickly. Especially when it comes to my dad. He's all I have left." Her voice caught.

Violet remembered hearing that Mary's mother had passed five or so years ago. "I'm sorry you lost your mom."

"I know everyone probably thinks it's ridiculous. I'm a grown woman and she died over five years ago. But they don't understand."

"Don't understand what?" Violet asked as gently as she could.

"It wasn't just that I lost my mom." Mary's face twisted in obvious pain. She placed her fork next to her plate and looked down at her lap.

"It's okay. You don't have to talk about it." She shouldn't push her. Kyle was right that she needed to let a thing go sometimes.

Mary looked out the window. "I was married. We had a little baby. Amelia. I called her Meme." A slight smile crossed her face at the mention of her baby's name. "She was born prematurely at twenty-two weeks. She only lived three days. Her little heart wasn't strong enough." She spoke without any emotional inflection. "Turns out, I have an unreliable cervix."

"I remember reading about that when I was pregnant."

"They didn't know until I went into premature labor. My mom died a few months later of a sudden heart attack. My marriage ended soon thereafter."

"Oh, God, Mary, I'm sorry. I can't imagine how hard that must be."

"It's hard to be around happy people. I'm jealous and bitter. I know that's awful, but it's true."

"Maybe you're just more honest with yourself than some of us are," Violet said. *I'm jealous. All the time.*

"What're you jealous about?" Mary asked.

She inwardly cringed. The wistfulness in Mary's voice was like being granted a secret entry into her friend's thoughts. Violet knew the unspoken words of her sentence. *What're you jealous about when you have Dakota?*

"I'm jealous of Honor and how smart and capable she is. I'm jealous of her relationship with Zane. I'm jealous of Kara and Brody and all their money, not to mention how in love they are. Let's see, what else? I wish a man would look at me the way Jackson looks at Maggie. I wish I had a talent like Maggie. *Any* talent other than annoying people with my causes. See? I'm awful and I don't even have a good reason. Losing a child is every mother's worst nightmare and I'm so sorry it happened to you." She shuddered and reached for Mary's hand.

Mary's chin quivered but she took in a deep breath, obviously trying not to cry. "Today she would've been six."

Violet moved around the table to sit next to Mary. "You poor thing," she said as she took Mary into her arms and let her sob into her shoulder.

This was why we must always be kind. One never knows what someone else has gone through. We can't intuitively know their heartbreak just by looking at them.

"Is there anything I can do?" Violet asked when Mary raised her head and gave her a weak smile.

"No. That's the thing. Nothing anyone does can ever take away the grief of losing a child."

"I can imagine," she said. "I don't want to, but I can."

Mary wiped her eyes with a napkin. "I know that Mollie's an innocent baby and I'm ashamed that all I could think of when I saw her was how unfair it was that Kyle should get a baby when mine didn't live."

"My first thought was about Honor and Zane. How did this womanizer deserve a baby when they won't be able to have one? But I've seen how Mollie's changed Kyle for the better. He embraced her without question. You won't believe it but he's been a loving and engaged father from day one. It's been amazing to see him change."

"I changed. But not for the better," Mary said.

"After what happened to you, no one could expect you to be all rainbows and sunshine."

To Violet's relief, Mary laughed. "I don't think anyone would describe me that way. Especially anyone here." She looked down at her salad and picked up her fork, then stabbed a roasted red pepper. It dangled from her fork like a worm on a hook.

"I need to move forward, but it feels impossible," Mary said.

"That's why I followed my dad here. Being without him was unbearable."

"Oh my gosh, I understand. Completely." Violet moved back to her original seat as Mary continued to pick at her food. "Do you regret coming here?"

"I don't know. I've felt more alone since my dad found Flora than I've ever felt in my life. I'm just a burden on them. They feel sorry for me, which is almost as bad as everyone else hating me."

"I don't hate you. I like you, as a matter of fact. Very much."

Mary tilted her head to the side and smiled back at her. "I like you too."

"I had no idea what you'd been through. It explains things."

"Like why I'm such a bitch?"

Violet grabbed her hand from across the table. "You're not a bitch, but you *do* put up a wall. I'm glad you let it down for me."

"Lance said the same thing to me recently," Mary said. "But, I mean, look at him. He's like the opposite of a wall. He's like a bowl of jello."

"From what I can see, he's just a genuinely nice guy," Violet said. "No wonder he's single."

"He's different from most guys, that's for sure."

"Like how?" Had Mary's voice softened at the mention of his name.

"He's impossible to alienate."

"Have you been trying to?" Violet asked.

"Oh, no, no. I just mean he likes me, even though I'm basically a cold bitch most of the time. Lance is kind, gentle. I can breathe when I'm with him."

"Maybe he sees beneath the surface to the real you," Violet said. "None of us are completely what we present to the outside world. Most of us are better."

"Do you think so? I'm a much worse person than people would even guess. Which is saying a lot."

"We can't expect ourselves to remain unaffected by loss or grief. I'm starting to think the trick to healing is to use our own hardships to become more empathetic to others. I'm trying to be more like Lance these days. Slower to judge based on outward appearance or persona. Unlike him, that quality doesn't come naturally."

"I've been pretty self-absorbed, so any of those tendencies have been dormant." Mary moved her gaze back to the window. A sparrow hopped between the bare branches of a tree. Holiday lights had been strung around the branches of the trees that lined the street. Later, they would sparkle in the dark night.

"I'm more connected to the characters in books than I am to people in real life," Mary said. "I was always like that a little, but after everything that happened, books were the only thing that saved me, the only way I could get through the day. Just lately, maybe Lance's influence, I've been a little more interested in living outside the pages of a book."

Violet scrutinized her new friend, looking for clues. Were there feelings developing between Lance and Mary? She wouldn't have put them together, but who knew the secrets of love? Certainly not her. "Are you interested in Lance? Is that what's making you interested in life?" She pretended to be absorbed in cutting a piece of chicken in her salad while she waited for Mary's answer.

"God, no. He would never be interested in me."

"Why do you say that?" Violet asked.

"He's in love with someone else."

"He is?"

"Someone from New York. She was the boss's daughter. *Married* daughter. He had an affair with her and it basically got him fired. That's why he decided to move out here."

Kyle had mentioned this to her one night during one of their chats. She hadn't gotten the impression Lance was still in love with her, but again, who could understand romance and all its complexities? "You don't think he's over her?"

"No, she's not the type of woman men forget easily. She's a Daisy."

"Daisy?"

"From The Great Gatsby."

"Ah. That's not good."

"Anyway, it's fine because I don't like him that way either. I'm not interested in dating or anything close. Since my divorce, there's no reason to believe there's anyone out there for me."

"Because he was so special?"

"No, because he was a George Wickham."

"I'm sorry?"

"From *Pride and Prejudice*. Remember how he told Elizabeth the lie about Darcy?

"Vaguely." Violet had watched the movie, but it had been a while. She really should read more fiction.

"Mr. Wickham was a liar, just like Chad. He was having an affair for months before I got pregnant. He tried to stop while I was pregnant, but he couldn't live without her. His words."

"You're kidding?" Violet asked, aghast.

"I wish I were. He left me for her and now they're married and have three kids. Healthy ones."

Poor Mary. No wonder she was bitter. "Lance is nothing like that, though. You said yourself he's different than most men."

"True. Regardless, I just don't see him that way. He's my first friend since my mom died and I wouldn't want to lose that. Plus, I learn so much from him. When he talks about other people, it's always something deeper than what most people would notice. Like, we were talking about you the other day and he said your energy and passion for this town had inspired him to buy the building and save the bookstore. He wants to make the bookstore profitable by changing it to meet customer demand, but in a way that respected the past. He said he learned that from you."

"No way! I had no idea."

"That's the thing, I guess. We never know how our actions influence others."

"Good or bad," Violet said. "Kyle told me I influenced some of his choices about the hotel, even though he hated me and my picket sign."

"Not that I listen to the Dogs and all their gossip, but I was surprised to hear you were working for Kyle." Mary said it a little too nonchalantly.

"I was too. But a desperate mother doesn't have many choices. The fact that it fell in my lap and would work so well with Dakota, I had to take it. And, well, it's not what I thought it would be. Kyle's not anything like I thought he was." *Kyle*. Every path led back to thoughts of Kyle.

"How so?"

"He's like you—there are difficult experiences from his past that have made him the way he is."

"Now you understand him," Mary said.

"Yes. And that complicates matters considerably."

Mary peered at Violet from across the table. "You like him?"

"I do. Too much."

"How much?"

"Let me put it to you this way. What's a story of unrequited love from one of your books? A woman in love with a man incapable of returning it?"

"*Remains of the Day*, maybe? It's about a housekeeper and a butler who love each other but are too frightened to admit it," Mary said.

"Something like that, yes."

"Not all books end unhappily, you know," Mary said.

"No, just the realistic ones."

* * *

Violet dreamt of Cole. They were in her apartment in Boston. Icicles hung from the windowpanes. Her stomach had the slightest bulge. *A baby. I'm going to have a baby.*

Cole's face darkened. *You stupid bitch.* He raised his hand and smacked her hard across her face. She fell to the floor.

I'm sorry. Forgive me?

She looked up at him. But it wasn't Cole. The face that stared down at her was Kyle. *Come on now, Lettie. Let's go build our house.*

Violet startled awake. Covered in sweat, she shivered. Two a.m. She got out of bed and changed into another pair of pajamas. Still shivering, she pulled on her warm robe. She wanted something warm to drink. Tea or hot milk. But Mel would be out there. She might even be awake.

Whatever. She couldn't be kept prisoner.

Violet opened her door and padded across the hallway to the entrance of the living room. Mel stood at the desk, looking through a stack of Kyle's mail from the basket he kept on the desk.

Clearly there wasn't anything interesting because Mel restacked the various envelopes and headed toward the bathroom. Violet waited until she had closed the door before scampering over to the desk. She peered into the basket. Most of it looked like junk. Credit card offers and the like—nothing important or private that Kyle wouldn't want Mel to see. However, one near the top of the pile caused her to pause and look more carefully. It was addressed to Daniel Kyle Hickman. Odd that the name was so close to Kyle Hicks. Was it possible he had two names? If so, why?

She left it on top of the stack where she'd found it and hurried back to her room. The hot drink would have to be forfeited. Once there, she took off her bathrobe and got back into bed. She longed to ask him about it, but if she did, she'd have to admit to going through the stack herself. Mel was nosy. But wasn't she guilty of the same?

It was probably nothing. If she found the right time to ask him about it, she would. Otherwise, she would keep her mouth shut. No need for him to know what a snoop she was. God forbid she was put into the same category as Mel.

She rolled over and closed her eyes but it was hours before she fell into a fitful sleep.

CHAPTER SEVEN

K<small>YLE</small>

THE REST OF the Dogs were already around the table in Brody's game room when Kyle arrived for poker night. Violet forced Kyle to leave Mollie with her and attend a poker night with the Dogs. Brody had a rare couple of days off and had come home for a quick visit. *Just go. You deserve a night out.* He could never say no to her, so off he went.

"The party may commence. I have arrived." He shrugged out of his coat and tossed it over the back of the couch.

The Dogs called out a greeting and told him to hurry up, he was late. Minnie, Brody and Kara's tuxedo cat, sauntered into the room, jumped onto the bar's counter, and curled up and went to sleep.

Kyle took his place at the table. Zane brought him a beer.

"Before you deal, we have to have a little talk." Jackson crossed his arms over his chest.

"More like an intervention." Zane dropped a round of beers on the table.

"Be gentle," Lance said. "I sense he's fragile."

"Are you talking about me?" Kyle asked.

"Kyle, you're not allowed to bring Mollie in to see Kara or me unless she's sick. Do you understand?"

"How will I know if she's sick, though?"

"You'll know. Violet will know." Jackson shot him a stern, doctorly type look from across the table. "Dude, you have to relax or you're the one who's going to end up sick. You're doing a great job. She's thriving."

"Thriving? Like more so than other babies, right?"

"Thriving, as in she's perfectly healthy and where she needs to be."

"But she's special, right? Like cuter and more alert than other babies her age?"

Jackson and Lance laughed. Brody rolled his eyes. Zane just shook his head and gave him that annoying know-it-all smirk.

"If I say yes, will you wait to bring her in again until her third month checkup?" Jackson asked.

"I'm waiting." Kyle tapped his fingers on the table and drew his eyebrows together.

"Mollie Blue Hicks is cuter and more alert than any baby I've ever seen," Jackson said.

"Was that so hard?" Kyle grinned as he shuffled the cards with a loud flourish.

"It was, actually. I took an oath," Jackson said.

Kyle dealt a round of cards and bets were placed. They played and talked simultaneously.

"Violet's parents came into the restaurant today," Zane said.

"They're back?" Kyle asked.

Zane nodded. "They've been back for weeks."

"Violet hasn't heard from them," Kyle said.

"That right?" Zane asked.

"Her old man's a jerk." Kyle folded. Terrible hand. "She and Dakota deserve so much better than the way he's treated her." He looked up to see Brody watching him from across the table.

"You and Violet are getting along better, huh?" Brody asked.

"She's phenomenal with Mollie." He smiled. "She has us all on a schedule."

Lance, sitting next to him, nudged him with his elbow. "The Doggiest of the Dogs on a schedule? That doesn't sound like you."

"Whatever. It's good. She makes sure I have time for my workout in the morning. When I get back, she always has my breakfast waiting. Coffee and an egg white omelet with avocado. She thinks avocados are good for you. I eat them, plus half of Dakota's bacon and pancakes when she's not looking."

They all stared at him like he was a strange animal at the zoo.

"Something I can help you with?" Kyle asked.

"Egg white? Avocados?" Lance asked. "Have you been invaded by an alien?"

"You guys are hilarious," Kyle said. He really needed to get them off this subject.

"Violet sounds like Kara," Brody said. "Women do that kind of stuff when they love us."

"Dude, she's my nanny." How did these guys always see right through him? It was beyond annoying.

"Wait a minute," Lance said. "You like her, don't you?"

"She's my nanny." Maybe if he repeated it enough he would convince them all, especially himself.

"I can't believe it. Honor was right," Zane said. "She totally called this."

"She did not," Kyle said.

"She did. Claims all that tension between you two is more than just an argument over politics."

"Fine. She's gorgeous. I'm into her. Are you happy?" Kyle handed the stack of cards to Lance for the next round. "Your deal."

"*How* into her?" Brody asked.

"It doesn't matter," Kyle said. "The last thing she needs is me. She deserves someone phenomenal. Like one of you guys."

"You *are* a well-established ass," Zane said, tossing a beer cap at him.

"My point exactly," Kyle said.

Jackson was looking at him with a contemplative tilt to his head. That was Jackson. Always thinking—the romantic, the philosopher of the group. Since Maggie had returned to him, the sadness in his blue eyes had changed to peaceful contentment. "How come you never talk about your childhood?" Jackson asked.

"What does that have to do with Violet?" Kyle asked.

"If you don't know, then you should be asking yourself why," Zane said.

"It's true, though," Lance said. "We know next to nothing about your past."

Kyle took a swig of his beer. "Nothing to tell. Normal stuff."

"You don't come to USC on a full ride as an emancipated adult if you had a normal childhood," Lance said.

Kyle pretended to study his cards. "I don't talk about the past. No reason to."

"Would you believe that talking about your past might change your future?" Jackson asked.

"God no," Kyle said.

"It did for me," Zane said. "Strangely, confronting my mother and my ex-fiancée was what I needed to fully move on with Honor."

Kyle slapped a card on the table. These guys needed to back off. "Did it? Did it really help to go back and meet your mother only to be rejected by her a second time? Once was enough for me, thanks very much."

"I wouldn't have thought so, but it did. In my case, I needed answers to be free." Zane paused, peeling the label from his beer bottle. "Man, I know it hurts."

"It doesn't hurt," Kyle said. "I hate her, but I'm not hurt."

No one said anything. Minnie woke from her nap and stretched. With a yawn, she jumped from the counter and headed toward Brody.

"My mother has nothing to do with anything. You guys know she left when I was young. My dad was a drunk. It was up to me to take care of my sister and brother after that."

Dead silence. Four pairs of eyes bored into him.

"What the hell? You have a sister and brother?" Brody asked.

"Dude, really?" Lance asked.

"I haven't seen them since I left home," Kyle said. He could kick himself. Why had he let that out of his mouth?

"Since you left for college?" Zane asked.

"Yeah," Kyle said.

"Why?" Jackson asked.

"Lots of reasons."

"Do you miss them?" Jackson asked.

"It doesn't matter if I miss them." Kyle got up from the table and grabbed another beer from the refrigerator. When he sat back down, he kept his eyes on his beer bottle. "They're better off without me."

"Did something happen between you guys?" Jackson asked.

Kyle looked up at him. "No, I just left and didn't want to go back. We weren't close, that's all. Nothing complex." He stood, knocking several plastic tokens off the table. "I better get home. Violet might need me. I shouldn't have left her alone with Mollie."

At the doorway, he looked back at their shocked faces. "Listen, can you not share this with the ladies? I don't want anyone else to know. I don't even know why I told you guys."

He didn't stay long enough to hear if they agreed or not. He had to get out into fresh air or his chest might explode.

When he was in his car, he sped out of Brody's driveway and down the road toward town. He turned the music on loud and tried to shut off his thoughts. All these years he'd kept his past a secret. What had possessed him to admit to having a brother and sister? They would ask him more questions now. He knew they wouldn't be able to let it go. What had he done?

* * *

When he arrived home, he found Mel on the couch with the plans for his house unfolded on the coffee table. Mollie was asleep in her crib. Violet must have gone to bed.

"Hey you," she said. "Good night?"

"Yeah. What're you doing with the plans to my house?"

"Just being nosy. I saw them on your desk and was too curious. It's going to be amazing."

"If I can get it built, sure," he said.

"It's a house for a full house. Get it, poker term. I know you went to play poker tonight."

"Did Violet tell you?"

"No, she hardly talks to me. Very unfriendly. Women sometimes react that way to me. I'm used to it." She fluttered her eyelashes at him like she was in a cartoon. There was definitely something wrong with this girl.

"How did you know I went to play poker if Violet didn't tell you?"

"Your calendar was open on your laptop. Says "poker night" right in there. You guys play at Brody Mullen's, right?"

"You ever hear curiosity killed the cat?"

She smiled. He could swear this girl turned into a cat the moment she left in the morning. Cats were nocturnal. Just right for night nanny positions.

He went to the table and picked up his plans. "Have a good night. I'm going to bed."

"Night. Sweet dreams." *A voice like a cat purr. Further evidence.*

When he got to his room, he stared at his phone. Would he wake Violet if he texted her? He really wanted to talk to her. One night without her and he was a mess. The night with the Dogs had been a disaster. They were probably totally bewildered and worried he was about to go off the deep end. They were used to fun Kyle, not dark Kyle. Not Pig.

I need to talk to Violet.

He took a chance and texted her.

You up?

A few seconds later, a response came through.

Yes. I'm hiding from Mel.

`She had my house plans out on the coffee`
`table and was staring at them with her cat`
`eyes like she wanted to commit them to`
`memory.`

She has ZERO boundaries.

`These young people are weird.` He pulled his shirt over his head and went to the window. There was no fog. The lights of town shone brightly.

She's not that much younger than me. I think SHE'S weird.

`I have a theory. She's a cat. Like for`
`real. One of those shifter deals. Think`
`about it.`

A second later, her response came in.

I concur with your theory. Cats are nocturnal. Perfect for a night nanny. We don't know what she does when she leaves here in the morning. Maybe prowls for mice. Spends some time at the sandbox in the park.

He shook with silent laughter as he texted back.

`That's exactly what I thought. And, ew, on`
`the sandbox. Remind me never to let Dakota`
`or Mollie play in one.`

I missed you tonight.

That surprised him. He stared at the screen for a moment, gathering himself.

I missed you too. I should have stayed home with you. I kind of made a mess of it with the Dogs.

Why?

I told them some things I shouldn't have and then clammed up and stormed out.

It's hard to believe they don't already know everything about you.

We're guys. We don't talk about real stuff.

Why is that?

Just because we're guys. I guess? How should I know? I'm a guy.

A pretty awesome guy, if you ask me.

He would text her all night if he could. She needed her rest, as did he. If only he could get some without tossing and turning and thinking about Violet. He texted back.

You're pretty awesome yourself. Anyway, I'll see you in morning. We should get some rest.

Night, Kyle.

Night, Violet.

He pushed his phone aside and sat on the edge of the bed. What was happening to him? This woman had him thinking and doing things he'd never done in his life. He *missed* her after only one evening apart. For heaven's sake, he'd seen her mere hours ago. The whole thing was silly.

Was this what falling in love felt like? This longing that ached in his chest and mimicked homesickness? A terrible spinning only alleviated by her presence? The leap of his heart when she walked into the room?

He brushed his teeth and got into bed. When he closed his eyes, he saw Violet's face, her brown eyes soft and her mouth turned slightly upward when he'd amused her but she didn't want to admit to it. He heard her tender voice as she murmured sweet nothings to Mollie. There in the dark room, he could almost detect the scent of her skin when she'd leaned close to take the baby from him. He'd never even held her hand, let alone touched her silky skin, yet he knew what she would feel like tucked into the crook of his arm as they drifted off to sleep.

Tomorrow would contain Violet. That's all he needed to know right now. Tomorrow would be here soon enough. Whether he fell for her or not didn't matter. He could not have her. After their year was up, he would go back to living the way he used to.

He drifted off to sleep and dreamt they danced under a starry sky by the sea with ocean breezes that smelled of jasmine.

* * *

Kyle drove Violet, Dakota, and Mollie out to Brody and Kara's for the football game. San Francisco was playing Los Angeles. He couldn't wait for this game.

They gathered in the Mullens' game room to watch. The Dogs, Honor, Maggie and Kara were there, along with six-year-old Jubie.

They all wore their Mullen jerseys, including the kids. He wondered if they made jerseys for babies. Mollie needed one.

Brody's Sharks won the coin toss and the game began with a failed pass to a receiver. A close up of Brody's face revealed his steely eyed game face.

Kara and Honor huddled together on the couch, ready to hold on to each other if Brody got sacked, or scream when the Sharks scored. Lance and Zane sat on the floor with their backs against the couch and a bowl of chips between them. Dakota and Jubie played together in the back of the room with Legos. Jackson and Maggie sat together in the oversized chair, holding hands. Violet stretched out like a cat in front of the fire, looking relaxed. And beautiful. She'd grown even prettier since she'd moved in with him, having gained a few pounds, which she'd desperately needed. The pinched look around her mouth had softened. Her skin glowed.

In his arms, Mollie arched her back and started in with her hungry cry. He knew it now like the back of his hand. Violet had been right. He could now decipher the various baby codes.

Usually Kyle didn't take his eyes from the game except to open another beer or fill his plate. Tonight, however, Mollie had other ideas for him. First, she had to have her bottle, half of which landed on his jersey during a burping session. Then she fussed until he picked her up and walked with her around the room patting her back until she let out a very unladylike toot. He missed both touchdowns in the first half, including an epic Brody Mullen fifty-yard pass. When Mollie finally fell asleep, he put her in her car seat. Turns out a baby could sleep anywhere in those things. He said a silent thank you to whomever had come up with the design, then grabbed a beer and plopped on the couch next to Honor. By that time, halftime had started.

Kara turned down the volume. All eyes turned to him.

"How's it going with the baby?" Kara asked.

"We're doing great." Kyle pointed at Violet. "Thanks to a certain person."

Violet ducked her head. Her hair fell over her cheek and glistened in the firelight. "Don't listen to him. He's taken to it like a champ."

"Never thought I'd see the day," Zane said.

"Me either," Kyle said. Every time he thought of his conversation with Zane where he'd tried to talk him out of adopting Jubie, shame rushed through him. Never say never and all that. He'd basically told Zane his life was over if he adopted a child. How ironic that less than two months later he was walking a crying baby around the room instead of watching their buddy play football. Zane had the decency to keep that point to himself.

His stomach growled. He couldn't remember the last time he ate. Had Violet eaten? He'd told her on the way out to relax and not be on duty tonight, but her eyes kept skirting over to the baby.

The women were distracted when Jubie and Dakota bounced over to ask if there was any dessert and could they have some. Kara smiled and rose from the couch. "I have a few frozen treats hidden in the freezer." She held out her hands and they each took one. "Juice bars okay with the mothers?"

"Fine with me," Violet said.

"Me too," Honor said.

Kara left with the kids. Honor moved to sit between Zane's legs. They looked good together. Like sunshine. A pang of jealousy twisted in his gut. Would he ever be able to make something work with a woman? *Not any woman, fool, Violet.*

Where had that voice come from?

I'm not ready.

So you say.

Kyle poked Violet's ankle with his foot. "Did you eat?"

She shook her head. "Not yet."

"You want me to fix you a plate?" he asked.

"I can do it," she said.

He got to his feet and offered his hand. "Come on. You can make sure I eat the kale salad."

"You'll like it," Violet said.

"Sure I will," he said.

As they passed, he glanced down to see Honor staring at him with one eyebrow lifted.

The third quarter was about to begin when Honor trapped him over by the bar. "You and Violet seem to have patched things up."

"We kind of had to."

"She's working out, then?"

"Better than working out. She's awesome," he said. "I'd be lost without her."

"Interesting."

"What does that mean?" Honestly, Honor was such a know-it-all sometimes.

"Nothing."

"Don't get any ideas. Just because you're in love doesn't mean everyone is."

"Who said anything about love?" Honor popped a raspberry in her mouth.

"You did."

"No, I didn't. But now that you bring it up, you two are seeming awfully domestic. Perfect little family unit."

He spoke with his teeth clenched. "Stop it. She'll hear you." He looked over to the other end of the room. Violet knelt on the carpet next to Maggie and Jackson's chair. Just then, she threw her head back and laughed. "She's my nanny and a damn good one. That's all there is to it."

"She looks gorgeous," Honor said. "Like a new person."

"Amazing what happens when the burden of money problems lessens."

"Preaching to the choir, brother." Honor picked up a baby carrot and shook it at him. "You two are good for each other. Ever think of that?"

"You really need to be quiet," he whispered. "Seriously."

"Sometimes situations happen for a reason. That's all I'm saying. It's beyond obvious how you feel about her. What's stopping you?"

"I love you, Honor. I do. But I swear to God, let this go."

She flinched and stepped backward. Her eyes sharpened into points that pierced through him. "Listen to me, Kyle Hicks. Whatever it is that has you hell bent on self-destruction and self-punishment—well, you need to work that out."

"You don't know anything about me."

She stepped closer and spoke right into his ear. "You're wrong, my friend. I know you. You think it's not like looking in a mirror? I know exactly what you're doing and why you're doing it. You may have the rest of our gang fooled, but I know you hate yourself. I don't know why exactly, but I can bet it's something from your childhood. It's time to figure it out and let go of whatever's haunting you or you're headed for a very lonely life. Do you hear me?"

"Stop. Just stop. You don't get to talk to me this way."

"You can bet your designer shoes I do. May I remind you who got into an actual physical altercation on my behalf when Zane was acting like an ass? That's right. I know about that. Brody told me about you two rolling around on the floor because you didn't think he was respecting me. I have just as much right to get into your business as you did mine. You know why?" She tapped him on the chest with her index finger. "I'll answer *for* you. Because we love each other and that's what friends do."

From the couch, Kara let out a scream. Kyle turned to look at the screen. Brody was flat on his back. A team of doctors and coaches rushed out to the field. From the television, the announcers described the scene.

"Brody Mullen on the ground here. A particularly brutal sack from defensive end Marty Shell."

"Yes, he seemed to come out of nowhere," the other announcer said.

"I can't tell for sure, but it seems like it might be a neck injury."

The footage of the incident replayed on the television. Shell slammed into Brody and knocked him several feet in the air. Brody's neck twisted as he hit the ground.

No, not this. Get up. You can do it. Just get up.

Cut back to present. Brody remained on the ground. Was he moving at all? Kyle held his breath. *Come on, man, move your legs.*

Kara stood before the television, her hands covering her mouth. Honor crossed the room to stand by her side.

They all waited.

Finally, Brody rose to his feet. The crowd cheered. Here, they watched in silence as the doctors helped him onto a cart that would take him off the field and into the locker room.

The announcers continued their commentary. "Brody Mullen on his feet there, but it looks like the doctors don't want him back on the field."

"He walked," Kara said. "He walked onto the cart. That's something."

No one needed clarification. They all knew the dangers of Brody's profession.

"Should I go to him now?" Kara asked. "Or wait for the call?"

Honor slipped her hand into Kara's. "Let's wait for the call. I'll take you into the city if he wants you there."

A few minutes later, Kara's cell phone rang. "It's him." She left the room as she answered. "Hi, babe."

No one said anything for a few seconds until Jackson said what they all feared. "That was a serious hit to his neck. I didn't know if he was going to get up and walk onto the cart."

Violet pulled her knees up to her chest. "That scared me so badly."

"Longest thirty seconds ever." Honor sank onto the couch. "Not gonna lie, I have a bad feeling about this."

"Didn't that player up in Washington have to retire from his neck injury last season?" Zane asked. "What's his name?"

"The defensive back?" Kyle asked.

"Gordon Thomas," Honor said. "He decided to retire after permanent nerve damage to his neck. Docs said it was too risky to play."

"But he's a quarterback," Maggie said. "Isn't it totally different?"

"A neck is a neck," Jackson said.

Kara came back into the room. "He's okay. He hasn't lost feeling anywhere, thank God, but best case he's probably out for the rest of the season."

"Best case?" Zane asked.

Kara nodded, her face bleached of color. "He said they're not sure the extent of the damage."

Honor swore under her breath. "Is he freaking out?"

"Yeah. Pretty much," Kara said. "I'm going to pack a few things and drive into the city to be with him."

"I'll drive you," Lance said.

"Jackson, he wants you to come tomorrow when he meets with the experts," Kara said.

"The Dogs should all go," Maggie said. "Just in case it's bad news."

Kara burst into tears. "Would you? Could you?"

If the news was bad for Brody it would be bad for all of them. Dogs stuck together. "Yes, we'll be there by morning," Kyle said.

"Ladies too?" Kara asked.

"Kyle, you go. I'll stay with the kids," Violet said. "Honor, Jubie can stay with me at the hotel."

"Flora would take the kids," Lance said. "She's dying to spend time with Mollie."

Kara reached out to Violet. "Please say you'll come. I need all my girls with me."

Violet looked over at Kyle. "Is it okay with you?"

"Yes, of course," Kyle said. Truth be told, he wanted Violet with him. "Flora will take great care of them. Mel can have the night off."

They went into planning mode. Lance called Flora and she promptly agreed to take all three of the children. Kara had three guestrooms, enough for Lance, Kyle, and Violet at their condo in the city. The couples would stay in a nearby hotel. When it was all settled, Kara left to pack and the rest of them dispersed to either help clean up or head home to get ready for the morning.

* * *

Fifteen minutes later, Kyle stood on Brody's balcony waiting for Violet to be ready to leave Kara and Brody's. She was huddled inside with the other women. Mist blanketed the yard. A breeze brought the scent of the ocean. Behind him, the doors off the kitchen opened and closed. It was Lance.

"Kara's not quite ready," Lance said. "Thought I'd get a little air before we start out." He came to stand beside Kyle. They both rested their forearms on the railing. "The days of our bachelor summer seem far away," Lance said.

"Yeah, sorry I haven't been around much. The baby keeps me busy."

"No need to apologize. I get it. Well, I don't totally get it, being childless and without any hope of ever finding a woman."

Kyle shook his head, chuckling. "Have you been trying to find a woman?"

"Not really. Still reeling from New York." Lance let out a deep breath. "Brody should go out now when he's on top. Think about a coaching career or broadcasting."

"You really think so?" Kyle asked. He couldn't imagine Brody was ready to retire at only thirty-one. But football was a young man's game. No question about that.

"I'm not saying he'll do it, but I think he should. He can continue to make money through endorsements and such," Lance said.

"It's not about the money," Kyle said. "It's about how he thinks about himself. His identity."

"You think?" Lance asked.

"Do you miss your work?" Kyle asked, referring to Lance's former career as a hedge fund manager.

"Not really. My eye's stopped twitching, so that's good."

"Come on, man. A bookstore? You're not going to be happy doing that."

"It's also a soda fountain and coffee shop," Lance said primly. "And I just own the building. Mary's doing the rest."

"Seems like every time I text, you're there."

"Mary's worried about things, so I stop in to answer questions and give advice. She's actually quite capable without my help, but she's trained as a librarian not a business owner."

"Has Mary loosened up any or is she still super uptight?" Kyle asked. *Uptight* was a kind word for her.

"She's just a quiet person. Cerebral," Lance said. "Once you get past her reticence, she's actually remarkably smart and interesting. But man, she's a sad girl."

"Sad?"

"Something happened to her. I don't know what, but it was bad. I've caught her crying in the back room a couple times."

Mary crying? "I can't stand to see a woman crying," Kyle said. "It's like I go on overload trying to fix whatever it is."

"I feel you. It's taken a lot of restraint not to ask her a bunch of questions when she comes into the shop with red eyes and dark circles. I know something's haunting her and yeah, I just want to fix it. I sense that deep down she's not at all what we thought at first."

"People aren't always what they first appear to be," Kyle said.

"Are you referring to Violet?"

"Maybe."

Lance continued to look out to the yard. Men. No eye contact when speaking of serious matters. "Listen, I'm not one to tell another man his business, but I think you need to look at yourself pretty hard and figure out what in the hell's the matter with you."

"Meaning?" Not Lance too? What was it about tonight?

"It's obvious that you and Violet are into each other and it's beyond me why you would purposely screw it up. Aren't you sick of prowling for women like you're still in college?"

"I haven't been prowling much," Kyle said.

"That's my point. Maybe it's time to grow up and admit to

yourself that you have feelings for an awesome woman. Someone you could build a life with."

"Has it ever occurred to you that she's better off without me?" Kyle asked.

"Sticking with that lame excuse. Okay. Good for you. Be an idiot. See if I care."

"Back off. Seriously," Kyle said.

"I'm sick of backing off when it comes to you. How could you have a brother and sister and never mention it to me?" Lance said. "I thought we were tight."

"We're not women painting each other's nails and talking about every single moment of our lives. There's some stuff I don't talk about."

"Let me give you a little advice. Take a look around you. You see how our buddies are happy? That could be you."

The door to the patio opened. Violet called out to them. "Kyle, we should probably go. It's way past Dakota's bedtime."

Kyle's stomach fluttered at the sound of her voice. "I'm ready whenever you are." *If only.* He brushed past Lance. "I'll see you tomorrow in the city."

"Don't think this conversation is over," Lance said.

"Dude." Kyle glowered and turned back to shove him with his shoulder.

They stared at each other for a moment, before Kyle turned away.

Violet held the door open for him. He smelled her perfume as he shuffled by her.

"What was that all about?" Violet asked.

"Nothing. Just the usual. A Dog can't seem to mind his own business."

* * *

When they arrived home, Mel was on the couch with her feet on the coffee table flipping through a magazine. "Hey guys," she said.

Kyle held a sleeping Dakota in his arms so he merely nodded hello. He carried him back to his bed in the closest and tucked him in between the blankets. Violet had remained behind to hand over Mollie to Mel. It was a little after ten, so the baby would need a bottle before she went down for the night. When he came out of Violet's bedroom, he paused before going into the sitting area, listening. Violet spoke sharply to Mel.

"It's none of your business," Violet said.

"I was just asking. Don't make a federal case out of it."

"The Mullens are very private people. Those of us in their inner circle know better than to gossip."

"It looked bad," Mel said. "I wondered, that's all."

"Don't."

"You're so bloody touchy," Mel said. "You need to loosen up."

Bloody? Had she picked that word up on her travels? Pretentious Mel. What in her past was she hiding that she had to put on these layers of forced sophistication?

He walked into the room. The minute she saw him, Mel's face lit up and she slid him a sultry smile. "Wouldn't you agree, Kyle, that Violet needs to lighten up." She was feeding Mollie a bottle from the armchair. Every time he saw Mel with the baby it gave him an uneasy feeling. He couldn't put his finger on it, but something about her looked odd with a baby in her arms.

He would ignore her question and keep it all business. That was the best way to deal with people who had no sense of boundaries. "Mel, there's an extra pair of pajamas in that diaper bag. Please dress her in them before you put her down."

"I'm going to bed," Violet said to Kyle.

He reminded her of his appointment in the morning and that he would swing by and get her after that.

"I'll be packed and ready."

"Great."

She said goodnight to them both and left for bed.

The moment she was out of the room, Mel asked him where they were going.

"We're going on a trip out of town overnight. You can have the night off. We have a friend looking after the kids."

"Overnight? Together?"

"That's right." He shoved his hands in his pockets. "You can have the night off tomorrow. The kids are going to Flora's."

"What's going on with you two anyway?" Mel asked.

"Who?"

"You and Violet."

"We're close friends." He walked over to the bar and poured himself a scotch. Most nights he went straight to bed when she arrived. Tonight, an instinct prickled the back of his neck. He wanted to watch her with the baby for a few minutes.

"So, you're available?" Mel grinned. "Asking for a friend."

What a strange girl she was.

"Depends on what you mean by that. I'm technically available, but I'm not looking for anyone. Mollie's my priority right now."

"My friend would find that sexy."

"You're barking up the wrong tree here," he said. "Trust me."

"I'll be sure to tell my friend." She went back to looking at Mollie.

"Do that." He drank his scotch and watched her. She was dangerous. Manipulative and conniving, the type to seduce a guy and sue him for sexual harassment. Was that what was going on here? Did she want to trap him and extort money out of him in exchange for her silence?

"I noticed you love country music. Do you ever go to concerts?" she asked.

"Sometimes. When I have time."

"Listening to live music is one of my favorite pastimes."

"Me too," he said absently. Time to get out of here.

"I'm going to a festival during the Thanksgiving weekend. The one at the stadium in San Francisco. You heard of it?"

"Sure. I thought about getting tickets before Mollie arrived. Things are different now, obviously." He finished his drink and turned away to put it in the sink at the wet bar.

"Does it make you sad?" she asked. "Not to have a life outside of the baby?"

He shrugged. "Sad is the wrong word. She's my life now, so everything's different."

"You need a woman by your side, Kyle Hicks." She smiled that cat smile that sent a shiver down his spine.

"Conventional wisdom would agree, but I think for myself."

He wanted to give Mollie a kiss goodnight but given that she was currently in Mel's arms, he decided to skip it tonight. "Goodnight, Mel."

"Night, Kyle. Sweet dreams."

* * *

He woke after seven the next morning. How had he slept so late? Mollie usually woke him by six. Alarmed, he rubbed his eyes and looked over to the baby monitor. The crib was empty. Violet must have gotten her. She'd let him sleep in.

He pulled on sweats and a t-shirt and padded out to the sitting area. Violet was with Mollie near the bank of windows. A weak autumn sun filtered through the glass and basked the room in a hazy light. Country music played softly from the speakers. Wearing nothing but a long t-shirt that hung to her midthigh, she cradled Mollie in the crook of one arm and danced in the muted light. He watched, mesmerized. She moved with graceful steps between the rays of sun. Her hair fell over her face as she gazed down at the baby. But it could not disguise her smile. The same smile she had for Dakota. A mother's smile for her child.

She loved Mollie.

And what about you, fool? Who do you love?

He loved the woman who loved his daughter. The truth almost brought him to his knees. He would do anything for the woman and the baby in her arms. His own life meant nothing if they were not safe and happy.

Dakota appeared, holding his blanket and dressed in his

Spider-Man pajamas. With tousled hair and cheeks pink from sleep, he ran to Kyle and wrapped his arms around his legs. An ache pressed against his chest. He loved Violet's son. Was it natural to love someone else's flesh and blood like they were your own? He didn't know. All he knew was that everything he would ever need was in this room.

A kernel of truth exploded inside his mind. Honor and Lance were right. He had to face his demons, his self-hatred, and come clean. If he were to have any chance with the woman who danced in the rays of light, he had to tell her everything. The Miller brothers. The accident. Daniel Kyle Hickman.

"Good morning, boys," Violet said.

"What's up with the country music?" Kyle asked.

"It's growing on me."

"I'm hungry for bacon," Dakota said.

"Agreed," Kyle said. "And pancakes."

"Don't you want your usual omelet?" Violet asked.

"Kale eats half my pancakes and bacon," Dakota said.

"He does?"

"Guilty," Kyle said.

"Every morning?" she asked.

"When you see a good thing, you stick with it," he said.

Like you. Everything he would ever need was right here in this room. But did they need him? Could Violet ever love him if she knew the truth?

CHAPTER EIGHT

Violet

VIOLET AND KYLE arrived in San Francisco around noon. Brody and Kara had gone to see the specialist that morning and were already home. Results of an MRI wouldn't be back until later that afternoon. Honor had suggested they take Kara shopping while the Dogs hung out at the condo. The doctors had warned Brody to take it easy. He was in a neck brace until they discovered the extent of his injuries. The Dogs had promised to do nothing but play poker.

Kyle had slipped some bills in Violet's hand as she and Kara were about to leave. "I don't want you to be the only one without shopping money."

She'd said no, but he insisted. "Consider it a bonus. I know you're paying down your debt with every cent you're making, and I want you to buy something nice for yourself. Please, let me do this for you."

It wasn't until they were in an Uber to the shopping district that she unfolded the wad of bills to discover ten one-hundred-dollar bills. She had fanned them out on her lap and told the other

141

ladies she couldn't possibly accept them. They disagreed, adamant she should take the bonus and buy herself some new clothes.

"Do it for me," Kara said. "It'll be so much fun to help you pick out some new things. Perfect distraction."

They spent the day in and out of shops, trying on clothes and looking at accessories. At the end of the afternoon, they all agreed that shopping was harder than it looked, and they couldn't wait to get home and go to dinner with the Dogs. If Kara was worried about Brody's test results, she didn't mention it.

Around five that afternoon, they rushed in with their packages, laughing and pink-cheeked from the cold. All five of the Dogs were in the living room. It was if a black cloud had entered the room. Brody was slouched in one of the armchairs with a bottle of whiskey in his lap. Jackson leaned against the wall with his arms crossed. Zane sat backward in a hardback chair. Kyle was on the floor with his back against the couch, peeling the label off a beer bottle. Lance paced around the room.

"What is it?" Kara's face drained of color. She dropped her bags on the floor. "What did the doctor say?"

"I'm done." Brody tugged on his neck brace like he wanted to peel it off.

"Done? For the season?" Kara asked.

"Forever," Brody said. "They said it's too risky. One wrong hit and I may never walk again."

Honor deposited her bags on the floor, speaking in an even tone. "What did they say exactly? Jackson, tell us in a way we can understand."

Jackson interpreted it for them, explaining that an injury this severe meant a risk of paralysis if he continued to play. "There's nothing that can be done. There's too much nerve damage."

Kara dropped to her knees near Brody's chair, obviously too shocked to speak.

Clearly no one knew what to say. Even Honor, who always knew how to wrangle any situation, seemed at a loss.

"But you'll be fine if you don't play, right?" Honor asked. "If you retire?"

"That's what the doctors said to me this afternoon. They were quite clear on it." Brody took a swig of whiskey. "Football has been my life. All my life. I don't know what to do without it."

"There's a whole world out there," Lance said. "You'll have time to actually explore it now."

Brody looked at his brother with blank eyes. "I don't want to. I want to play football."

"This doesn't mean you have to leave the sport," Lance said. "You could coach or go into announcing like Dad. You've had a good run. It's time, with or without the injury."

"It's not time," Brody said. "Not like this."

Zane perched on the arm of the sofa. "You won a Super Bowl. Everything you set out to do, you've done."

"I didn't want to go out like this. Not injured. I wanted to go out on my own terms, not because I have to," Brody said.

"Take it easy on the whiskey," Kara said. "You haven't had a drink all season."

"You've been disciplined and driven for a long time," Jackson said. "You'll have the chance to have a life without so much pressure. You can take Kara places. Have a family. Spend time doing normal stuff like the rest of us."

"My life was football," Brody said.

"I thought I was your life," Kara said.

"Baby, you are. Of course, you are. You know what I mean."

"I do," Kara said. "You knew eventually this was going to happen. Like Lance said, you've played longer than most. It's not like we need more money."

"It's not about the money," Brody said.

It was about identity. Violet understood. She wrestled with this very thing when she had to close the store. Who was she without her shop? She looked over at Kyle. He hadn't said anything this entire time. What was he thinking?

"What about Honor?" Brody directed the question at Kara like it was her fault. "She's suddenly out of a job."

"Not really," Honor said. "You're going to remain a hot commodity for years to come. I'll still be figuring out ways for you to make more money than you know what to do with. Anyway, you don't owe me anything. I'm perfectly capable of working for someone else. We know everyone in this business, and I have a good reputation."

"I don't want you working for anyone else," Brody said.

"You're not responsible for everyone on the planet," Zane said. "Honor's the queen of her own castle."

"I'll always be grateful, Brody, you know that. But you don't have to take care of me," Honor said. "You've done so much for me already."

"And I could use your help with the brewery plans, to tell you the truth," Zane said to Brody.

"I know what you guys are trying to do here, but I'm not buying it. Help out with the brewery plans? You don't need help. The only thing I know is football. Who am I if I'm not a quarterback? I've been one since I was in seventh grade."

"You're a husband, brother, friend," Kara said. "Hopefully a father soon."

"A Dog," Zane said. "You'll always be the quarterback of this motley crew." He gestured around the room.

Maggie stepped forward. "Brody, I understand this better than anyone. When they told me I couldn't dance any more it felt like my life was over. Who was I if not a song and dance girl? But it was just the beginning of something great. Different, but equally wonderful. I know it's impossible to see now, but you *will* get through this and come out the other side."

For the first time, Brody's stubborn expression softened. "I forgot that part of your story."

"I got through it. You will too. And like the Dogs said, we're all here for you." Maggie still clutched her bags to her chest like they were a life jacket.

Kyle spoke for the first time. "Man, you've been my hero since the day I met you. Not because of your game but because of who you are down deep. You'll figure out what to do next and you'll do it like you've played football—with grace and integrity and hard work. It's a blow. I get that. But we've all had setbacks and got right back up to try again. You taught us how to do that better than anyone."

"Thanks, man," Brody said, wiping his eyes. "I just need some time."

They should leave. Give the couple some time to talk. "We should maybe let Brody and Kara talk alone," Violet said.

Jackson nodded. "We can go down to the bar. Give you guys some alone time."

The other Dogs quickly rallied, gathering coats and wallets. Before she knew it, all seven of them were crammed in the elevator headed down to the lobby. No one spoke until they reached the first floor. Then, they stood huddled together, unsure of what to do.

"What do we do now?" Kyle asked.

"Crap, I don't know," Honor said.

"Should we go home?" Jackson asked.

"*We* can't. I have a meeting in the morning," Maggie said.

"Right. I knew that. Sorry, I'm shaken up," Jackson said.

"Me too," Zane said. "I've never seen him like that."

"He'll recover," Lance said. "Tomorrow he's going to be majorly hungover. But he won't be down for long. He'll rally. You'll see. He'll be in the broadcasting booth by this time next year. In the long run, this is better for Kara. She worries herself sick over him every single practice and game."

"It did have to happen eventually," Honor said. "I thought he should've retired after last season, but he wouldn't even consider it."

"Kara misses him a lot when he's on the road," Jackson said. "And I know she'd prefer to work more at our office. She keeps saying her nurse practitioner degree is being wasted as the invisible partner to a famous football player."

"I never thought of it from that angle," Zane said. "Come on, let's get some food and drinks. Let's toast our favorite quarterback of all time."

Violet ended up sitting next to Kyle. They were seated in the largest booth in the restaurant. She and Kyle were on one end, with Jackson and Maggie on the other and Zane and Honor in the middle. Lance had grabbed an extra chair from another table.

"Did you get some pretty things?" Kyle asked, leaning close to speak into her ear.

"You gave me too much money."

"Did you get some pretty things?" he repeated, smiling indulgently.

"Yes. I spent the whole amount. I'm disgusted with myself."

He chuckled. "Good. You've made me happy."

"Flora texted and said everyone was doing well and behaving themselves. Jubie hasn't left the baby for a moment, which made Dakota jealous. Flora was able to distract him by making cookies and buying him a new truck at the toy store."

"Well played, Dakota," Kyle said.

They ordered dinner and drinks, more subdued than usual, given Brody's situation. Finally, Lance broke the mood by ordering a round of shots. "Listen to me, you guys. Brody's basically lived a charmed life. He got to play football for most of it. Yes, it's a bummer he's forced to quit, but we need to keep this in perspective. He's rich and he's married to a beautiful and smart woman who worships him. We don't need to feel too sorry for him. He'll bounce back. Our dad did after he retired. Now, let's have some fun."

"To Brody and the future," Jackson said.

"Down the hatch," Honor said.

They all did as they were told. Violet almost gagged, not used to hard alcohol. "You okay?" Kyle asked.

"Strong." She coughed. Everyone laughed.

A DJ played music from the corner of the restaurant while they were eating. The lights were dimmed and a disco ball hanging from the ceiling cast sparkles on the walls and floor. A woman came over and asked Lance to dance, which he reluctantly agreed to. The others got up to dance as well, leaving Violet alone with Kyle.

"We could dance, if you wanted to," Kyle said.

"Do you?"

"It's perilous," he said.

"Yeah."

"But so is sitting this close to you, so we may as well go for it."

"Fine."

She scooted out of the booth. He followed her to the dance floor. A ballad was playing. The place wasn't busy, with only a few others besides their friends on the dance floor. Kyle held out his arms and she walked into them. He was taller than her by about five or six inches, but in her high-heeled boots, she could easily spread her hands in his hair. Not that she would, of course. His spicy cologne was enough to make her want to take a bite out of his ear.

A man at the bar with a thick neck and square head was staring at her. She avoided looking at him again by concentrating on Kyle. The way his hair curled just above the collar of his sweater made her fingers itch.

"That guy's staring at you," Kyle said.

"Maybe he's staring at you."

"It's not that kind of bar."

"Doesn't he see I'm with you?"

"Clearly not. He reminds me of someone I once knew," Kyle said under his breath.

"Just ignore him."

"Good idea. I'd rather look at you anyway," he said.

After a few songs, they decided to go the bar and order a drink. Kyle asked if she'd order him a scotch, neat, while he used the restroom.

"I know what you want," she said.

He tucked her hair behind one ear and looked right into her eyes. "Do you?"

She held her breath, as if that would squelch the rush of desire that coursed through every nerve ending.

"I meant what you like to drink," she said.

"I know. I'm just teasing you." His hand lingered on her arm for a moment, warm and dry.

She watched him walk away, his hard body visible through the tight knit sweater. What was she going to do about this man? She knew what she wanted to do to him, which was unfortunate. She ordered Kyle's drink and asked for a white wine for herself. The bartender, a slight, balding man with a bored expression told her he needed to grab a few bottles of wine from the storage area. She perched on a barstool, nervous to be left alone at the bar with only the thick-necked man. The others were still on the dance floor. Seconds later, the guy started toward her. She looked down, pretending to be interested in the coaster. He slid onto the barstool next to her, close enough to look down her blouse.

"What're you drinking?" His words slurred. He was drunk. *Great.* She'd never get rid of him. He tipped toward her. One wrong move and he'd be on her lap.

"I'm with someone."

"With gay boy?"

"Please, just leave me alone. I'm not interested." She looked away. The bartender had yet to return.

"Why's that? You think you're too good for me." He sneered and put his face close to hers. His breath would light the whole place on fire if someone struck a match.

"No, I told you, I'm here with someone." She slid from the other side of the stool. Considering how intoxicated he was, the man moved quickly, pinning her against the counter with the bulk of his body.

His hands were as thick and large as his neck. He placed them on her shoulders. Something hard pressed against her stomach. She gagged, realizing it was his erection.

"Get off me." She tried to push him away, but he trapped her hands in his fat ones and twisted her arms behind her back. And then he was gone. Kyle had lifted the man and thrown him three feet across the room. Before he could get to his feet, Kyle was on top of him, pummeling the guy's face.

She screamed for help. Her friends were already there by then. Jackson and Zane, both strong from years of surfing, managed to pull Kyle off the guy, whose face was bloodied and already starting to swell. The bartender finally appeared with two bottles of wine in his arms.

"Oh, for Christ's sake. Go. Before anyone calls the cops," he said with the same bored expression as before. "I'll take care of this one."

Jackson and Zane each held one of Kyle's arms as he struggled to get away from them. "Calm down, buddy," Jackson said.

"Let me go." Kyle panted, flushed with anger. "I'll kill that asshole, I swear to God."

"Please, Kyle, we should go," Violet said. "I don't want you to get in trouble."

Her voice seemed to calm him. He nodded and followed Jackson out the door and onto the street. Violet and the others followed. Within minutes they were back in the lobby of Brody's building. No one spoke as they headed up in the elevator. Maggie's face was white and scared. Honor looked mad. Other than Kyle, the men, strangely, seemed amused.

They entered the empty living room quietly. Hopefully Kara had gotten Brody to bed with some water and pain killers.

Once they were safely inside, Honor said something about Kyle's hands. Violet hadn't noticed before, but they were bloodied and bruised. "I'll get something to clean up your knuckles," Honor said.

Violet froze in the middle of the room. Cold after the rush of adrenaline, she started to shake.

Jackson took her by the hand and led her over to the sofa. "Here, just sit. I'll get you something to calm your nerves."

"Better get one for him too," Zane said, pointing at Kyle.

"Make it a double," Kyle said.

Maggie sat next to Violet on the couch and took her hand. Violet rested her head against Maggie's shoulder, happy for the warmth of her friend's body next to hers. "It's okay now," Maggie whispered. "You're safe with us."

"What the hell happened?" Zane asked.

"He had Violet pinned against the bar with his hands all over her." Kyle winced as Honor placed a damp cloth on his hands.

Violet shuddered. "He had me trapped."

"That piece of shit deserved everything he got," Kyle said.

Jackson handed Violet a glass of whiskey.

"No, I'm fine," Violet said.

"Drink up," Maggie said. "It'll warm you."

Violet did as she was asked. The whiskey helped even though it tasted terrible. Kyle was on his feet, pacing between the fireplace and the sofa, looking like a thundercloud.

Lance planted a drink and a plastic bag of ice on the coffee table. "Kyle, come sit. You need to relax. It's over now."

Kyle picked up the drink but remained standing and talked about her as if she weren't in the room. "I shouldn't have left her alone. It was my fault." He downed his drink in one gulp. "I saw that asshat looking at her earlier. I know his type. I grew up with a dozen guys just like him." He turned to Violet. "I should've stayed with you."

"It wasn't your fault. The bartender went to the back and the guy just pounced on me." Her voice shook almost as hard as her trembling hands.

He crossed over to the couch and sat beside her. "Are you okay? Did he hurt you?"

"I'm fine. Just shook up, that's all."

Jackson announced that it was time for him to get Maggie back to their hotel room for her meeting tomorrow. Zane and Honor agreed that it was time for them to go as well, leaving Violet alone with Kyle and Lance.

"I'm going to bed," Lance said. "You two should get some rest."

After he was gone, Kyle took her hand. His knuckles were red and bruised. "You sure you're all right?" he asked.

"I will be. He scared me. You scared me too. I thought you were going to kill him."

"Seeing him with his hands on you made me lose my mind."

She smiled. "My knight in shining armor?"

"Hardly." He rose to his feet and brought her with him. "Let's get you to bed."

They walked down the hallway. Her room was on the left, just off the living room. His was further down the hall. They stopped in front of her door.

She didn't want him to leave her.

"Goodnight," she said. *Don't go.*

"You all right to be alone tonight? Because I can stay with you. I'll sleep on the floor."

She looked up into his eyes. "Would you?"

"If you want me to, yes, of course I will."

Dangerous. He was dangerous. But her need for his presence outweighed the risk.

"I'll go brush my teeth," he said. "That'll give you a chance to change, then I'll come join you."

She nodded and went inside her room. Numbly, she brushed her teeth and put on a pair of flannel pajamas. Surely they couldn't get into any trouble if she was wearing these.

When he returned, he'd changed into sweats and a t-shirt, and carried a stack of blankets and a pillow. She crawled into the king-sized bed and pulled the covers up to her chin.

"Are you still cold?" Kyle spread a blanket onto the floor next to the bed.

She nodded.

"You'll be warm in a minute. Especially in those granny pajamas."

"They're not granny pajamas," she said.

"You rock them." He plopped onto the floor.

She rolled to her side to get a better view of him. His blue eyes looked up at her.

"How's the floor?" she asked.

"Hard."

"You should just come up here. This is a huge bed. There's room for both of us."

"You sure?"

"If you promise to keep to your side of the bed and not steal all the covers, then yes."

He grinned. "Deal."

She scooted to the other side of the bed. He slipped under the covers. *This is what it's like to have a man in my bed.*

They lay there for a moment. From the street below, a siren interrupted the silence. She shuddered, remembering how they had to pull Kyle off the man.

"Are you still shivering?" he asked.

"Yes."

"Come here," he said. "I'll warm you up."

Her heart pounded. Kyle's arms around her? Could she allow it? She closed her eyes and took in a deep breath before deciding.

CHAPTER NINE

KYLE

KYLE THOUGHT SHE'D say no to his offer. The minute it was out of his mouth he regretted saying it. For what seemed like minutes, he lay there holding his breath and waited for her rejection.

Instead, she moved closer. He put his arms around her and brought her to his chest. Her hair tickled his nose. She snuggled against him, like it was the most natural thing in the world. "Better?"

"Yes."

He stroked her hair. "I'm sorry I scared you tonight. The thought of anyone hurting you made me temporarily insane."

"If anyone tried to hurt you, I'd be the same way. That's what friends do."

He let that sink in for a moment. What did that mean? Friends? Yes, he would have done the same if it had been any of the other women in his life. But would rage have consumed him like it had tonight? Or was it just because of the way he felt about Lettie? *I have to keep her safe.*

"Have you ever talked so much to another person in your life?"

she asked. "We never run out of things to say, have you noticed that?"

"I have, yeah. But I bet there's a lot more to know," he said. "I bet we could come up with some questions."

"Okay. What did you ask Santa for when you were in third grade?"

"Same thing I asked for every year. A train set. I never got one. Christmases were lean around our house."

"That makes me sad."

"I'm making up for it now with fast cars." He smoothed her hair away from his nose. "You?"

"Third grade? A baby doll. The kind that ate and drank and you had to change their diapers."

"I gave you one of those a couple months ago," he said.

She laughed. "Yes, and she's way cuter than the baby wetsy or whatever her name was."

"What was your favorite subject in school?"

"That's easy. History."

"I should've guessed that one. Math for me."

"What was your major?"

"Business. Kind of boring when you think about it, but it served its purpose," he said.

"I didn't finish college. My dad cut me off when I changed majors from religion to environmental sciences."

"Do you ever think about going back to finish your degree?"

"Not since Dakota. No time or money."

"Would you, if you could?"

"Maybe. Probably not. I don't know what's wrong with me, but I don't seem to have much ambition anymore. Since I lost the shop, I feel so deflated. I like being your nanny. Being with Dakota and Mollie every day gives me a better sense of purpose than I've had in a long time. After our year is done, I don't know what I'll do. Honestly, nothing sounds appealing."

He knew what he wanted her to do. *Stay with me and Mollie. Let us be your purpose.*

"Why did you stop teaching yoga?" he asked.

"I couldn't make it work with Dakota's schedule. The only time slots they had were in the early mornings and evenings." She played with the sleeve of his shirt. "I feel bad about myself. Compared to Maggie and Kara and Honor, I'm such a loser."

"That's not true. You ran a business. Sure, it didn't work, but that doesn't mean you can't figure out something else to do. You've had Dakota all by yourself. Jeez, one night alone with Mollie and I was a mess. Seriously, I don't know how you've done it alone."

"Okay, next question."

"If you could go anywhere in the world where would it be?" He breathed in the scent of her hair. God, she smelled so good. *Focus on the questions before something happens below.*

"Europe. All over, so don't make me choose. Like the trip Kara and Brody took."

His heart hurt as he realized how hard it must be for her. All her closest friends were having careers and trips and money dripping from trees and here she was without even the joy of teaching her yoga classes. He would change that. Dammit, he would. This woman would have everything she wanted.

"How about you?" she asked.

"I'd like to go to Europe. And maybe Africa and see an elephant. I love them."

"Me too. When I was a kid we took a trip to the San Diego zoo, and the night before we got there, a baby elephant had died. They didn't know what was wrong with him. The mother was out in the open that day and I could see how sad she was that she'd lost her baby. She was listless and wouldn't eat. That broke my heart."

"They have burial grounds where they visit their ancestors," he said. "I always thought that was so cool."

"They have a great sense of family."

He chuckled. "No wonder we're drawn to them."

"Because we don't have any?"

"Something like that."

"Have you ever been in love?" she asked.

Sheri Swanson. With her green eyes and blond curls and a face like an angel, it would have been easy for her to be a mean girl. But she wasn't. She was the only one in school who called him by his real name. His name was Daniel back then. Daniel, not Pig like everyone else. Her voice had been like a feather trailing his skin. She smelled of flowers and sunshine.

Pig.

"There was a girl. Sheri Swanson. When we were little, she was the only one who would sit with me on the bus. I loved her, but sadly it was unrequited."

"She just thought of you as a friend?" Violet asked.

"It was more complicated than that." The friend zone was something for normal people, not Pig. "She looked out for me, even though she was beautiful and rich. There was no reason she had to be nice, but she couldn't stand cruelty to any living creature. She stood by her principles, which made her brave. Like you."

Violet sighed against him.

"Her family was probably the wealthiest in town. They had this big white house with pillars and a wraparound porch." He closed his eyes, seeing Sheri walk up the steps of her front porch—her pigtails and those shiny black shoes—the bows in her hair that matched the pink hydrangeas. "Their house, it was like this symbol to me of the American dream. The perfect house and family."

"Do you know what happened to her?" Violet asked.

"Yeah, I know." He swallowed, remembering their last conversation. *I'm going somewhere no one can hurt me.* "Turns out she didn't have the perfect family. There was a reason she always wore long sleeves."

Her breath caught. "Oh no."

"I worked at the diner in town and she used to come see me almost every day. The ladies I worked for always let me give her a free soda. One day she came in, crying. I'd never seen her cry. I remember just standing there feeling helpless and small. When I asked her what was wrong, she lifted the long sleeves of her shirt all the way up to her shoulders. Cigarette burns on the inside of her upper arms. So many. New ones. And scars and scars of old ones."

"Her dad?"

"Her mom."

"No."

"She told me she was going somewhere no one could hurt her. She'd come to say goodbye."

"Did she run away?" Violet asked.

"She took a bottle of her mother's sleeping pills and never woke up."

"Oh no. That's what she meant by a place no one could hurt her."

He nodded, unable to speak.

"I'm sorry, Kyle."

"It was a long time ago."

"Is she one of the things you wanted to forget?" she asked.

"Yes. But I never could. When someone is kind to you and loves you for who you are under all the scars and dirt and poverty, you never forget them."

"It makes you think, though, doesn't it?" Violet asked. "What we assume about people's lives."

"Everything that glitters is not gold," he said.

"There's more to my family than people knew. Things no one would believe." She grew still in his arms, her breath moving the hairs on his arm. "My dad's an angry person. I'm not sure why. Nothing I did was ever good enough. He never hurt me physically or anything like that, but there were punishments inappropriate for the crimes."

"Like what?" His stomach clenched. What had he done?

"His favorite was to deny me food for twenty-four hours. I had to stay in my room, stomach growling, as the scent of my mother's Sunday dinner crept up the stairs."

"Wow," Kyle said.

"Any small failing riled him. A 'B' on my report card, smiling at a boy in church, spreading too much butter on my bread. I couldn't go to any of the dances at school or join any clubs, regardless if I had good grades or not. Strangely, he wanted me to be a cheerleader. He insisted that I try out. If I hadn't made the squad, I don't know what would have happened."

"That doesn't make sense."

"I know. That's how he was. Irrational and manic. I was so anxious all through high school that my hair started falling out. When I left for college, I thought I might be free, but it was the same. After he cut me off, I went to work for Cole Lund's church, hoping to make enough for tuition. But you know how that turned out."

"Why did you come back to Cliffside Bay? Wouldn't it have been better to stay away from them?"

"If you can believe it, I actually thought they'd want me to come home...that they'd want to be part of Dakota's life. No matter what, I still wanted them to love me."

He tightened his arms around her and kissed the top of her head. "It's their loss."

"This town was my home, not my family. I see that now."

This town was my home. No wonder she didn't want it to change. She needed some aspect of her life to be steady and loyal. *I can be her home.*

Could he? Was he strong enough to be her rock? Dakota's dad?

He didn't know the answers to those questions. All he knew was that everything in his world had changed the moment Mollie came into his life. She'd brought Violet and Dakota to him. She'd changed his heart.

With everything in him, he wanted to be the kind of father the other Dogs had, but what tools did he have? An image of his sister's mangled body came to him, followed by the article in the local paper about Sheri. He hadn't been able to shelter either of them from harm. How did he think he could do it now?

If she knew the truth about the accident would she be able to love him?

Violet's breathing had changed. She was asleep. "Goodnight, my sweet Lettie."

He stared at the ceiling, wide awake, ashamed of his earlier behavior, not for beating the crap out of that jerk but for scaring her. She deserved a nice night out with dancing and drinks, not an escort who acted like a lunatic. Furthermore, he shouldn't have left her alone. He knew better.

For the first time in years, he prayed.

Please God, give me the strength to do right by this woman. Give me the courage to tell her everything.

When he finally fell asleep, he dreamt of Violet and Sheri hand-in-hand, pink bows in their hair. From the window of the bus, he watched as they walked up the stairs to Sheri's front door. The door opened. A black cloud of smoke sucked them inside the house. He banged on the bus window, shouting for them. It was too late. They were gone. The bus pulled away.

CHAPTER TEN

VIOLET

A WEEK LATER, Violet sipped a mineral water in the parlor of a couture wedding dress shop in the city with Maggie and Kara beside her. Honor was currently inside the dressing room, with an attendant, trying on the first dress of the day.

"I'm so glad you could come with us," Maggie said.

"Me too," Violet said.

"Kyle's a softie. Who knew?" Kara asked.

After learning that Violet had told Honor she had to work and therefore couldn't go into the city to help find Honor a dress, Kyle had demanded she go with the rest of the girls to San Francisco. "The maid of honor has to go dress shopping. End of story."

He'd even offered to take a day off and stay with the kids. Since the night they'd slept in the same bed together, life had gone on as usual, only Kyle seemed distant. Not avoiding her exactly, but more like something weighed heavy on his mind. Last night, he'd seemed antsy and agitated, like he wanted to tell her something but couldn't quite get it out. He'd stopped and started a few times with vague references to events in his past he'd like to share with her. They'd been interrupted when Mel arrived early. Of course. She had impeccable timing.

"Hey, what're you thinking about?" Maggie asked, pulling Violet from her musings.

"That I can't wait to see what Honor picks out." One little white lie never hurt anyone, right?

"Nothing like waiting until the last minute," Kara said with a laugh. "She's going to pay a fortune for rush alterations."

"I told her not to order that short one," Maggie said. "It had no romance to it."

"So did I," Kara said. "But she never listens."

"I can hear you," Honor called out from the dressing room. "This is why Violet's my maid of honor and not one of you bitches."

They all doubled over in a fit of giggles.

The original dress Honor had ordered online arrived two days ago. She'd called Violet in a panic. "It's awful. Like the worst ever." Apparently, the short skirt she'd thought she wanted turned out to be exactly opposite of what she imagined it would be. "I thought it would be all flirty and whimsical and great on my small frame, but it looks like a prom dress for a slutty chick."

The ladies had quickly hatched a plan to go into the city. Kara insisted they go high end or they'd never find one that didn't need a hundred alterations. Violet wasn't so sure. From what she could tell this shop was filled with dresses covered in elaborate lace or layers of tulle. They wouldn't be easy to alter.

The wedding was scheduled for three days before Christmas. Brody and Kara had offered their house. After convincing Zane to have it there rather than a church, Kara and Honor had jumped into arranging every detail. The guest list was small. Just the Dogs, Doc and Janet Mullen, Flora and Dax Hansen, plus Mary and Sophie.

"It's official that Doc's officiating," Kara said. "He ordered his license over the internet."

"Something about that seems wrong," Maggie said.

"And yet so right," Kara said.

"Was Brody touched that Honor asked him to walk her down the aisle?" Maggie asked Kara.

"There might have been tears, but I'm sworn to secrecy," Kara said.

"Speaking of guys that cry." Maggie rolled her eyes. "Jackson's taking his best man role way too seriously. He's been working on his speech for weeks."

"That's adorable," Kara said.

"Not after the seventh or eighth time you've heard variations of the same speech," Maggie said.

Kara went on to tell them she'd hired a group to decorate the house for the wedding. "Trey recommended them. They have every type of decoration you can imagine and just come in and do it all at once." The interior designer, Trey Mattson was everywhere lately. He'd decorated Maggie and Jackson's remodeled home and was currently working on Lance's beach house on the Mullen property.

"Wait, that's someone's job?" Violet asked. "Just to decorate for the holidays?"

Kara nodded, as if it was the most natural thing in the world to have your house decked out for Christmas by a professional. "We're doing two huge trees and garland and sparkles everywhere. Honor wanted silver and cranberry for her colors, so that's what she's going to have." She lowered her voice. "I told them to spare no expense. We want the best for our girl."

Honor came out of the dressing room wearing the first dress of the day. The attendant helped her onto the raised platform situated in front of a long mirror. The dress had an enormous skirt with a tight bodice.

"It's pretty," Kara said.

"But not quite right," Honor said. "I feel like I'm playing dress up in my mother's clothes."

"Or on a plantation with Rhett Butler," Maggie said.

"You're too petite for it," Violet said. "That's the problem."

The next one had a tight bodice and a mermaid skirt with a slit that went up to the top of Honor's thigh.

"What in the world? How is this a wedding dress?" Kara asked. "You can't get married with your butt hanging out."

"You cannot get married to 'yes ma'am Zane' in *that* dress," Maggie said. "Even though you look hotter than hot."

"I agree. I can't wear this one. I'm someone's mother now," Honor said.

"If that's the case you're going to have to take half your wardrobe to the Goodwill," Violet said.

"I do love this one though," Honor said.

"You don't *really* like it?" Kara asked.

"It's killing me not to buy it right here and now." Honor grinned.

Kara waved her hands in front of her face like a traffic cop at an intersection. "I'm going to pretend like you don't mean that."

"You're such a prude," Honor said. "Honestly, you're like from the 1950s or something."

The third dress was the color of blush with a mermaid skirt and a beaded sleeveless bodice.

"No way," Kara said. "You need white."

"I'm not exactly a virgin," Honor said.

"The dress has to be white," Maggie said. "Traditional, like Zane."

"But I want him to gasp when he sees me," Honor said. "I can't be *too* conservative."

"The one with the slit all the way up to your butt would make him gasp," Violet said.

"In horror. He'd probably run down the aisle and tie his jacket around my waist," Honor said, laughing.

The fourth and fifth dresses were no good. One had puffy sleeves. The other was made of a silky material that clung to all the wrong places. Violet lost count after that.

Finally, they found *the one*. When Honor came out of the dressing room, they all let out a collective happy sigh. Sparkly beads adorned the fitted, strapless bodice. The skirt was made from layers of tulle with a lace overlay. With the three-foot train and filmy veil, it seemed as if the whole ensemble floated and moved like a graceful breeze.

The attendant fanned the train over the edge of the platform. Honor's eyes sparkled in the mirror. "This is it."

"Can you guys have it ready in four weeks?" Kara asked.

"It's possible. With the right frame of mind," the attendant said.

"Meaning if I'm willing to pay?" Honor asked.

"Precisely."

"I'm willing. For this dress, anything."

Afterward, they all went to dinner at one of Honor's favorite restaurants in the city. It wasn't until they were seated that Violet learned why.

"This is the restaurant Hugh took me to when I graduated from college," Honor said. "It was the first time I ever ate someplace fancy. I come here when I'm in the city whenever I can. To remember him and that night."

Violet looked around the glittering restaurant. It was not the type of establishment she could imagine Hugh Shaw enjoying. He'd been so down to earth and casual. Here the staff were dressed in black and described the food like they'd written the recipe. All the tables had crisp white napkins and tablecloths. Any fallen crumbs were whisked away by the server.

"I had no idea what to do with all the utensils," Honor said.

"I wouldn't have either," Maggie said.

Violet's parents had sent her to a course on dinner etiquette. She knew the use for every fork, spoon, and knife. "I would've. My dad beat that kind of thing into me."

They ordered wine and appetizers to share. "All the best stuff is on the appetizer list," Honor said.

"Always," Kara said.

While they waited for their wine to arrive, they talked about the details of the wedding reception. Although engaged in the conversation, Kara kept glancing at her phone, obviously worried about Brody. Honor must have noticed because she steered the conversation toward a light topic.

Honor tore off a piece of bread from the loaf on the table and passed it over to Maggie. "You know what's bugging me. Why don't we have a name for our group like the Dogs do?"

"We *should* have one," Maggie said.

"Even though it's cheesy as hell," Honor said.

"I think it's cute, not cheesy," Maggie said.

"Grown men with a summer camp name is not cute," Honor said. "It's like it should be hung over the door of their cabin. The Dogs. Cabin B."

"It's kind of sad, in a way," Maggie said. "Jackson told me Kyle thought of it as well as the ritual of their Friday night poker games. He wanted desperately to belong to a group to make up for his lack of family."

"I get that," Honor said.

"Me too," Maggie said.

Kara and Violet nodded in agreement.

"Besides Brody and Lance, none of us have any family," Kara said. "Maybe that's why we're all so close."

"That and we're awesome," Honor said.

A server appeared with a bottle of white wine. Honor nodded approval and he poured glasses for each of them. Violet detected aromas of butterscotch and melon as she swirled the wine around her glass.

Honor raised her glass. "Thank you, ladies, for being my family. Sharing this wedding stuff, although almost embarrassing, is super fun."

They all clinked glasses.

"If the boys are Dogs, we could be the Cats," Kara said, taking up the thread from earlier.

"Too on the nose," Maggie said.

"On the nose?" Violet asked.

"Obvious," Maggie said. "Like in a bad script."

They paused the conversation as the server brought their trays of appetizers. While the food was passed around, Kara looked at her phone again. Violet caught Honor's eye and they silently agreed to continue with the distraction technique.

"What makes a dog wag its tail?" Honor asked. "Because that's what we do."

"You always make everything dirty." Kara put aside her phone and placed a piece of fig and pear flatbread on her plate.

"But am I right?"

"We make *something* wag," Maggie said.

"Thank God." Honor wriggled a limp pickled asparagus.

"I do love a hard breadstick." Maggie picked up a breadstick wrapped in prosciutto and twirled it like a baton then took a bite out of one end. They collapsed into laughter.

"Ladies, really?" Kara asked, wiping her eyes. "Are we twelve?"

"Kind of," Honor said.

They ate in silence for a few minutes. "Dogs like walks, right?" Kara asked.

"We can't be the Walks. That sounds dumb," Honor said.

"And the opposite of feminism," Violet said.

"Like they walk all over us? I don't think so," Honor said.

"No, that won't do," Kara said.

"Dinner. Dogs like dinner," Violet said.

"Everyone likes dinner." Honor cut into a meatball. "Especially me."

"The Dinners? No, just no," Kara said.

"Treats make a dog wag its tail," Maggie said.

"The Treats? Does that sound right?" Kara asked.

"I feel like it needs a jazz hand movement to go with it," Maggie said, demonstrating like only a former dancer could.

"We're not *cupcakes*. That's a treat," Honor said.

"What about simply the Wags?" Violet asked.

"It has a nice ring to it," Honor said.

"Brody wants to have a baby," Kara said, out of the blue.

The table hushed.

"You don't want to?" Maggie asked, finally.

Kara shook her head. "Not to fill some hole he has now that football's done. He has to want one for the right reason."

"What would that be exactly?" Maggie asked.

"I don't know. This deep desire to make a family together," Kara said.

"He has that," Honor said. "But I understand what you're saying. He's reeling right now, and this seems like a knee jerk reaction."

Kara nodded with a grateful smile. "Yes, exactly. They always say not to make any life altering decisions when you're in crisis mode."

"Jackson wants to have a baby in the worst way," Maggie said. "I'm not ready. My career is finally taking off."

"Is he supportive?" Violet asked.

"Yes, of course. It's Jackson we're talking about. But the way he was looking at Mollie the other night told me everything I need to know."

"Wait a year or two. It's fine," Honor said. "Enjoy each other. Zane and I will never have the chance to be just us since we have Jubie. I'm kind of jealous. Not that I would trade Jubie for anything."

Maggie sobered. With a mournful expression, she turned to Honor. "Does it bother you that we're talking about babies?"

"What? No. Am I sad that I can't have a baby? Yes. Does that mean I can't be happy for others? No."

"You're a better person than me," Maggie said.

"We all know that's not true," Honor said.

Kara dropped her fork onto her plate, as if it was suddenly hot. "I'm worried about Brody."

"He's going to be okay," Honor said. "Like Lance said, he'll bounce back. He's not the first football player to have to retire."

Kara pushed food around on her plate. "I wanted him to retire. Secretly. I would never have told him that, but I swear to God, every game I sat there terrified. I'm a medical professional. I know what can happen. And then it did. Am I a bad wife?"

"Oh gosh, no," Maggie said. "I would be the exact same way if it were Jackson."

"I was nervous for him too," Honor said. "It just means we love him."

The subject changed to what Brody might do next, including that Honor had organized meetings for him to meet with the producers of several sports networks. Violet listened, fighting the sadness that slithered into her like suffocating smoke.

During a pause in the conversation, the words slipped out of her mouth. "Do you have to be married to a Dog to be a Wag?" She ripped a piece of bread in two, afraid she might cry.

"Of course not," Kara said.

Violet's throat ached. "Good, because there's only two Dogs left and I'm certain neither of them are marrying me."

"You sure about that?" Honor raised one eyebrow and cocked her head to the side. "Because none of us are."

"After what we saw the other night, we're all pretty sure how Kyle feels about you," Maggie said gently.

"Yeah, beating the crap out of the guy at the bar pretty much told us what we needed to know," Honor said.

Violet made a fuss of buttering a piece of her torn bread, afraid to look at anyone. "We've spent a lot of time together in our little cocoon. We've talked about everything. I've told him things I've never told anyone. He's opened up to me about his past—most of it anyway. There's a closeness between us that I never would have seen coming, not in a million years."

"I couldn't help but notice he came out of your bedroom the other night," Kara said.

"What?" Honor said. "You didn't tell us that."

"I wasn't sure it was my place," Kara said.

"This is key information," Honor said. "Fess up, Violet."

Violet flushed as she told them how he'd offered to stay with her and she'd accepted. "We just talked. Like we always do." *For heaven's sake, just admit it.* There was no reason to keep the truth from them. She buried her face in her hands. "I'm in love with him. It's so stupid. So juvenile."

"It's not stupid, sweetie," Maggie said. "Your feelings are your feelings."

"Yeah, how is it stupid?" Honor asked.

"He's damaged," Violet said. "I don't think he'll ever want what I want."

Honor picked up her glass and paused for a moment, as if thinking through what she wanted to say. "He's a man with something to prove. All the women, the fast cars, making deals like the devil's chasing him—they're all just an attempt to prove his worth. He has some gigantic demons. I'm not sure what happened to him when he was young, but I know it was bad. I can spot a *walking wounded* a mile away. I know from my own experience the only way to work through those demons is through love. Hugh was the first person to show me love, then Brody, then you ladies, and now Zane. Kyle has the Dogs. Now he needs the right woman."

Maggie wiped at the corners of her eyes with a napkin. "That's beautiful, Honor. I feel a new song coming on."

"You need to fight for him," Honor said to Violet. "It's hard to put yourself out there, but if anyone can conquer Kyle Hicks, it's you."

"What do I do?" Violet asked.

"Tell him how you feel," Maggie said. "I saw him the other night. There's no way that man isn't in love with you."

"You're such a romantic," Violet said.

Maggie smiled and picked up her wineglass. "Let's have a toast. To romance."

"To kicking fear's ass," Honor said.

"To the opposite of fear," Kara said. "To love."

* * *

The next night, Kyle came home from work looking like a kid on Christmas morning. "I found us a house," he said.

Violet sat cross-legged on the floor, dressed in loose jeans and a sweater. Dakota had been sent to his room for a *time out* after refusing to pick up his toys. Next to her, Mollie kicked and squirmed under a mobile made of red and black farm animals. "I don't believe it."

He rubbed his hands together. "You underestimate my magical powers."

"Magical powers?" She laughed. Why did her heart leap at the sight of him?

"Actually, Honor found it for us. She met a couple who need renters while they travel for a year. They want to leave all the furniture and household items, so it's perfect for us. It's gorgeous. And, get this—it's right down the street from Honor and Zane."

"Which house is it?"

"The Burnside house. Do you know it?"

The Burnside house was large and pristine with a view of the ocean. "Do they know we have a three-year-old?" Why had she said it like that? They were not a *we*.

"A fat security deposit made their worries disappear. I cleared everything with them." He pulled her to her feet. "Don't worry so much." For a second, she thought he might pull her into an embrace. Instead, they stared at each other until Violet knelt next to the baby, pretending she needed to adjust Mollie's onesie.

He joined her on the floor and lifted Mollie into his arms, kissing her forehead. "Hello, sweet girl." To Violet he said, "I never thought I'd be this excited to move into a real house."

"What about your pack-and-play life?" she asked.

"Overrated." He grinned.

Mollie looked up at her daddy's face, then matched his grin.

"Did you see that? Was that a smile?" Kyle asked.

"That was a smile."

"Holy crap," he said.

She wouldn't tell him, but Mollie had smiled at her earlier that day. Let him believe her first smile was for him. Violet reached over and stroked Mollie's cheek. She was rewarded with another smile. "She takes my breath away sometimes."

"Totally," he said.

I love her. I love him. She loved them both like they belonged to her. But they didn't. The path out of here was paved with one heartbreak too many.

How had this happened?

"What is it?" Kyle asked. "You got sad."

She blinked to focus on his face. He watched her with a wary look in his eyes, like she was a wild cat sure to bolt out of the room. "I'm going to miss Mollie when our year is done. That's all."

"That's all?" His brow furrowed.

"What else could it be?" She peaked up at him through her lashes.

"I don't know. Maybe her dad? A little?"

Her heart turned over in her chest, swear to God. "Do you want me to miss you?"

"I don't want you to go anywhere. That way you don't have to miss me."

CHAPTER ELEVEN

KYLE

KYLE TURNED IN to Zane and Honor's driveway. In the back seat, Dakota grinned. "Kale, are we going to Jubie's?"

"Just for a few minutes," Kyle said.

"How come?"

"I want to talk to Jubie's parents."

He parked and then lifted Dakota out of his car seat and onto the driveway. Dakota ran up to the front door and rang the bell. Jubie answered right away and jumped up and down with excitement when she saw it was Dakota standing there. She folded him into a hug. When Jubie had first arrived, she'd looked malnourished and sickly. Those attributes were nowhere to be seen in the vibrant six-year-old currently taking Dakota by the hand.

"You wanna see the kitties?" she asked.

Dakota squealed a happy *yes* in response and the two of them ran across the living room and up the stairs. Honor appeared, looking downright domestic with an apron over her jeans and sweater. "Kyle, what's up?" She hugged him. "Come on in."

"Sorry to come by unannounced but I needed to talk to you. And Zane too, if he's around."

"Sure. He's in the kitchen. We're just finishing up our coffee."

He followed her across the spacious front room into her modern farm-style kitchen. Zane was at the table with a cup of coffee and his laptop.

"Good to see you, bud. What's going on?" Zane asked after they'd greeted each other with a slap on the shoulders.

"Where's the baby?" Honor asked.

"She's with Violet. Dakota wanted to go with me to the store."

He sank into a chair at the table. Without asking, Honor brought him a cup of coffee.

"You look like hell," Zane said. "Rough night?"

"Something like that." Kyle glanced out the window. The rain had started again. "I can't sleep lately."

Honor joined them at the table. "I've never seen you unshaven before." She never missed a detail.

"I have a problem," Kyle said.

"You? You don't have problems," Zane said. "You have to have a heart to have problems."

Kyle sighed and rubbed his eyes. He didn't have it in him to spar with Zane today.

"Whoa, what's the matter?" Honor asked. "Is Mollie all right?"

"Yes, Mollie's fine. Really good. Violet takes such good care of her. The woman can make a home wherever she is."

Honor narrowed her eyes. "Say her name again."

"Mollie?"

"No, Violet," Honor said.

"Why?"

"Just do it."

Kyle glanced over at Zane. He shrugged as if to say, *don't bother to question her, just do what she says.*

"Violet." Kyle placed his hands on the table. Why did his chest ache like that when he said her name?

"You slept with her," Zane said. "Didn't you?"

"I didn't. I swear. But I want to," Kyle said. "In the worst way."

"It's more than that," Honor said. "You have feelings for her."

"No wonder you can't sleep," Zane said.

Kyle tried like hell to remain stoic, but every muscle in his face twitched and flexed with the effort. Finally, he gave in and let himself crumble. "I'm in trouble."

"By trouble do you mean you've fallen for her?" Honor asked.

"I think so," Kyle said.

"I knew it when I fell for Honor," Zane said. "The reason you feel messed up is because you're trying to run from it."

"I'm not this guy." He gestured toward Zane. "I can't just instantly become a family guy."

"Mollie instantly made you a family guy," Honor said.

"And that little boy looks pretty attached to you," Zane said.

"You seem to be that guy, whether you see it or not," Honor said.

"We all see it, man," Zane said.

"See what?" Kyle asked.

"How you look at the baby. How you look at Violet," Honor said. "The way you and Dakota are glued at the hip."

Was it true? Had he become the guy they needed without realizing it?

"I'm afraid I won't be enough."

"This all boils down to fear," Honor said. "Zane and I know all about that, don't we?"

"We almost let it ruin us before we even got started." Zane patted Kyle's shoulder. "Just give into it, buddy. Resistance is futile."

"Unless you *want* to be miserable," Honor said.

"What if my old instincts kick in and I run away? Or what if she decides I'm not the guy for her? I don't know if I can take it. I'm not strong like she is. We all know I'm not good enough for her." He tugged at the collar of his shirt, hot. Everything was spinning out of control. *He* was out of control.

"Can you tell how she feels about you?" Zane asked without a hint of his usual ribbing.

"I make her laugh. We talk constantly. She fell asleep in my arms the other night."

"She has major feelings for you," Honor said. "Trust me."

"I can't think of anything but her."

"You've got it bad," Honor said. "Just admit it."

"Fine. I'm in love with her. Crap." Kyle made a tent with his fingers blew into them, embarrassed.

Zane grinned. "That's great, man. Welcome to the club."

"The club?" Kyle asked.

"The love club." Honor tossed her hair behind her shoulders and flashed him a facetious grin.

"*This* is what it feels like? Because I don't like it. I'm out of control. Like spinning."

"Just take a deep breath," Zane said. "You'll get used to the spinning. Pretty soon it slows down to a nice, slow churn and you'll see that everything is brighter, sweeter, softer."

"I don't have one quality that can make this work," Kyle said. "Not one."

"Kyle, we've been kicked around and fought for everything we have," Honor said. "With that comes a lot of layers of Teflon. We're hard to love. We fight loving someone like it's the plague instead of a miracle. If someone can see through all that to the real you, then she's the one for you. Letting someone in, who has earned the right to be there, will set you free. You'll amaze yourself at your capacity to love. Take it from me."

He looked at her, dazed. "I don't get it. Why would Violet want me?"

"The question is not why, but *how*," Honor said. "You're going to have to teach her how to love a formerly abused dog."

"I don't get it," Kyle said.

One corner of Honor's mouth lifted in a sad smile. "You have this look in your eyes sometimes that reminds me of an abused dog—wary and sure you're about to be kicked. You're always ready to fight. I was like that my whole life. I get it. But you survived. Whatever or whoever it was that gave you that look in your eyes, you beat them. This is the prize at the end."

"They called me Pig." Kyle swiped at the tears that leaked from his eyes.

"Who did?" Honor asked softly.

"The kids," he whispered. "Because I smelled bad. We were so poor and dirty. I got beat up almost every day. No one would sit by me at lunch."

"Oh, Kyle," Honor said, her voice breaking. She wiped her eyes with the bottom of her apron.

"For years I had these episodes. I don't know how to explain them or even what triggers them, but I scrubbed my skin as hard as I could. Just trying to get clean. I never told anyone about how bad it was."

Kyle sagged against his friend. Zane wrapped his arm around his shoulders and held him close, like a man comforting a small child.

Honor stood beside them, her hand on the back of his neck. "You lived. You made this life for yourself. You won. Not the bullies. Not the poverty. Not the past. You."

"You can let it all go," Zane said. "It's all over now."

Sobs rose from Kyle's chest. He no longer cared. Letting go was a relief.

"You're a Dog, not a pig," Zane said. "I love you, buddy. We all do."

"Kale?"

He lifted his head from Zane's shoulder to see Dakota standing there. "Hey little man." He wiped his eyes and held out his arms.

Dakota climbed onto his lap and pressed his fat hands against both Kyle's cheeks. "I love you, Kale."

"I love you too, buddy." He looked up at Honor and managed a weak smile.

Honor blew him a kiss. "You won."

* * *

Kyle stared at the television. An old western played, but he wasn't really watching. Everything was off tonight.

Violet had gone out with Honor for something wedding related. Dakota was staying the night at Zane's.

Honor had promised him she wouldn't say anything to Violet about his feelings. He wanted to tell her himself, but he had to tell her the rest of his story first. Tonight was the night. If she would ever get home.

He glanced at his watch. Again. It was nearing ten and Violet wasn't home. How long did this wedding errand take? She'd said something about grabbing dinner at The Oar later. The dress she had on when she left was black and tight, showing every inch of her sexy body. Men would be all over her. A Friday night always brought in the crowds. Who knew how many men were hitting on her?

A few minutes after ten, Mel came in, looking flushed and disheveled. "I'm sorry I'm late." She unbuttoned her coat and tossed in over the back of the couch. "My car wouldn't start. I had to beg a ride from a friend." She fixed her cat eyes on him. "Where's Violet?"

"She went out."

"Good for her. She needs to do that more often."

"Why do you say that?" he asked.

"She needs to get laid."

He flinched and stared at her, speechless.

"It appears you're not going to do it, so she needs to find someone who will."

This girl was outrageous.

Mel kicked off her shoes and sat opposite him, dangling her feet over the arm of the chair. "How was your day?"

He wanted to wait up for Violet but not if Mel was in his living room. This girl annoyed him, like a pesky mosquito, always buzzing around looking for blood.

"I had a good day," he said. "You?"

"I slept most of it."

Right, another bout of stomach sickness. This time she'd called in sick with the flu instead of food poisoning. Zane had mentioned that he'd seen her at The Oar last night when she was supposedly sick. Violet had been right. She was always right. Just for fun he baited Mel. Would she confess? "You've recovered quickly."

"I may as well tell you the truth. There are no secrets in this town. I was invited out with some of my new friends and I just couldn't say no. We were at The Oar. Zane was working, so I figured he'd tell you."

"It's best not to lie in this town," he said.

She crossed her ankles, legs still slung over the arm of the couch. "You won't hold it against me forever, will you?"

"We probably won't need you much longer," he said. "So, no."

Her face fell. "Really?"

"A couple more weeks, I'd say." He was totally making this up. A sudden urge to have her out of their lives had seized his better judgment.

"Mollie's still waking up twice a night." She unfolded from the chair and crossed over to the couch. "But if I'm no longer working for you, does that mean we can be friends?"

"Friends?" He swallowed. This girl was about to make a pass at him. One night without Violet and she pounced.

Mel sat on the arm of the couch. He remained where he was on the other end, unsure what to do.

"This may come as a surprise to you, but I'm into you. I'd like to know where you stand. I mean, I know you stare at me, so I'm pretty sure we're on the same page."

"The same page? I don't think so."

Like a cat, she leapt from her position on one end of the couch to land between his legs. She teased the cuff of his shirt with her fingertips. "You want me. Admit it."

The old Kyle would have. He would already have her in the bedroom. Not anymore. There was nothing for him here but trouble. For weeks he hadn't even looked at another woman other than Violet. Certainly not this one with her feline ways. *Lettie, come home. Save me.*

"I'm not interested, Mel. I've never been, and I won't be."

She jumped onto his lap, wrapped her arms around his neck, and pressed her mouth to his. He shot to his feet and her tossed her aside. Like a limp ragdoll, she fell backward onto the couch. "What in the hell are you doing?" he asked.

"Playing hard to get is so hot," she said.

Her lipstick had smeared all over his face. He rubbed it from his mouth. He was about to tell her to *get out* when he heard the front door open and Violet appeared. She froze when she saw them. Mel slid from the couch, straightening her blouse like they'd been fooling around. Mel had missed her calling. She should be on the stage.

"Hey, Lettie. Did you have fun?" Not sure why that question had come out of his mouth.

"I did, yes."

"Where did you go?" Mel asked. "Any hot guys?"

Violet turned to look at her, her eyes like hard candies. "I left a new container of formula under Mollie's crib. You'll need it for tonight."

Mel smiled like she'd won a prize. "You're always so on top of it, Violet. The perfect nanny."

Violet's gaze slid to him with an expression he'd never seen before. Did she think they'd been fooling around? Was she angry? Sad? He could practically hear her mind churning. After coming to some conclusion, she crossed the room, high heels clicking on the cold floor. She linked her arm in his and flashed him a flirtatious smile. His stomach fluttered like the leaves of a birch tree in a spring breeze.

She straightened the collar of his shirt. *Subtext, he belongs to me.* "You ready for that drink I promised you earlier?"

"Sure. Yes," he said, almost stammering.

Violet turned to Mel. "Dakota's staying the night with friends, so we're taking the opportunity to go out. We'll be quiet when we come in so we don't wake you."

Mel tossed her hair behind her shoulders and subtly, but not enough to go unnoticed, wiped the smeared lipstick from under her bottom lip. "Just so you know, you didn't interrupt anything just now."

"Excuse me?" Violet linked her arm into his and glared at Mel.

"We were just talking." How was it possible to sound the exact opposite of the words coming out of your mouth? *We were about to have hot sex on the carpet.*

"I have no idea what you mean," Violet said.

"When you came in, you know, it might've looked like we were, how shall I say, having a moment," Mel said.

"I saw Kyle leap up like you'd scorched him with a hot poker. Is that the moment you're referring to?"

Mel flushed as red as the aforementioned hot poker. The large vein that ran across her forehead pulsed. "It's not what it looked like." This time it was more of a mumble than the sexy purr of earlier.

"I know, sweetie. Don't you worry for a second. I'm quite confident that this man here has no interest in you. Because he belongs to me." With that, she turned to him and wrapped her arms around his neck and kissed him. He pulled her closer and kissed her back. The world shifted.

Mollie had reopened every unsuppressed memory of his past. Her presence was like jagged shards of glass, beautiful but full of sharp edges that slid down his skin, threatening to cut him wide open. She made him see how inadequate he was, how one wrong move could ruin her like he'd ruined his sister. But this. This woman. Her kiss. She stitched him back together so that he was no longer adrift and afraid.

When they parted, Violet flashed a smile that held the essence of that kiss. *We are a team.* "Come on, baby. Mama needs a drink."

They held their laughter in until they got in the elevator. "*Mama* needs a drink? Where did that come from?" he asked.

She buried her face in her hands, shoulders shaking. "I don't know. She just looked so evil and self-confident; I couldn't help it."

"Your laugh's like chamomile tea with two teaspoons of honey," he said.

"You don't drink tea."

"I might. If you made it for me," he said.

She rewarded him with one of her eye rolls. "Unlikely. Anyway, what happened before I got there?"

He shuddered. "She jumped me. I told her I wasn't interested, but she wouldn't take no for an answer. She pounced on me like a cat on a giant bird."

"*I* jumped you just now," Violet said. "Do you feel used?"

"You can use me anytime if it involves a kiss like that. Honestly, I almost fell over. I did *not* see that coming."

"I'm so sorry. I've never done anything like that in my life. Mel brings out the worst in me."

"No need to apologize," he said. "Unless you never plan on ever doing it again."

She blinked. "Oh."

He drew close to her and traced the outline of her lips with his fingertip. "I've never been kissed like that in my whole life. And now I want another."

"Just one?"

The elevator doors opened before he could either kiss her or answer the question. They stepped out into a nearly empty lobby. Several front desk staff talked quietly behind their computers. The fountain babbled, like notes of encouragement. *You can do it, you can do it.*

Upstairs the lights of the bar beckoned him. "Should we have that drink for real?" he asked.

"We can't go back upstairs. Not now anyway."

The bartender greeted them when they walked into the bar. "Evening Mr. Hicks. Miss Ellis."

"Hey Rufus," Kyle said. "How are your college courses going?"

"Good, sir, thank you."

They ordered their usual, scotch and white wine, and sat in the booth in the back. The atmosphere soothed his nerves somewhat. Trey, his interior designer, had suggested they give this bar an aura of an exclusive club. Walnut wainscoting, dim lights, and deep green cushions on the booths and chairs gave the bar a feeling of an old boy's club from times past. Now, after everything that had happened, he could see that the idea for the décor had appealed to him on a level not entirely emotionally healthy. Yet another example of his neurotic need to purge Pig. *See here, suckers? I made this bar. Me. Kyle Hicks, formerly known as Pig.*

There were several other couples scattered around the room, as well as a large group that looked like a birthday celebration.

"We're going to have to let Mel go." Kyle chose the easy subject first. "She scares me. I'm afraid she's going to say I forced myself on her or some other lie. You know how a scandal like that can ruin a career."

Violet frowned and brought her fingers to her mouth. "I hadn't thought of that."

"She obviously has issues," he said.

"She's the type who will turn on us if we fire her. She'll tell lies to anyone who'll listen."

Rufus brought their drinks and a bowl of pretzels and nuts, then scurried off to help another customer.

"I thought you might have gotten the wrong impression when you walked in tonight," he said.

"Wiping your mouth in obvious disgust told me everything I needed to know." Her eyes reflected the soft lights that hung above the table.

"I would never touch her."

"I'm surprised but pleased."

"I would've maybe. In another lifetime. Before Mollie."

She moved a cocktail napkin from one end of the table to the other. "Is Mollie the only reason?"

"No, she's not the only reason." He hesitated, unsure of what to say next. This was his opportunity. *Tell her how you feel. Don't be a coward.* He stayed quiet a second too long. The moment was lost. She spoke, breaking the silence.

"I saw my parents again tonight," she said. "Through the window at The Oar. They were having dinner."

"Did you go in anyway?"

"Yes. Honor made me. She said they were not *allowed* to ruin our night. We sat in the bar. If they saw me, they didn't acknowledge me."

Laughter from the large table interrupted whatever she was going to say next. She sipped from her glass, seemingly lost in thought.

"Where'd you go?" he asked.

She looked up and blinked. "Nowhere really. I was just thinking it's weird to see your own parents and not have them acknowledge your presence. I don't know what I ever did to deserve this."

"You didn't do anything," Kyle said. "It's them."

"The night I told them I was pregnant, he called me a whore."

Kyle stomach turned. What kind of man said that to his daughter? "It's only a word."

"A very hurtful word," she said.

"But so far from the truth."

"No kidding." She smiled. "*Very* far."

"Has it really been since Lund?" he asked.

She lifted her chin. "It's been my choice."

He straightened slightly and whistled under his breath. "God, girl, you're depriving mankind."

"It has to be right this time. I won't compromise again." She bit her bottom lip. He called on every ounce of self-control to keep himself from dragging her across the table and kissing her until she begged him to take her upstairs.

I will not be a compromise. I will be everything you need.

A great pressure pushed against his chest. *Now. Tell her now.*

"Lettie, I have something I want to tell you."

She went perfectly still.

183

"It's the thing I've tried to forget. The memory I've been running from." He ran his thumb around the rim of his glass. "I'm afraid to tell you."

"Don't be. You can tell me anything."

"My real name isn't Kyle Hicks. It's Daniel Kyle Hickman. I have a brother and a sister. Stone and Autumn who are two and four years younger than I am. After our mom left, I took care of them. By the time I was in junior high, my dad was either out of it or off on some binge with one of his skanky friends. He'd lost so many jobs we lost count. Money was tighter than ever. When I was thirteen, I got a job at the local diner after school, so we could eat and have hot water. We functioned like a team. I helped them with homework. Stone did most of the outside work, cutting trees for firewood and making sure the roof was repaired. Autumn kept the house clean and cooked all our meals.

"By the time Stone entered ninth grade, he was six feet tall and weighed a hundred and eighty-five pounds. All muscle. I was still scrawny Pig. Stone was determined to beat the crap out of anyone who bullied me. The news quickly spread. Mess with Daniel Hickman and Stone Hickman would beat you to within an inch of your life."

His mouth seemed full of cotton. He drank from his water glass.

"There were these brothers. The Millers. They're the ones who gave me the nickname." He told her the details of their torture that started when he was six. "They were the instigators of most of the bullying. But Stone put a stop to that."

She nodded, watching him.

"One day Stone saw them corner me under the bleachers. He went crazy. They left with split lips, black eyes, and a few less teeth. After that, they left me alone. But they were just biding their time, waiting for revenge. One day, they got it."

He shut his eyes, seeing the events unfold in his mind. "It was late spring. I was eighteen. Autumn was fourteen. In a few months I planned to head to USC but until then it was life as usual. It was my payday, so I took Autumn into town to shop for groceries."

He told her the story, as succinctly as possible but with all the details. She must know everything.

Rain fell hard and fast that day. By late afternoon the tender tulips and daffodils in the pots that lined the main street of town were bent and broken. Later, he would think of those flowers as a symbol of his sister. Autumn had started the day as a perfect, newly bloomed flower. By the end of that day, she was as bent and broken as the flowers so carefully planted by the women of their town.

He and Autumn exited the grocery store, each clutching a bag. They ran across the parking lot, damp by the time they reached their car. Kyle unlocked the trunk. He hadn't noticed their truck until he saw the Miller boys start toward them.

"Get in the car," he said to his sister.

Too late. They were near them now. The older one, Tim, had a knife in his hand. Jason, younger but bigger than his brother, with an oversized, round head and maniacal grin that reminded Kyle of a jack-o-lantern, held a bottle of whiskey. Kyle dropped the grocery bag inside the trunk and turned to face them.

"Look who it is. Pig and his hot sister."

"What do you want?" Kyle asked.

"Where's your moose of a brother, huh?" Tim shoved Kyle and he staggered against the bumper of the car. Jason knocked the grocery bag out of Autumn's arms and grabbed her. With his free arm, he pulled her against him. "Hey pretty thing. You want to go for a ride?" Autumn looked over at Kyle, obviously paralyzed with fear.

"Let go of her." Kyle lunged forward, but Tim shoved him against the back of the car and pressed the knife's blade against his neck. The sharp edge pierced his skin. For a split second, everything went numb, followed by a sharp sting, almost like a burn. Blood trickled down his neck and onto the collar of his shirt. Tim's hot breath smelled of cheap whiskey.

What would Stone do?

Fight like hell. Fight dirty.

With every ounce of muscle in his scrawny frame, he called upon the ravine of rage that had built up inside him for years and years. He shoved his knee into Tim's crotch with the force of his anger and fear. The knife flew out of Tim's hand and tumbled onto the concrete. The boy fell to the ground, screaming and clutching his groin. Jason, perhaps surprised by this sudden turn, let go of Autumn and stumbled toward his brother.

They're drunk. This had not been obvious at first. Drunk people were unsteady on their feet. He knew this well enough.

"Autumn, get in the car." Kyle shouted to her, but he needn't have. She was already half way around the car.

He reached into the bag of groceries he'd put in the trunk and pulled out a can of cleaning spray. Using it like a bat, he swung it hard against the side of Jason's head.

"What the hell?" Jason touched his hand to the side of his head. Without wasting a second, Kyle sprayed the cleansing agent into Jason's eyes. He yelped and stumbled backward. Kyle shoved the butt of the can into Jason's chest, knocking him to his knees, then sprayed again.

Tim continued to writhe on the ground. Kyle kicked him four times in the ribs, then did the same to Jason. "Get out of the way or I'll run you over."

Kyle slammed the trunk closed and ran to the driver's side door and slipped behind the wheel. He started the engine. The Miller boys were on their feet, staggering toward their truck. Kyle backed up and out of the parking space. He would have made it out before the Millers if there hadn't been an old lady crossing from her car to the front door. By the time she was safely out of his path, the Miller boys were right behind them.

The truck slammed into the back of their car. He and Autumn lurched forward in their seats. "Hold on tight." Kyle pressed his foot on the gas and sped out of the parking lot and onto the main street of town. The Millers followed.

Kyle increased his speed as he drove through town. The Millers stayed close. They hit the back of Kyle's car again just as they exited town and onto the highway that would take them home. Would they follow them all the way home? Stone was there. A shotgun hung over the door. Stone would use it if he had to.

He pushed the gas pedal down to the floor. They barreled down the highway at just under a hundred, the Miller boys behind him. The windshield wipers were no match for the falling rain. The road blurred into a soppy impressionist painting. He didn't see the sharp turn in the road near the Foster's farm. Too late, he slammed on his brakes. They slid on the slick road and spun in a full circle, then stalled. The Millers' truck hurled toward them. Autumn screamed.

The Millers' truck plunged nose first into the passenger side of the car. Blackness.

He woke on a stretcher in the middle of the road. "Autumn. Where's Autumn?" The car. Where was the car? He thrashed and pushed against the strap that held him down, searching for the car. Oh God. The whole right side had folded in like the tin cans they picked up on the side of the road. How could she have survived? "My sister. Where's my sister?"

"She's in the other ambulance. Relax now. We're going to take good care of her."

"I'm not hurt. Let me ride with her." He tried to sit up but couldn't. Straps kept him flat on his back. "Is she going to live?"

"She's going to fine, young man. Just rest. We'll take care of her."

They took care of her as best they could. But a girl as broken as Autumn couldn't be perfectly put back together.

He had cuts and lacerations. Nothing serious. Autumn had not fared as well. The right side of her beautiful face had been slashed by a piece of metal. It had missed her eye but would leave a significant scar. Both legs had been crushed and would require surgery and months in the hospital. She would never walk without braces again, they'd told him. *Best case scenario.*

They were right. After her long stint in the hospital, she came home with braces on her legs, needing canes to help her walk. The scar ran from just under her eye to the middle of her cheek.

His sister never complained. He never even heard her cry. By the time he left for college, she had mastered the braces and was making it around well enough that she would be able to start high school as planned. No more dance team. No more boys drooling over her when she walked by. She was now the girl with the braces and the scar.

"I'll never forgive himself," he said to Violet, whose eyes glittered like the brightest star in the sky. "I promised Stone I'd get them out of there. I've done that. Once I made money, I set them both up financially through trusts. But the day I left town, I disappeared. I changed my name so there was no way they could ever find me. It's +like Daniel Hickman never existed."

"But why? Why would you leave your sister and brother?"

Kyle stared back at her. Adrenaline rushed into his system. He must tell her the truth. Could he? Would it ruin her opinion of him? If she knew what a coward he was, would she run?

He thought back to the day Mollie came to him. Paulina had said it hurt too much to look at Katy's baby. She was a reminder of her dead friend.

"Here it is." He placed his hands on the surface of the table. "Seeing Autumn scarred and crippled hurt too much." His temples throbbed, like pangs of guilt were trying to escape. "I was too weak to face her. All I could see when I looked at her was how I'd failed her and ruined her life. So I left. All these years I've tried to forget."

"But it didn't work?"

"No. No matter what I do, it haunts me." He raked his hands through his hair. "You're the first person I've told since I became Kyle Hicks."

"Why me?"

"I want you to know the truth about who I am."

"But why?" she asked.

"You need all the information…all the data…so you can decide if I'm worthy of you."

"Did you think this would change my opinion of you?"

Was she incredulous or disgusted?

"How could it not?" he asked.

"It doesn't. The accident wasn't your fault. You were being chased by monsters. If anything, it explains so much about you." He watched as she worked through it all, piecing together the missing pieces to the puzzle of Kyle. "You never had a chance, Kyle. But you made it out anyway. Do you know how much I admire that?"

His eyes filled. He pressed against them with a napkin. Relief tugged and loosened the guilt that throbbed between his ears. Could Lettie love him despite everything he'd done?

Her warm hand circled his wrist. "Please, you must let go of the guilt. It's going to eat away at you for the rest of your life. You deserve to feel joy."

He looked into her warm eyes. She cared about him. He'd shown her everything and she still cared.

Go deep. Tell her everything.

"There's something else. Over the years I've had these episodes." He described them and what he believed triggered the last one he had. "I might have one again. I just don't know. It's something I can't seem to control."

"Of course not. It's a delayed reaction to the abuse. You were bullied every day of your childhood. How could you not have lasting effects?"

"I just wanted you to know, in case that changes anything." He took in a deep breath. "I have feelings for you. I've fought against it. But it's time to come clean. I've been happy. Happier than I've ever been. I love being Mollie's dad. I love how Dakota runs to greet me when I come home from work, like I'm a rock star. But it's not just the kids. You wreck me. I think I'm falling for you."

"You think?" she whispered.

He tugged at his ear. "No, I said it wrong. There's no thinking. I have to say it exactly right, so you understand. I've fallen for you. I'm in love with you."

"Oh. In love with me?"

"Yes. I love you." The second time was easier. He'd try another. "I'm hopelessly in love with you."

She gazed at him for a long moment. His heart pounded, waiting to hear what she would say next, fully expecting her to reject him. There was no room in her heart for him. Not for Pig.

"I kept telling myself you were everything I should protect myself from. I thought I knew how men like you operate."

That hurt. *Men like you.* She was right. He was exactly like she described. *That was before. Before you.*

"But you're nothing like I thought. I see now that you're like Honor. The outer polish hides inner wounds." She placed her hands over his. "These past few months have been the happiest of my life, other than I felt sure I was headed into heartbreak. Being with the children all day and having the luxury of a life without constant money worries have been great gifts. But it's you that matters most. If we lived in a shack on the side of the road, my heart would still beat faster when you walked through the door. If I could spend every moment of the day with you, I would. Don't you see? There's nothing from your past that would ever change my opinion of you. I adore you. I love you." She looked down at her hands. Did he imagine that her gaze had skirted to the ring finger of her left hand? "But I want everything."

"The white picket fence?"

"And backyard barbeques. A father for my son. A *husband*. I can't play around. I'm not a pack-and-play kind of girl."

"Lettie, don't you see? I want to give it all to you. I love knowing you'll be there when I get home. I'm like a country song these days. Just itching to get home to my…" He wet his upper lip with the tip of his tongue. Dare he say it?

"To your what?" she whispered. "What are we?"

"I can't wait to get home to my family." He caressed her wedding ring finger with his thumb. "We've done all this backward and upside down. You deserve dates and wooing. I have every intention of winning your forever heart."

"I'm scared," she said. "Please don't change your mind."

"Lettie, losing you would kill me."

"I won't hurt you. I just want to love you. If you'll let me."

"I will. I promise."

He moved to sit beside her, inhaling the scent of her perfume. The smell of his one true love—jasmine and spice and a hint of citrus. "Do you know how beautiful you are to me?"

"I think so."

He placed his hands on either side of her face. "Are you ready for the kiss we're going to tell our children about? The kiss that sealed our future?"

She nodded with a slight smile.

He lowered his mouth to hers and kissed her gently. His heart pounded and his throat ached. *This is what it is to kiss the woman I love.*

CHAPTER TWELVE

Violet

THEY MOVED INTO the Burnside house the next day. The moment she saw the cathedral ceilings, marble floors, and everything in shades of white, Violet's immediate concern was Dakota and his sticky fingers. Those fears were waylaid by the four bedrooms and state of the art kitchen. She hadn't thought it possible, but she missed cooking.

Last night still seemed like a dream. When they had arrived back upstairs to the suite, Mel was asleep on the couch. They had agreed it was too weird to sleep together with Mel in the other room, so they went off to their separate bedrooms. Violet had scarcely slept, thinking of Kyle, wishing she was there with him. All day they'd been busy with the kids and moving. They hadn't had much time to talk. Or kiss.

Now, she put Dakota down for the night in his new, temporary bedroom and went downstairs to the kitchen to finish cleaning up from their pasta dinner. It was already done. The counters gleamed. There wasn't a dish in sight. On the video baby monitor, she could see Mollie had already been put down. *Super dad.*

Kyle was on the deck, looking out toward the sea.

She stood near the sofa in the family room and stared at his back. The dark November evening kept the view from being anything more than a black abyss. She wondered what he saw. What did he think about when he stared out to sea on a night like this?

The transitory nature of the hotel had made their living arrangement seem more natural, like they were on a trip away from reality. They were in a cocoon, an escape from real life. Tonight, they were in a house where a real family had lived. Ghosts of that happy family lingered. Children's heights and ages were written on the inside of the pantry door, documented from the time they could stand to be measured. As if on cue, the ceiling creaked like a background melody in a movie, reminding her that a family belonged in a house like this.

The doorbell rang. She glanced at the clock. Nearing eight. Usually she would think—two hours until Mel arrived and broke up their night. But Kyle had called her earlier and asked if she would come by for a chat. She agreed, sounding defeated. "She knows it's coming," Violet said.

But as they sat down with her, she seemed her usual perky self. Wearing skin tight jeans, a plunging sweater, and thick makeup, she was like a poster child for women who take those sexy selfies and post them all over their social media accounts.

"What's up?" she asked.

Kyle had agreed to take the lead. "So, Mollie's pretty much sleeping through the night these days. As far as we can tell, she just wakes up at four now. We're ready to take the helm."

"You're letting me go?" Incredulous and wide-eyed, she clasped her hands together on her lap. "Before the holidays?"

"We'll pay you another three weeks. That should give you time to find another job," Kyle said.

"Is this because of what happened?" Mel asked. "Our little moment?"

"It wasn't a moment," Kyle said.

Big crocodile tears spilled from her coal-lined eyes. "I'll miss Mollie so much."

"I'm sure Nora can find you another position," Violet said.

Mel's eyes fixed on Violet and for a split second she detected anger and hatred coming out of those cat eyes. Mel disguised it as quickly as it had come. "I'm sure she will."

They walked her to the door. "Oh, jeez, I have to pee super bad. Do you mind if I use your bathroom?" Mel asked.

Violet pointed to the kitchen. "It's the door next to the built-in desk."

They stood awkwardly waiting for her to return. After a few minutes, she did.

"It's been real, guys. Thanks for everything." She bounced out the door with a brief wave.

They stood against the door after she left. "Why do I feel like we just dodged a bullet?" Kyle asked.

"Because we did."

"We're free. The creep nanny has left the building." He grabbed her into his arms and danced her into the kitchen. "Let's celebrate."

Kyle went into the family room to grab a wine opener and some glasses from the hutch. Her phone buzzed on the counter. It was her mother. *Really? After all these weeks of silence?* Why would she call now?

Her heart thudded hard in her chest as she answered. "Hi Mom."

"Violet, how are you?"

"I'm fine."

"We're in town."

"I know."

A ripe silence greeted her from the other end of the phone before her mother finally spoke. "I'm sorry I haven't called. Your father made me promise I wouldn't, and you know how he is— constantly monitoring my every move. But he's out tonight."

"So, you called. How nice."

"There's no need for sarcasm. We heard you're living with a man at a hotel."

"I'm working for Kyle Hicks as a nanny. I look after his baby daughter while he's at work. I'm not living with him like you think." *Always assuming the worst.*

"That's not the word about town. The bridge ladies said you're living with him in the penthouse suite. He's a rich playboy and he's seduced you. Someone saw you kissing him in a bar."

Good God, word traveled fast in this town.

"We just moved into a rental house today." She'd ignore the playboy accusations and the kissing. "What do you want, Mom?" Violet shivered and pulled her sweater tighter.

"I'd like to see my grandson."

"If you want to be part of our lives, you have to tell Dad. Dakota and I won't be your dirty secret."

Her mother blathered on about how it wasn't that simple. Violet's father was from a different time and his belief in the words of the bible led him, not the trappings of this world. Kyle came in from the patio and shot her a questioning look. She mouthed the words, *my mom.*

His eyes widened as he crossed the family room toward the kitchen. She would know his stride anywhere, so sure and steady, as if he knew exactly where he was headed. He came to stand on the opposite side of the kitchen island. "Stay strong," he whispered.

She put the call on speaker. "My job is to protect my little boy from heartbreak. If Dad can't accept me for what I am, then neither of you get to be part of Dakota's life. That's the end of it."

"I'm sorry you feel that way." Her voice sounded thick with tears. What did she have to cry about? Other than being spineless? "If you would apologize to him, we could put this whole thing to rest."

"Mom, I have nothing to apologize for. He's the one who wanted me out of his life." She stared at the granite countertop, looking for a pattern but found only chaos. Not one section was the same as the other. This was the work of nature, not man.

"But your temper—you wounded his pride. He would forgive you if you would soften. You two are so much alike—sure of your position on everything. Do you realize your stubbornness ruins relationships? No wonder you don't have a man."

"I'm not like him. I would never push away someone I love because of some ideal." Was that true? Her picketing and militant stance on the environment had almost kept her from Kyle. "You're my parents. You're supposed to love me unconditionally."

"We *do* love you. You were awful to him, Violet. You know you were." Her mother was in full tears now, replete with sniffles and sobs. Violet looked up at the ceiling, wavering between pity and anger. Kyle circled around the island and put his arm around her shoulders.

She let her weight sag against him, gathering strength from his warmth.

"Mom, I really have to go. You know how to reach me if you and Dad change your mind." She clicked off before her mother could say anything further. She pushed the phone across the shiny granite countertop. It stopped just before falling off the other side, like a car on a snowy cliff. "I shouldn't have answered the phone. But there's always this part of me that believes this time might be different."

Kyle loosened his embrace and brushed the tears gathered at the corners of her eyes. "You did well." He gave her one last squeeze before stepping aside. He rested his elbows on the countertop, looking at her. "When you remove yourself from the drama, it takes away their power. You're in control of your life. You know what's best for Dakota."

"Did you hear what she said? That I'm just like him—that I let my ideals outweigh my personal relationships."

"Went right for the jugular on that one."

"Do you think that's true?" she asked.

He hesitated a split second too long.

"You do?"

"No, I don't think that."

"Then why did you hesitate?" she asked.

"I was thinking about how to explain why not."

She hugged herself, waiting.

"I was thinking of you and me, actually," he said. "You put aside your intense dislike of me to take care of Mollie. That's perfect evidence that you're exactly opposite of what she said."

She let out a long, slow breath. Mary's words about Lance came back to her. *He makes it so I can breathe.*

"I can breathe when you're here," she said.

"Me too."

She clung to him as he kissed her.

They went to the window over the sink and looked up at the night sky. The clouds shifted to let a sliver of starry sky peek onto the horizon.

He stood behind her with his arms loosely around her waist. "I think your parents want to reconcile. That's why your mom called."

She gripped the sink with her hands and hung her head. Did she want them in her life?

"We could have Thanksgiving here instead of going out to Maggie and Jackson's," he said. "We could invite your parents. An olive branch."

She turned around to face him and gripped the steel muscles of his upper arms. "You'd do that for me? Give up seeing the Dogs on Thanksgiving?"

"I would do anything for you. A roasted turkey seems like a small thing."

"You don't know my parents."

"Whatever you want, I support," he said.

"I'd have to apologize to my dad to get them to come."

"You know what I've learned since Mollie Blue showed up?" he asked.

TESS THOMPSON

"That we do whatever it takes to give our children what they need?"

"Something like that, yes."

"I don't know. Do I even want them in Dakota's life?"

"It seems to me that you feel something's missing without them," he said. "Who knows, maybe your dad would be a better grandfather than he was a father."

"I'm scared to call him."

"I'll stay right by your side," he said.

"Can I have wine?"

He grinned that wolfish grin that made her stomach do flips. "Whatever the lady wants, she shall have."

She fetched her phone and followed him into the family room. Kyle opened a bottle of red and poured two glasses. The glow from the gas fireplace cast a warm orange light. Still, she shivered as she dialed her mother's number.

"Violet?"

"Hi again. I was thinking…maybe you guys would want to come over for Thanksgiving dinner."

"At that man's house?"

She caught Kyle's eyes. "Yes. At the house we're renting."

"I don't know if your dad will agree to it."

"You can ask him, can't you? If he says no, then so be it. I tried." She glanced at Kyle. He made a gesture like he was stabbing a sword into his chest and then leaned forward.

She almost laughed. "Tell him I want to reconcile. For Dakota's sake."

"I'll ask him and get back to you."

"It's been too long, Mom. Do it for Dakota."

Her mother sniffed, obviously crying on the other end. "I'm glad you called back."

After they hung up, Violet accepted the glass of wine from Kyle. "She said she'd let me know."

"Soon, I hope? We need to buy a turkey."

Her phone buzzed with a text from her mother.

He won't come, but I will.

"Oh my God, she says she'll come without him."
"You're kidding?" Kyle asked. "Tell her fine."

That's fine. Please come around 4:00.

I'll bring the pies. I know they're a little much for you.

She shook her head in disgust and showed Kyle the text. "Translation. Your pies are awful."

He laughed. "I don't care about your pies. I'm proud of you for calling."

Tell Dad that I would like him to come. And that I'll apologize.

I'll try.

"I hope I don't regret this." Dread crept into her stomach and curled up like a heavy snake.

"I'll be there. We'll make it fun. First thing tomorrow, I'll go out and get a turkey. If there are any fresh ones left, that is. Otherwise, we'll do chicken."

"Or one of those Tofu turkeys."

He groaned. "Please, no. I'll do anything."

"I'm just kidding."

They wandered over to the couch and took their positions on opposite ends just like they had at the hotel.

She watched his long fingers wrap around the stem of the wineglass and stifled a shiver as she imagined them traveling up the length of her legs.

"What is it?" he asked.

"Huh? Nothing."

He grinned. "You were staring at me."

"I was not." She uncurled her legs and stretched them out

along the length of the couch. He tossed her a pillow that she put under her head.

He draped an arm across the back of the couch and spread his long legs out to rest on the coffee table without taking his gaze from her. "You look so good tonight. So damn good. Those jeans."

Her mouth went completely dry. She'd dressed in skinny jeans and a t-shirt that clung to her slender waist and small, round breasts. Knowing he liked it, she'd worn her hair down.

His gaze landed on her feet and stayed there. "You're always barefooted. Why is that?"

"I hate shoes. They're hot." She wriggled her toes at him.

"But it's cold outside."

"Not to my feet."

"Are you hot at night too? Do you like to have the windows open or the air conditioning blasting when you sleep?"

"Windows. Air conditioning is bad for the environment." She said it to evoke an eye roll, but he didn't sway from the subject of her sleeping routine.

"Do you take off your flannel pajamas before you get into bed?" he asked.

"Depends on how warm it is."

"So, I should imagine you in the summer months."

She sucked in a deep breath and held it in as a surge of desire slapped her hard.

He put aside his wine and reached out to one of her feet. His finger brushed the inside of her arch. Every nerve in her body popped to life.

A few more inches and her feet would be in his lap.

"Lettie, this is impossible."

"What is?" she whispered, afraid to move.

"Thinking of anything but how badly I want to take you upstairs." He moved closer and lifted her legs onto his lap. He reached under the cuff of her jeans to stroke her ankle. "And about all the things I want to do to you."

She withdrew her legs from his lap and sat up, cross-legged, staring at him, breathing hard. "I thought we were taking it slow?" She could barely able to choke the words from her dry mouth.

"You should take pity on me. Think of all the sleep I've lost imagining you in my bed," he said.

"I've lost a lot of sleep too."

"Come here," he said softly. "Put me out of my misery." He reached out and pulled her onto his lap.

She wrapped her legs around his middle, straddling him. Her hands went into his thick hair.

He pressed into the small of her back and placed his mouth against her neck, his breath hot on her skin. "I'm going crazy. Concentrating on work is nearly impossible." Kyle's voice deepened in tone but lowered in volume. His words were like strokes of his tongue on her body. "My mind won't shut off, thinking about you."

She couldn't breathe. If she did, she might wake up from this dream.

He lifted his head to look into her eyes. "I don't know how much longer I can take it."

She barely recognized her own voice. Was it possible for speech to drip with desire? "I haven't been with anyone but Cole. You should know that."

"I don't care if you've been with a hundred men or none. I intend to make you mine." He reached under her t-shirt and unfastened her bra with a quick flick of his thumb and fingers.

I'm already yours.

"You're not just one of my conquests. This has to be what you want, on your terms." He kissed her neck. "Do you want me to take you upstairs?"

"What if you lose interest after sex? That happens. I've heard it happens, anyway."

"Trust me. I'm not going to lose interest."

"Then take me upstairs and do all those things you promised," she whispered in his ear.

"Jesus, Lettie." He kissed her again.

She opened her mouth to let him inside, darting her tongue against his upper lip.

"Not fair. So not fair."

She moaned. "You're the one who isn't fair."

"The things I want to do to you are better demonstrated in the bedroom." With her legs still wrapped around him, he stood and carried her across the room to the bottom of the stairs.

"Please God, just let Mollie keep sleeping," he muttered as he pushed her against the wall and kissed her.

"Upstairs, now," she said.

He set her onto her feet. They hustled up the stairs, taking the steps two at a time.

When they reached the door to the master bedroom, he looked down at her with a gentle smile. "You sure about this? Once you step into this room, there's no going back."

"I'm ready. I've *been* ready."

"You're killing me." He scooped her into his arms and crossed into the bedroom. The door closed behind them. A lamp from the desk threw shadows in the dim room.

"Wait, lock the door," she said. "Just in case Dakota wakes up."

"Good call. Rookie mistake." He kissed her before sprinting across the room and twisting the lock. On the way back, like there were skates on his feet, he slid across the floor in his socks and fell onto the bed.

She squealed with laughter as he pulled her under him.

"You like my skating moves?" he asked.

She wrapped her arms around his neck. "I like all your moves. Turn out the lamp."

He brushed her hair away from her face and looked into her eyes. "No, I want to see all of you."

"I've never done it with the lights on." She might burst into flames under his gaze.

"There's no shame in it. Not when I feel the way I do about you."

"I'm afraid you won't like what you see."

"That's not something you should ever worry about. With or without your clothes, I see exactly how lovely you are." He tapped her chest. "Because I see what's in there and it's the most beautiful thing I've ever seen. Don't be afraid. We'll go nice and slow."

"Not too slow." She closed her eyes and lifted her mouth to his.

CHAPTER THIRTEEN

KYLE

KYLE DREAMT OF the dirt road that led to their trailer. He chased after his little sister. She screamed and laughed with delight until she tripped and fell. *Daniel, help me.* He woke with a start.

A woman slept beside him, curled into a fetal position. *Lettie.*

She was in his bed. Her hair covered her face and the covers were pulled up to her chin. He'd made a study of every curve last night, every soft and hard part of her. He warmed, remembering how she'd opened her body and heart to him.

After, she'd clung to his damp chest.

I've never had one before. I mean, never with a man.

Really?

Really.

He'd felt her mouth against his chest turn upward into a smile.

It was amazing.

Let's have another then, shall we?

For the first time in his life, he hadn't merely had sex with a woman. What happened between them went beyond the physical. She'd been so vulnerable that he'd had no choice but to match her level of intimacy. This love pulled him under like a strong riptide. No chance of escape. There was nothing to be done. He couldn't stop loving her even if he wanted to. And he didn't.

Rolling to his side, he watched her sleep. This is what it would be like if she were his wife. Every day he would wake up to her by his side.

She stirred next to him. He turned on his side to look at her.

"Hi." She brushed her hair out of her eyes. Pillow marks had left indentations on her left cheek. He wanted to press his lips to them, to mark them with his own indent.

"Morning. How'd you sleep?"

"Fine." She yawned. "I feel like I ran a marathon. Every muscle in my body hurts."

He grinned as he recalled their athletic lovemaking. He'd never been with a woman as physically strong or flexible. "I have a newfound love for yoga."

"I'm pretty fond of CrossFit," she said. "What time was it when we finally fell asleep?"

"Just after one. Mollie was up at four, but you slept through it."

"Lucky me." She flashed a dreamy smile at him.

God, that smile of hers—so trusting and guileless. He caressed her upper arm. "How do you feel about morning sex?"

"I've never had it, but in theory it sounds good." She flushed.

"Let's test that theory."

"If you insist."

* * *

After he showered and dressed, he offered to take Dakota with him to do the shopping. The little guy was getting into his coat when Kyle noticed his keys were missing from the desk. He felt sure he'd put them there last night.

Violet hadn't noticed them, she said as she popped a few pieces of bread into the toaster.

"The new house key was on there too," he said. "But I have an extra pair of car keys." He sprinted upstairs to fetch them. When he returned, Violet was feeding Mollie her bottle in the kitchen.

"It's not like me to misplace my keys," he said.

"I'm sure they'll turn up," she said. "It was chaotic yesterday."

"I must have put them somewhere else and not remembered. I was distracted yesterday by someone. I won't mention any names."

She smiled. "Remember the day I came to work for you? I'd lost my keys that day too."

"Maybe missing keys brings good fortune." He leaned down and kissed her quickly before calling for Dakota.

When they were in the car and headed down the hill toward town, Dakota called out to him from the backseat. "Kale, are you and Mama getting married?"

"Why do you ask?"

"Because I saw you kissing."

"Can you keep a secret?"

"Maybe."

"I'm going to ask your mom to marry me. But I have to get a ring first."

"Will you be my dad then?"

"Yes. Would you like that?"

"I sure would."

Kyle glanced at him from the rearview mirror. Dakota gazed out the window with a dreamy expression. What did he wish for? What did he see?

"We'll be a family," Kyle said, more to himself than the little boy who'd stolen his heart.

"Kale, we already are."

CHAPTER FOURTEEN

VIOLET WAS IN the kitchen when she heard the garage door open and then Dakota's footsteps running across the floor. He burst into the kitchen and threw his arms around her legs. "Mama, we got a turkey—the most giantest turkey in the whole store."

Kyle arrived with several bags of groceries. He dropped them on the counter and turned to look at her. His expression softened. "Hello, beautiful."

"Hey."

"We got everything you asked for. I'll go back to the car to get the turkey."

"Dakota says it's a big one."

"Wait until you see it," he said.

After he left, she knelt on her knees to talk to Dakota. "I have a surprise. My mom, your grandmother, is coming to turkey dinner tomorrow. Isn't that exciting?"

"I guess so." His blue eyes widened. "Does she know me?"

"You met her last year. Do you remember her?"

He shook his head. His forehead wrinkled like he was suddenly worried. "Mama, Kale will be here, right? And Mollie?"

"Yes, we're all having dinner."

Kyle was back, carrying a big turkey. "This sucker weighs twenty-one pounds." He plopped it into the sink.

"Kale's strong, Mama. He carried it like a ball."

"Hey bud, will you do me a favor and go play in your room for a little bit?" Kyle asked. "I need to talk to your mama."

"Okay." Without a backward glance, he scampered off.

He pushed her against the sink and kissed her like it was the first and last thing he would ever do.

Mollie's cry came through the baby monitor. He laughed. "Mollie needs better timing. I'll work with her on that. You keep that in mind for later. I can't wait to do all the things I did to you last night all over again."

The doorbell rang.

"Are you expecting someone?" Violet asked.

"No. Maybe it's Lance. He said he might stop by and say hello."

They walked together to the doorway. When Kyle opened the door, a young woman with hair the color of a copper penny and a light dusting of freckles on her fair skin stood under the light of the front porch. In her left hand she carried a walking cane.

"Hi Daniel." A tight, shy smile lifted the corners of her mouth. A barely visible scar on the right side of her face spoiled her almost perfect complexion.

Beside Violet, Kyle flinched.

"Autumn?" Kyle sounded like his mouth had filled with sand.

"I wasn't sure you would know me." A soft voice matched her shy smile. She turned to Violet. "I'm Autumn. Daniel's sister."

Kyle seemed to have frozen beside her. Autumn was here. How had she found him? What would he do? Violet stepped forward and introduced herself. "I'm Violet."

"May I come in, Daniel?" Autumn asked. "I came a long way to see you."

"Yes, please." Violet gently pulled Kyle into the foyer to give his sister room to pass.

"May I take your coat?" Violet asked.

Autumn nodded and shrugged out of a white peacoat. "The dampness works its way into a person's bones, doesn't it? What a lovely home," Autumn said.

"We're renting," Violet said. She glanced at Kyle. His complexion had gone from its usual ruddiness to the color of white chalk. As much as she'd studied him the past few weeks, she couldn't read him now.

"Our house growing up was the dark, small, and dirty variety," Autumn said. "Very popular back then."

Quick witted like her brother.

They walked into the family room. Violet turned on the gas fireplace.

"What a cozy room," Autumn said.

"We're terrified of all the whites and grays," Violet said. "Because of my son. He's three and perpetually sticky."

Autumn smiled. "This would be a better room for a single girl like me."

"Would you like something to eat or drink?" Violet asked. "We have some leftover pizza."

"I've eaten, but I wouldn't turn down a generous glass of scotch." Autumn leaned on her cane as she crossed the room, bearing the weight of her left leg. With the aid of her right hand, she lowered herself onto one end of the couch.

"I'd like one too, Lettie," Kyle said, his voice odd and strangled as he sank into one of the gray armchairs.

"Sure." Violet scooted over to the bar and busied herself pouring them both a glass of scotch. Behind her, the siblings were quiet. Silence had a sound of its own just then, like the pained throbbing of a broken heart.

Drinks in hand, she returned to the sitting area.

"Did you fly here from Denver?" Kyle asked.

"That's right." Autumn hands fluttered in her lap. "You know where I live?"

"I do." Kyle said. He didn't look up when Violet handed him the drink.

Conversely, Autumn thanked her with a smile, then gripped her glass with both hands. White knuckles gave her away. Kyle watched Autumn like a man in fear for his life.

Violet hesitated, unsure if she should stay or go. "I should let you two talk. I'm sure you have a lot of things to catch up on."

"Stay." Kyle lifted his face to look up at her. "Please." His eyelids fluttered ever so slightly. She knew that panicked, humbled look in his eyes. He'd had it the first night they had Mollie.

Autumn took a sip of her drink and closed her eyes for a split second. "This is just what I need. I had an early flight this morning and then drove here from San Francisco."

Violet studied her. The siblings looked nothing alike, other than the intense way they peered at someone or something. Violet had once thought Kyle's intense glittering stare was meant to intimidate, but she knew now that it was a deep curiosity from a man who remained an outsider despite appearances to the contrary. Under the designer clothes and expensive cologne, Kyle remained the little boy who gawked at the big white house and dreamt of the girl inside. When one was unseen and disposable and dismissed, the world was experienced through a distance, like a detective gathering information.

"How'd you find me?" Kyle asked.

"I read about the opening of Cliffside Bay Lodge in a travel magazine. They had your photograph. I knew it was you, despite your name being slightly changed. I've looked for you for a long time. This was the first lead I had. I took a chance I might find you at the resort, but your staff wouldn't tell me anything. I decided to head into town and ask around. A woman at the grocery store said to head over to The Oar and ask Zane Shaw for information." A flash of pain crossed her face. "It took a photograph to convince him I was your sister. He said you guys go way back."

Kyle didn't respond, other than to cross one leg over the other.

Autumn reached into her handbag and pulled out an old photograph. She deposited it on the glass coffee table and flicked it with her finger toward the chair where Kyle sat as still as a statue. "Fortunately, I had this one. He said he knew it was you right away."

Embarrassed by his lack of response, Violet reached out for the photograph. It was of a little girl around two and a rough little boy of about six. She grinned into the camera, but the boy's expression was stoic bordering on hostile. The way he glared at the camera reminded her of photographs from the late 1800s of people on the frontier. No one ever smiled in those photos. She'd always wondered why. No question, however, that this was a young Kyle. He had the same sharp features and dark hair. Unlike now, his hair was cut unevenly and stood up on one side in a ratted tangle. Both faces were smeared with grime. An old rusted truck behind them made a dreary backdrop.

"Where did you get this?" Kyle asked from behind Violet.

She jumped. Enthralled in the photograph, she had not seen Kyle get up from his chair.

"From the house after Dad died. I found it in a book," Autumn said. "It was stuck in one of those paperback books Mom used to read."

"You can't possibly remember that. You were only six when she left."

"I vaguely remember her sitting in that orange chair reading," Autumn said. "Stone tells me about her when I ask. He said she read all day to escape."

"Until she left," Kyle said. "The ultimate escape."

"Until then, yes," Autumn said.

Kyle returned to his seat without taking the photograph. Violet held it for a moment before leaving it on the table.

"It's the only one I have of the two of us." Autumn turned to Violet. "Our brother Stone is between us in age. There aren't any photos of the three of us together, unfortunately."

Violet crossed over to the bar and poured herself a glass of wine. Afterward, she perched on the edge of the couch, unsure what to say or do.

"You look so different," Autumn said. "He was always so thin."

"The word is scrawny," Kyle said.

"You wouldn't know it now," Autumn said. "The lodge is beautiful too. You always had a flair for making beautiful things out of nothing."

"Isn't it the opposite?" he asked.

"It wasn't your fault," Autumn said.

They looked at each other like two kids in a staring contest.

"Zane told me you have a baby daughter," Autumn said. "But he didn't mention a wife."

No response from Kyle.

"I'm not Mollie's mother. Or his wife," Violet said.

"We're together," Kyle said hoarsely.

"Does Mollie have a mother?" Autumn said.

Kyle drank from his glass. "She died."

"I'm sorry." Autumn's gaze remained on her brother. She must be curious, but how did one ask about the sudden appearance of a baby?

"Her mother and I weren't together. I met her in a bar—it was a casual encounter," Kyle said.

"I'm still sorry. For the baby, especially."

"Kyle learned of Mollie's existence after she was born," Violet said.

"And you didn't mind?" Autumn asked.

"I don't mind." Violet smiled to hide her embarrassment. "It was before me."

"I'm sure it's a shock to see me," Autumn said.

"Yes," Kyle said.

"You did a great job disappearing." Two bright pink spots blazed on Autumn's cheeks.

"You guys were better off without me."

"We disagree." She drank the rest of her scotch and put the glass aside. "Like I said, Stone and I have been searching for you for some time now."

"Why?" Kyle asked.

"Because it devastated us when you left. Stone joined the Marines after high school."

"I know," Kyle said.

She looked surprised but didn't ask how. "He's had some problems since he got back from Afghanistan. Seeing you would help him. His psychologist thinks it would be good for him to have closure. Even if it's only to explain why you disappeared out of our lives. She believes it would help him to move forward. He's stuck. Depressed. Anxious. He saw things over there no one should have to see." She pulled a card from a pocket and pushed it across the table. "Here's my contact information. We're staying at the resort for the long weekend. If you decide you'd like to see us and talk, we'd welcome it."

"I'll think about it," Kyle said.

"Please do. We don't want anything from you. We're both fine financially. I'm a pharmacist. But maybe you know that too?"

"I do."

"You've checked up on us but haven't given us the chance to do the same? It makes no sense," Autumn said.

"The scar's less visible," Kyle said.

"Your money paid for a plastic surgeon." Autumn placed her fingertips over the scar.

"They did a good job," Kyle said.

"As good as it gets," Autumn said. "After I got insurance through work, I had an operation on my legs. They reset the bones and used some pins and various other techniques. After physical therapy, I'm able to walk without pain. My right leg's almost normal, but my left can't take too much weight. But my friend here helps." She wrapped her right hand around the head of the cane and stood. "It's better than those awful braces. Remember those?"

A terrible darkness seemed to cloud Kyle's face. "Do you really think I could ever forget?"

Autumn shook her head as if suddenly weary. "The Miller boys did this, not you."

"I was driving," he said. "I took that corner too fast."

"They were right behind us," Autumn said. "We were scared for our lives. Those boys tortured you for most of your childhood. Don't forget that part."

"If I hadn't been such a pathetic loser, then they wouldn't have come after me in the first place."

"Daniel, for heavens' sake, you were barely eighteen years old and taking care of the entire family. You were trying to protect me, like always."

Kyle downed his drink and slammed it down on the coffee table. "Do you know how many times I've gone through that moment in my head? If only I'd done this or that or the other thing?"

"They were chasing us. You did the only thing you could do." Autumn looked over at Violet. "The roads were slick from rain."

Kyle put his hand out like a traffic cop. "We're not doing this. I don't revisit the past. Ever." He leapt to his feet and headed toward the bar. "Seeing you is just a reminder of all the ways I failed you."

"Is that why you left?" Autumn had started to cry. "Because you couldn't stand to look at me."

Kyle turned back to look at her. "I ruined your life. You're better off without me. You know that."

"My life wasn't ruined," Autumn said, her voice just above a whisper. "I don't even remember what it was like before."

"You mean before your legs were mangled and your perfect face scarred?"

"Yes, that. This is my life. I'd rather it be different, but hey, it got me out of P.E. the last few years of high school." Autumn wiped under her eyes. "How could you leave us?"

"When I left home it was for good. I started fresh," Kyle said.

"But what about Stone and me? You left just like Mom did. Nothing. Just evaporated."

Kyle buried his face in his hands and let out a long, shuddering sigh. "It's what I had to do to save myself. I had to save myself to save you guys."

"Why couldn't you do that and stay in our lives? Is it because of me?"

The second hand on the clock above the mantel clicked away the seconds. Finally, he answered. "Yes. It kills me that I did this to you. All I ever wanted was to make sure you guys were okay. I failed you."

"The only way you failed us was to disappear. Stone needs you. Please, can we see you? Talk things through?"

"You could come to Thanksgiving dinner tomorrow," Violet said. Why had she said that? It just slipped out of her mouth. Kyle glared at her. She looked away, flushed.

"I'd like that. Very much," Autumn said.

The sound of Mollie crying through the monitor interrupted them. Violet stood, but Kyle shook his head. "No, I'll get her." He rose from the chair. "Yes, come tomorrow. Bring Stone."

"I will." Autumn smiled.

"I'll see you tomorrow." Kyle headed out the door. His footsteps echoed through the house.

Autumn picked up the photograph from the table and stared at it like she'd never seen it before. "Do you know how many hours I've spent staring at this picture? I could have circled the earth twice on foot." She looked up and over at Violet. "I should go."

"I'll walk you out," Violet said.

When they reached the front door, she helped Autumn into her coat and escorted her out to the driveway where a rental car was parked next to Kyle's Lexus.

At the car, Autumn opened the driver's side door and placed her cane inside before sitting. She looked up at Violet. "Do you think he's all right? I mean, for real. Is he happy?"

Violet gripped the top of the car door. "I think so."

"He has friends?"

"Yes. The best kind."

"He basically raised us after our mom left," Autumn said. "Until he left for college, he took care of everything." Her voice softened. "I missed him more than I can say. Stone wouldn't admit it, but he did too. We never missed our mom much because we were so young when she left, but Kyle, well, that was hard. I would never have predicted he was the leaving kind. I guess he got that from our mother."

"I'm sorry. My family's estranged too."

"This was more like abandonment, not estrangement."

"Kyle's complex. He has demons, clearly." *More so than I could even imagine.*

"I'm one of them," Autumn said.

So it seems.

Autumn started the engine. The driveway filled with the smell of engine fumes. She rolled down the window. "Are you guys in love?"

Violet nodded. "Very much so."

"Be careful. Kyle will leave when you least expect it and break your heart."

"People change," Violet said.

Autumn looked up at her with a sad smile that didn't reach her eyes. "I hope so. Was it dumb to come? Are my hopes for reconciliation futile?"

"I don't know. But you have to try."

"Yes, I do. Thanks for the invitation to dinner. I have a feeling you may have to pay for that," Autumn said.

"Sometimes you have to take a risk for someone you love." Violet pulled her sweater tighter around her waist. "Honestly, it slipped out. But my gut tells me this is the right thing. For all of us."

"I hope so. I'll see you tomorrow."

Violet shivered in the night air as she watched the car back out of the driveway and onto the street. When the lights were no longer visible, she looked up at the moonless sky. A few stars twinkled between the clouds. The roar of the car's engine faded, replaced by the sound of waves crashing to shore. She wrapped her arms around her middle and closed her eyes. *Please God, help them forgive and become the family they're meant to be. Please help Kyle forgive himself.*

If he didn't, would he ever be free of his demons? Without forgiveness would he be able to love her and the children the way he should? Was it true that one must love themselves before they could love others?

Love. It was all a leap of faith that required great courage. Kyle loved her. She loved him. With that pact came the responsibility to stand by the other during moments of weakness and uncertainty. She looked back to the sky, to the twinkling stars that pushed aside the clouds to shine. Tonight, I'll be the strong one. I'll shine with such intensity that he will melt into forgiveness.

She walked into the house, determined to wake the sleeping lion named Courage that resided in the deepest part of her.

CHAPTER FIFTEEN

KYLE

KYLE WAS HUNCHED over in the armchair in the master bedroom with a drink in his hand when Violet appeared in the doorway. Every muscle and organ in his body ached. He couldn't shake the weight that wanted to cut him off at the knees and make him fall apart.

"Drink?" he asked.

"No thanks."

"Don't give me that look," he said.

"I didn't say anything. You're a grown-up. You can have another drink if you want."

She moved nearer to the fireplace with her arms wrapped around her waist like she did when she was cold. "I'm sorry I asked your sister to dinner. It just slipped out. She looked so sad and I thought about my parents and how I wished they were in my life and I got carried away. I know it wasn't my place."

"It's okay." He blinked, and she came into focus. How was he supposed to stay angry at her? An apology stole the fury from him. He tried to conjure a little more anger, but nothing came.

Instead, a sadness crept into the lining of his stomach. He drank from his glass.

She moved toward him almost on her tiptoes, like he was a frightened animal and she the benevolent zoo keeper. Her over-sized sweater made her seem small, almost fragile. He knew differently. She was made of steel. When she reached him, she took the glass from his hands and situated it on the bedside table.

An image of Autumn on the ground, bloody and mangled flashed through his mind. *I can't do this. I can't feel all this at once.* Black spots danced before his eyes.

I just want to feel numb, to forget.

She slipped between his legs and splayed her fingers through his hair before forcing his chin upward so that she could peer directly into his eyes. "Did you hear what I said?"

"No." Kyle breathed in the heady scent of her perfume like it would ease the tightening of his chest. It didn't. He fixated on her small mouth, those perfect lips that made him think of pink daisies. If he could kiss her the ache might leave for a moment. But the anguish would come back. It always did.

Violet knelt on the floor beside him and placed her hands on his knees. She stared up at him with those eyes that saw through every layer of skin to his heart. "You're the only one who thinks the accident was your fault. She doesn't. Stone doesn't."

"My temper and ego fueled the flame. If I'd been a better man I would've just walked away. But I couldn't. I was an irresponsible, selfish boy who let his sister get smashed to bits."

"You fought dirty, just like Stone told you to do. Because you had to. You don't know what they would have done to Autumn had you not gotten her out of there. Think about that for a second."

"Her face, Lettie. Her beautiful face."

"She's still beautiful. Maybe more so because of what she went through."

"I made sure they got out. I made sure. That's all that mattered." Words were hard to conjure. *Too much scotch.* And still he wasn't numb. The pain was a heavy cloak dragging him deeper into darkness.

"If you're under the impression that people would rather have your money than you, you're wrong," she said.

"Money makes a person like me seem a lot better than I really am."

Violet shook her head so violently that one of her earrings fell out and flew across the room. She didn't appear to notice. "Your money isn't you, Kyle. Of all people, *you* should know that."

"I'm dark and selfish. All the women, all the business deals to prove I'm worthy—they all add up to one thing. I'm no good for you or anyone."

"Do you really hate yourself that much? Do you really think disappearing from their lives was the best thing for any of you?"

"When I was a kid that was everyone's wish. Make Daniel disappear. Pig stinks." His voice was ragged in the quiet room. "When I wake up in the middle of the night and it's all dark, I remember. I remember it all. The torture. The ridicule. The accident. With them, I'll always be the one who ruined my sister's life, the boy who smells like a pig farm, the kid whose own mother didn't want him."

"Is that what you've been doing all this time? Running from your old self? Because I have news for you—there's no way you can ever succeed. You're still going to wake up with yourself in the morning."

"That's just it. No matter what I do, Pig still lives inside me."

She looked up at him in that way she did with the tilted head and her mouth slightly parted and those eyes that swallowed him whole. "You can't wish away the little boy you were. Maybe you shouldn't even want to. Do you think you would be this version of yourself without those hard times? They made you into the man I love." Her eyes filled. One teardrop clung to the bottom lashes of her left eye.

In that teardrop, another Kyle lived. The one who could make her his wife and give her that picket fence she wanted. He wanted so desperately to live there forever. But could he?

"You don't have to punish yourself any longer for a crime you didn't commit. You can let people love you. You can love yourself."

"How? How do I do that?" The words strangled in the back of his throat.

She wiped his cheeks with her thumbs. Was he crying?

"Do you love me?" she asked.

"I do."

"Say it."

"I love you," he whispered.

"It's as easy and hard as that."

"Loving you isn't hard. It's the easiest thing in the world."

She finished his sentence. "But how do you love yourself?"" She paused. "Close your eyes."

He followed her instruction.

"Now think of the little boy in that photograph, the one with the dirty face and ragged clothes. He's an innocent child, hungry and sad. Did he deserve love?"

"Yes," he whispered.

"You're still that little boy. A child who deserves love and affection and a full stomach. You did your best in a terrible situation. But we're not our circumstances. Can you find it in your heart to forgive the little boy who did his best to protect his sister and brother?"

He opened his eyes. "I think so."

"What do you see when you look into my eyes?"

"Love."

"Absorb it. Let it heal all the broken parts. Use it to absolve yourself. We can't ever make the past disappear, but we can use it to inform how we live now. The hardships you went through made you strong and determined. But now it's time to reconcile your past with your present. They have to merge. Otherwise you'll never have peace. Your sister and brother have come back to you for a reason."

"I don't know if I can do this—maybe it's too late to have a relationship with them."

"They're here. It's a start. And, I'll be there for you tomorrow and the day after that. When one of us is weak, the other can be strong. We don't have to carry our burdens alone."

He kissed her, cleansing the last of the grime that remained under his skin and in those nearly impossible to reach crevices. It was Violet's smell now that permeated every part of him. Jasmine and sunshine and the scent of her hair splashed over him like no bottle of expensive cologne ever could.

CHAPTER SIXTEEN

THANKSGIVING DAY, THE doorbell rang at exactly four. Kyle and Dakota were by her side as she took in a deep breath. Whatever happened today didn't matter as much as the two people right here with her. As if he knew she needed it, Dakota slipped his hand into hers just before she opened the door.

To her surprise, both of her parents stood on the porch. "Hi Mom. Hi Dad." Violet's voice sounded high pitched, or was it the buzzing in her ears? Dakota had slipped behind her and peeked out from behind her skirt.

She gestured for them to come inside and accepted her mother's hug.

"This is Kyle Hicks." Violet's voice sounded like a child's, even to herself. She was eight years old the minute he walked in the door.

"Terry Ellis." The men shook hands.

"Good to meet you," Kyle said. "Thanks for coming."

Violet gently pushed Dakota forward. "And this is Dakota."

"Nice to meet you, young man," her dad said.

Her mother crouched low to take Dakota into her arms. "You've gotten so big."

Dakota escaped from his grandmother's tight embrace and smiled politely. "Kale says I have to eat meat to get big like him."

"The boy doesn't look a thing like our family," her dad said, almost under his breath. *We all heard you, Dad.*

"I don't, Mama?" Dakota asked.

"You look like yourself," Kyle said. "And that's just right."

Dakota grinned. "Just right." He turned back to his grandmother. "We have a baby here too. Mollie Blue."

Her mother nodded and smiled. "Your mom told me about Mollie Blue."

"A nanny job," her dad said. "This is what happens when you don't finish your degree."

"Terry," her mother said. "Please."

"What was that, Rose?" Her father glared at his wife. A warning. *Don't cross me in front of others.* Violet knew that one all too well.

"Would anyone care for a cocktail?" Kyle asked.

"I would," Violet said.

"Some wine might be nice," her mother said.

"Do you know how to make a dry martini?" her dad asked.

"One of my best friends is a bartender. I've picked up a few tricks over the years." Kyle smiled but it didn't match the steely glint in his eyes.

Kyle led them all into the living room and asked them all to sit while he fixed drinks. "My brother and sister will be here soon and then we'll eat. Violet and I have been cooking all day."

"She cooks now?" Her father raised his eyebrows before turning to Kyle. "She never had much interest in that when she lived at home. Seemed to think meals were delivered by a magical fairy."

Violet stifled a sigh. *Here we go.*

"Well, she lived with you when she was a *child*, so that sounds about right," Kyle said.

"She was a pampered princess. Enough said," her dad said.

This was a mistake. Why had she weakened? He was the same. Toxic and awful.

The doorbell rang before Kyle finished mixing her dad's martini.

"I'll finish up," she said. "If you want to get the door."

"Sure. Wish me luck." He kissed her cheek before disappearing into the hallway.

"You don't know how to make a martini. Move over. I'll do it." Her dad picked up the bottle of vodka and poured a good dose into the shaker.

Violet poured two glasses of white wine and handed one to her mother who was now sitting with Dakota on the couch, listening to one of his stories about his favorite train.

Her dad approached, having fixed his drink. "What's going on here? I thought he was your boss."

"He was. Now he's my boyfriend."

"For heaven's sake. You are shacked up with him," her mother said. "My friends were right."

"Your mother told me about the store. I knew that hippie idea wouldn't work. Not in this town, especially."

She was saved from responding when Kyle came into the room with his siblings. Autumn looked beautiful in a light blue dress and ballerina flats. Stone wore a pair of khakis and a cranberry colored sweater over a button-down shirt. He was taller and wider than Kyle by several inches in every direction. Their faces were similar, with the same dark blue eyes and strong jawline. He held out his hand to Violet the moment he came into the room. "Thank you for having me. It smells delicious."

"Thank you. I'm glad you could come."

"I'm never one to turn down a homecooked meal." His voice was soft and low-pitched, which belied his tall, muscular frame.

Dakota approached, looking up at Stone with a timid smile.

"Who's this now?" Stone asked.

"I'm Dakota."

"I'm Kyle's little brother," Stone said.

"But you're bigger than him," Dakota said.

Stone reached into the pocket of his sports coat and pulled out a toy car. "I brought this for you. It's a Corvette."

"Thank you," Dakota said. "I love cars."

"Me too," Stone said.

"That was very thoughtful," Violet said.

"It's nothing," Stone said. "We're pretty darned excited to meet you all."

"Do you want to see my truck?" Dakota asked. "It's over there." He pointed to a corner of the family room where his truck was parked next to a potted plant.

"I'd love to," Stone said. With a wink at Violet, he took Dakota's hand and followed him to the truck.

* * *

The afternoon passed without incident. Everyone was polite during the meal with benign conversation ranging from the weather to movies. Kyle and his siblings were quiet for the most part, only chiming in when asked a question. Still, she breathed a sigh of relief when the meal was finished. As they cleared the table, the sun peeked through the clouds, prompting her mother to offer to take Dakota out to the patio to play with his new car. Kyle and his siblings went out for a walk.

She had just put the last Tupperware container away when her father walked into the kitchen.

He crossed his arms and leaned against the counter. A familiar pose from her childhood. It was the pose that indicated she'd displeased him somehow. "Your mother says you have something to say to me."

She turned to him, hiding her shaking hands behind her back. "I did, yes. I wanted to say I'm sorry for our fight and the things I said. I was feeling hurt and rejected and I lashed out."

"You've always had a temper."

"I'm a work in progress, yes." Her skin burned under her dress. How dare he chastise her? He was the one who should apologize. But no. She must not let him get under her skin.

"A nanny. Really?"

"I love being with the kids," she said. "It's the first time since he was born that I don't have to take Dakota to daycare. It's a gift to be home with him."

"If you had a husband, it would make more sense."

She took in a deep breath and busied herself at the sink. There was no way in hell she would cry in front of him. He needed to leave and not come back.

"What happened with the store?"

"It didn't do well. That's all. So, I cut my losses before it got any worse."

"I told you not to open that hippie store," he said.

"I know." *God, please don't let me cry. I have to be strong.*

"What'd you do, just start sleeping with this Hicks guy for the fun of it? Like you do?"

"We're close."

"Where's the baby's mother?"

"She passed away," she said.

He rested his arms over his plump belly.

"What's the nature of your relationship with this guy?"

"We're close, like I said."

"I know his kind. Charming. Always says the right thing. But under all that is a lack of character."

She folded a dishcloth in three and hung it on the refrigerator. "Dad, it's really none of your business."

"You bet it's my business. You're exposing my grandson to sin."

"How you can even call him that is beyond me. You've never even met Dakota until today."

She turned to look at her father. He was a mean man, overly critical and disloyal. All her life she'd tried to please him to no avail. The way her mother tiptoed and groveled made her physically ill. *No wonder I'm a mess.* Cole Lund popped into her mind. Her low self-esteem had caused her to be taken in by him. She had wanted so desperately to be loved that she'd fallen for his act.

"Mark my words. This man is trouble. What's with his family showing up out of the blue? White trash. They show up once they know he's rich."

"They grew up poor, Dad, but they got themselves out of it. You're the one always talking about how hard work will get you everywhere in America. They're perfect examples."

"If you say so," he said.

"I do say so. And as far as Kyle goes, he's the reason they were both able to get a jump start in life."

"Come on now. He's the type who got lucky. I've seen it a million times. Trust me, he's like one of those lottery winners who blows all the money in five years."

"You're wrong, Dad. He owns property and buildings up and down the coast. You should see everything he's accomplished."

"If that monstrosity of a lodge is any indication, I'm not interested."

"The lodge brought jobs, Dad. Isn't that what you're always preaching? All these freeloaders need to get a job and do their part instead of living off the taxpayers? It's a heck of a lot easier when there's a business in town where they can work."

"I did a little research on him before I came over here," her dad said. "There's more to him than you know."

"I know him, Dad."

"Did you know he's being sued over one of his business deals?"

"So what? That happens in business," she said.

"I asked around town and the man's known for his womanizing. You think there's a future with this guy? I highly doubt it. He's never going to settle down with a girl like you."

"A girl like me?"

"An unmarried mother. We all know what you did to get in this predicament. You think he has any respect for you?"

"He doesn't care about that. Plus, he loves Dakota."

"You two aren't fit to raise a cat. We want Dakota to live with us. We can give him the stability he needs."

She gasped, then swallowed the massive lump in her throat. If she could punch something she would. Instead she tried to breathe like her years of yoga had taught her. "He's stable with us. I'm a good mother."

"You're sleeping with your boss. How is that stable?"

"We...we're together. Like a family."

"He is *not* your family. He's some loser who got a girl pregnant and now wants you to raise his baby, so he can go back to what he does best. Womanizing and dirty business deals."

Kyle appeared in the doorway. "I want you out of my house." Red-faced, he strode over to her father and shoved him against the counter. "If you come so much as five feet from Violet or Dakota, I'll make sure you regret it."

"Who do you think you are? Get your hands off me. She's my daughter. Dakota's my grandson." Her father shoved his hands into Kyle's chest, but he was no match for his young and muscular adversary.

Kyle kept hold of her father's collar and with gritted teeth spoke right in his face. "She's *my* fiancée."

Violet's mouth dropped open. *My fiancée?*

"Furthermore, Dakota's going to be my son when the adoption paperwork is completed. You will never see either one of them again if I have anything to do with it."

Her mother came running into the kitchen. Had she been standing outside the door listening the entire time? "Fiancée? Is this true, Violet?"

"You bet it's true," Kyle said. "We weren't ready to share it with anyone yet. Our best friends are getting married in three weeks and we didn't want to take the focus away from them."

Violet stared at him, amazed. How had he come up with that so quickly?

"Where's the ring?" her mother asked.

Kyle crossed over to Violet and wrapped his arms around her shoulders. "I haven't gotten her a ring yet. We've been busy with the babies."

"You've been the guy's nanny and now suddenly you're getting married to him? Do you really think your son deserves more turmoil when you two obviously mismatched people get divorced?" Her father's face had turned a shade of purple Violet had never seen before. Of all the times she'd made him angry in her life, this was the most enraged she'd ever seen him.

"Get out of my house," Kyle said again.

"You won't see me again, Violet. Know that."

"Dad, I love you. I've tried my whole life to please you, but it's impossible. I'm tired. I'm sorry I've been a disappointment, but I can't do toxic relationships and be a good mother to my children. You make me feel terrible about myself. Kyle's the first man who's treated me like I deserve to be treated. I want you to leave."

Her mother was crying silently with her hand over her mouth. Violet knew she would not argue or plead. Once her father decided something, there was no convincing him otherwise.

"I pity you," her dad said. "When this charlatan leaves you and you want to come running back to us, we won't be there for you. Not again."

"When have you ever been there for me?" Violet asked. "Not four years ago when Cole Lund seduced me and left me pregnant."

"What did you say?" Her mother's tears vanished as her eyes widened with shock.

She hadn't meant to say it.

"Cole Lund?" her mother asked. "He's Dakota's father?"

"Why would you make up such a heinous lie?" Her father's voice matched his enraged complexion.

"She's not lying," Kyle said. "That married bastard took advantage of a lonely young woman who had never been loved properly by any man in her life, most especially you. When you're adding up who's at fault here, you can look in the mirror."

"How dare you."

"Get out of my house or I'll physically remove you myself." Kyle let go of Violet's shoulders and stepped closer to the older man. "Now."

Her mother was back to weeping as her husband dragged her from the kitchen. Violet remained standing at the sink. Kyle followed them out. Seconds later, she heard the front door bang shut. She sank to the floor and hugged her knees to her chest. Instead of grief, a numb calmness settled over her. It was done. This was the last time. There would be no more hoping or wishing things were different, no more trying to please them. Her life was with Kyle now. Kyle and the children were her family. Their friends were her extended family.

Kyle strode into the kitchen and rushed to her. He knelt next to her on the floor and held her hand. "I'm sorry, Lettie."

"I'm okay." She buried her face in his neck. "It's over."

"What did you tell me last night? When one of us feels weak the other is strong?"

"How did you come up with the pretend engagement so quickly?"

"It's not pretend. I want to marry you and not for the reasons he said. Not to care for Mollie, but rather to care for me. We're the perfect combination. I'm going to give you that white picket fence and the whole yard that goes with it."

She looked up at him. His blue eyes smiled at her. "But it's so fast."

"Do you love me?"

"Yes. So much."

"Do you want to be my wife and Mollie's mom?"

"Yes."

"Good because I want to be your husband and Dakota's dad."

"Is this really happening?"

"I'll get you a ring as soon as I can. A big fat one."

"No, not a diamond. The mines are ruining the environment.

And don't even get me started on the corruption and exploitation of people."

"You've got to be kidding me. I'm getting you a diamond, so get over it."

"A vintage one, maybe? They're already made so we can't do any damage with one already made, right?"

"Yes. I'll find a vintage ring for you. God, you're a pain."

She smiled up at him. "Or a different kind of stone? Maybe blue topaz to match your eyes?"

"Well now you're just trying to distract me with flattery."

"Kiss me," she said.

His demanding mouth on hers made her forget all about diamonds or topaz or even how cold the marble floor felt against her backside.

"I love you," he whispered against her mouth. "Don't ever forget it."

CHAPTER SEVENTEEN

K<small>YLE</small>

KYLE FOUND BOTH Stone and Autumn in the living room. "How much of that did you hear?"

"Enough to know that guy's an asshole," Stone said.

During their walk, they'd talked of surface things, catching up on the past twelve years, filling one another in on Kyle's business decisions, Stone's tours, and Autumn's decision to become a pharmacist. The harder discussion had not yet come. Kyle figured it was about to start.

"Where's Violet now?" Autumn asked.

"She went upstairs to bed," he said. "This was a long day for her."

"With her dad, no kidding," Stone said.

"She's strong, but that man is awful. I don't know how she turned out so well," Autumn said.

You and me both.

"You guys want anything to drink?" Kyle asked.

"No, I'm fine," Autumn said.

Stone asked for a beer. Kyle grabbed two from the refrigerator in the kitchen. When he returned to the living room, Stone was by the fire, warming his hands.

Autumn sat on the couch, her cane next to her legs. "Is it true? Are you and Violet getting married?"

"Yeah. I need to do it right first. She needs a down on my knee proposal and I plan to give her one. But I couldn't listen to that idiot berate her like that."

"I don't blame you," Stone said. "But you guys seem crazy in love, which is cool. Very cool."

"Yeah, we are. What about you? You have a girl?" Kyle asked.

"Nah," Stone said. "I'm not the settling down type."

"How about you?" Kyle asked Autumn.

"I was with someone for a few years," Autumn said. "But it didn't work out."

"The guy was a first-class shit," Stone said.

"Stone, stop. That's unkind." Autumn shot him the disapproving sister look Kyle remembered so well. Autumn was the heart of their family. The trio: Heart, Body, Brain.

"Who gives a crap?" Stone said. "We don't have to be kind when it comes to him. In fact, I'd love to beat the crap out of him. I will if I ever run into him. Tell him what he said to you."

"He was drunk one night and said he could never marry a cripple," Autumn said. "I kicked him out the next day."

Bile rose to the back of Kyle's throat.

Could never marry a cripple. I did that to her.

"It did occur to me to ask him how it was possible to have sex with a cripple for two years since I was apparently so disgusting to him." Autumn smiled and shrugged her shoulders. "He didn't have an answer for me."

"The guy was a loser," Stone said. "He wasn't good enough for you and he knew it."

"I'm sorry you had to hear that from someone you loved," Kyle said.

Autumn looked over at him. "Stop it. Don't go there. It wasn't your fault."

"It was the Miller boys. You know that," Stone said. "They were chasing you. Autumn and I were always exactly clear on what went down. You did what you had to do to protect Autumn."

"But I didn't. I hurt her instead."

Stone sat in a chair and leaned forward with his hands on his knees. He looked directly at Kyle. "We're going to talk through all this. Now. Nothing left unsaid."

Kyle couldn't help but smile. Stone was never one to mess around. Right to the point without any worry over social conventions. "All right."

"My understanding is that you left us because you felt a ton of guilt over what happened with Autumn. Is that right?"

"In a nutshell, yes." A thousand tiny pricks of regret stung his eyes.

"I can understand that," Stone said.

"You can?" Kyle asked.

"I couldn't. Not for a long time. But some stuff went down overseas that made me realize why you did what you did."

When he didn't elaborate, Autumn explained. "Stone's best friend was killed in Afghanistan."

"Our truck got hit one day. I lived. He didn't. I torment myself. What if I'd done this differently or that differently. You know, the kind of bullshit you think about in the middle of the night?"

"Yeah, I know," Kyle said.

"I'm not going to sit here and lie to you. When you disappeared, it devastated us. We were a team and you bailed. For years I didn't want anything to do with you. Autumn kept trying to find you and I was like, why? He left us just like Mom did."

Kyle's chest was so tight he could barely breathe. He sank into a chair.

Stone continued. "But then I lost my buddy and I went a little crazy—a self-destructive kind of thing. I won't go into all that. They have me seeing the shrink. I have to say, I've learned a lot about myself. Enough to understand that you felt guilty and your response was to flee. You're either punishing yourself or running from the past because it's too painful to face—or a combination of both."

"It felt like the only thing I could do and keep breathing," Kyle said.

"Honestly, bro, I get it. I mean, you were dead wrong, but I get it. That doesn't mean I'm not still pissed at you."

"But you can forgive him, right?" Autumn asked.

"I don't really know what that means," Stone said. "All I know is that I'd like to figure out a way to let go of all the bullshit and move forward. I'm not saying I know how. But I'd like to try."

"Is it possible?" Autumn asked. "Daniel, do you even want to be part of our lives? Can you be in the same room with me without hurting?"

Kyle ran his hand through his hair before looking over at his sister. She had her hands clasped in her lap. For a second, she looked like the little girl she once was, all eyes and heart. "I didn't think you'd want to be in my life."

"You were wrong," she said.

"I'm working on forgiving myself," Kyle said. "Knowing that you don't blame me helps."

"I never blamed you," she said.

"I've hated myself for a long time," Kyle said. "Walking away from you two was a mistake. Cowardly and weak. I'm not trying to make excuses, but growing up in that town messed me up." His voice cracked. He drew in a shaky breath. "The bullying took its toll—made me cold and calculating and self-preserving. It's taken a long time to stop thinking of myself as Pig. The name change, running from you guys, it was all my attempt to wash away the bad smell."

Autumn's cheeks shone with tears. "We know."

Stone nodded. "No one knows like we do."

"I'm sorry. That's all I can say. I'm sorry I left you guys. I never stopped loving you. Ever. Not one day went by that I didn't think about you. I kept track of you both over the years and I've been so proud of your accomplishments."

"We knew you still loved us or you wouldn't have continued to send money," Autumn said.

"But we couldn't get how you could do that but not want to see us," Stone said.

"I was wrong," Kyle said.

They all sat there for a moment.

"What do we do now?" Kyle asked.

"Make up for lost time?" Stone asked.

"Can you two stick around for a while?" Kyle asked.

"I have to get back to work on Monday," Autumn said. "But we could come back for Christmas."

"And for the wedding," Stone said. "Whenever that is."

They talked for a few minutes about logistics, making plans for another visit. Stone admitted he wasn't sure where he would end up next now that he was out of the Marines. "I got my contractor license, so now I just have to bite the bullet and start my business."

"You could stay. Build my house," Kyle said.

"You serious?" Stone asked.

"I have the land and the house plans. I just need it built. As soon as possible."

"You'd trust me?"

"Who better than my own brother?"

"It's not like I have anything in Denver, other than Autumn. But to tell you the truth, I think she's sick of me. I've been living with her for six months."

"I'm not sick of you, but this would be a great opportunity for you," Autumn said.

"Move to California? I don't know." Stone ran his hand over the top of his closely cut hair. "Maybe I should grow my hair out like yours," he said to Kyle. "Go all metrosexual like my big brother."

"Metrosexual?" Kyle rolled his eyes. "No way."

"What do you call this?" He gestured toward Kyle's outfit of black designer jeans, cashmere sweater, and Italian loafers.

Kyle shook his head and laughed. "You could use a date with my personal shopper."

"Nah. Chicks dig my look."

"I don't think that's a look," Kyle said. "More like something you pulled out of the bottom of a laundry basket."

"Personal shopper? California's ruined you, man." Stone smiled and raised his beer bottle. "You did good, brother. Successful. Rich. All bulked up. I'm proud of you."

"I did it for you guys," Kyle said. "To make sure you had a chance."

"We made it out," Autumn said. "Just like we said we would."

"Turns out you guys didn't need me anyway," Kyle said.

"We didn't need your money," Stone said. "But we needed you. Still do."

"I'm here and I'm not going anywhere. Not again," Kyle said.

"There's something we wanted to ask you," Autumn said. "Something about the Miller boys."

He swallowed the bile that rose to his throat at the mention of their name. "What about them?"

"A few months after you left, they died in a house fire. It was determined the fire was caused by arson, but they never found the killer," Autumn said.

"I heard about it when it happened," Kyle said. "I always figured Karma's a bitch."

"We wondered if you had anything to do with it," Autumn said.

Kyle laughed, a bitter cackle that sounded like a branch breaking in a dark forest. "As much as I wished them dead, I wouldn't have risked getting caught. My focus was on providing for you two long term, not revenge."

"I told you," Stone said.

"You thought I did it?" Kyle asked. "Autumn, I'm not a killer."

"You were so angry," Autumn said. "I thought you might have gone temporarily insane due to rage."

Kyle shook his head. "No. Wasn't me."

"Who else would've wanted them dead?" Autumn asked. "Besides us?"

"There was a long list of people who hated them," Stone said. "Maybe it was one of them."

"The local police didn't look too hard for the killer," Autumn said. "After what happened to me, I don't think there was anyone in town who didn't think they deserved it."

"But still, I wonder," Stone said. "I guess we'll never know."

"Maybe Dad did it," Kyle said.

"I don't think he had it in him." Autumn tightened her sweater around her chest. "He was a docile drunk."

"True," Stone said.

"Did he suffer at the end?" Kyle asked.

"Nah. Died in his sleep," Stone said. "Kind of like he lived."

"I guess he did the best he could," Kyle said.

"Most people do," Autumn said.

"The problem is," Stone said, "some people's best sucks."

CHAPTER EIGHTEEN

VIOLET

Violet spent the week before Christmas helping Kara with last-minute details for Honor and Zane's wedding. Because Honor was busy with Brody's affairs, helping him negotiate changes in endorsements and contracts since the announcement of his retirement, Kara and Violet agreed to take over the last-minute details. Brody had insisted on paying for the wedding. Kara had spared no expense, even ordering a heated tent for the outdoor reception. With fewer than twenty guests, it was an extravagant event, but Kara insisted that Honor have the best.

Now, Violet sat with Kara in the Mullens' kitchen. The wedding was five short days away. They'd finalized everything with the wedding planner and were now having a cup of coffee before Violet left for Christmas shopping with Kyle in the city.

"We're staying overnight," Violet told Kara. "He won't tell me where we're going, only to pack a nice dress."

"Flora called this morning to tell me how excited she was to have the kids again," Kara said. "She has a new purpose now that Zane and Kyle have kids."

"It's nice to have someone we can trust."

"Do you think Kyle's going to propose while you're away?" Kara asked.

"It did cross my mind."

"You'll say yes, right?"

"Oh, gosh, yes. I'm so in love with him it's ridiculous."

"Isn't it amazing when you find the right person?" Kara asked.

"It is. You and Brody are happy, right?"

"Very much so. We've had to go deep the past few weeks. Ending his career has knocked him for a serious loop. Football was his life."

"Giving up my store felt like I was dying, so I can only imagine."

"But he's getting used to the idea. He's starting to see the positives now. In a weird way, it's brought us closer. Besides losing his dad, he's lived a charmed life. I had to give up everything I knew and come out here. He's tried to understand but up until recently he couldn't empathize."

"Is he still talking about having a baby?"

"Yes." Kara gazed out the window. Drops of rain water slid down the glass, like they were chasing one another. "I was close with my mom. When she died I lost all sense of what it's like to have a family. I missed her so much it hurt. I still do. To have a child terrifies me."

"You mean because you could lose them?" Violet flashed upon her conversation with Mary about the loss of her baby. Kara was right to be terrified.

"Yes."

"That's true of all love, though, isn't it?"

"I suppose it is." Kara drew an imaginary circle on the table. "Sometimes I dream my friend Jessica is still alive. We're doing the most ordinary things like cooking pasta together and laughing. It feels so real and then I wake up and remember she's gone."

Violet squeezed her hand and said how sorry she was, even though she knew how inadequate it was.

"Thanks for being my friend," Kara said.

"Back at you."

Kyle came into the kitchen with Brody right behind him. Both wore mischievous expressions, like two boys up to no good.

"You ready to go, Lettie?" Kyle asked. "I want to get to the bike shop before noon."

"Dakota asked for a big boy bike from Santa," Violet said. "We're picking it up today."

"Scoot along then," Kara said. "Brody's going to keep me company this afternoon while the decorator comes. By the time you guys get back, it will be a winter wonderland fit for Queen Honor's wedding."

* * *

"Thank God he didn't ask for a puppy," Violet said.

Kyle laughed as he put the bicycle in the back of car. "I need a bigger car."

They were parked in a lot near a busy section of shops, including the bicycle shop where they'd just purchased Dakota's gift. Shoppers scurried past them carrying packages and bags. The sound of a Salvation Army bell rang out into the cold evening. White lights decorated the trees and lampposts. "I love the holidays," she said.

"I do now that I have you and the kids." Kyle took her hand and they crossed the street to the toy store Kyle had spotted earlier. They stood in front of the display window where a Christmas train circled a three-foot tree.

"I want that," Kyle said.

"The train?"

"I always wanted a train when I was a kid," he said.

"I remember." She'd remembered it all right. The train set she'd ordered from an online store had already arrived at the house.

"I'm getting this." The lights hung in the window reflected in his eyes as he looked down at her. "We'll put it around the tree like in the movies."

"But you don't want that one, do you? I mean, you'd only be able to use it once a year."

"For the entire time the Christmas tree is up," he said. "Like a month."

She almost laughed. "We have yet to put up a tree this year and Christmas is in a week."

"We're late this time, but next year Dakota and I will put it up with this train the day after Thanksgiving."

She brought her gloved fingers to her mouth. Next year. Would there really be a next year?

"Why did you sigh?" he asked.

"Did I? I was thinking about next year. What it will be like."

"I hope we'll be moved into the new house by then."

Something cold hit her on the forehead. "What's that?" She looked up toward the sky. Hail fell in hard pebbles that smacked the sidewalk.

"Where did it come from?" Violet tugged her knit hat over her ears.

Kyle pulled a small box from inside his coat. He dropped to one knee. "I was going to do this later, but when the sky opens and dumps hail, it's a sign." Pieces of hail caught in his dark hair looked like white sprinkles on a chocolate cupcake. "Lettie, you came into my life just like this hail, without warning and changed everything. You're the finest person I've ever known. That you love a dope like me is a miracle. I love you. I adore you. I want to make sure you're always by my side now and forever. Will you marry me?" He opened the box and presented the ring to her. Tiny diamonds encircled a center diamond the size of her knuckle. A scroll motif gallery and diamond-set shoulders made it sparkle from every angle. "I swear the ring is vintage. Edwardian period, according to the jeweler. He purchased it from an estate sale. Brody found it for us. The guy knows all kinds of rich people."

"It must've been a large estate. I know a little about antiques and this must've cost you a small fortune."

"Can we stay focused on the question?" He gazed up at her, still on one knee. The hail stopped as suddenly as it started. He brushed his hair back with his fingers. A small crowd had gathered around them, all waiting for her answer.

She flushed and took off her gloves. "I'm sorry. What I mean to say is yes. Yes, yes, yes!" She threw her head back and laughed as she held her hand out to him. He slipped the ring onto her finger. It was the perfect fit. "How did you know my size?"

"Honor told me. She knows everything." Kyle rose to his feet and lifted her in his arms. "You've made me the happiest man in the world." He spun her in a circle. The sidewalk was slick. Down they went, falling in a heap together, Violet on top. The crowd went silent, waiting to see if Kyle had hurt himself. He lifted an arm. "Nothing to see here." The crowd clapped. Violet laughed with her head buried in the scarf around his neck.

"Way to make a scene," she said.

"Can we buy the Christmas train now?"

She looked down at his chiseled, gorgeous face. *My husband. My love.* He peered up at her with those eyes the color of the twilight sky and she saw the little boy who wanted a train and never got one. She would give him a thousand trains if she could. "We can get the train."

"The big one with extra track?"

She kissed him. "The biggest and best they have."

* * *

The next day, they sat Dakota down to tell him the news. She showed him her ring. "While we were away, Kyle asked me to marry him. I said yes."

Dakota stared at Kyle but didn't say anything.

"What do you think, little man?" Kyle asked. "Can I marry your mom?"

"I think it's a very good idea." Dakota scooted from his chair and crossed over to them. He kissed Violet's cheek before crawling onto Kyle's lap snuggling into his chest. "This means we stay together forever, right?"

"That's right," Kyle said. "Forever and ever."

"Until you grow up," Violet said. "Which is a long, long time from now."

"I don't want to grow up," Dakota said.

"That makes two of us." Violet sighed and nestled closer to Kyle and Dakota. How was it possible that she could be this content?

"Can we have bacon at the wedding?" Dakota asked.

Kyle laughed. "What's a wedding without bacon?"

* * *

In one of the guest rooms at Brody and Kara's, Violet fastened the veil onto Honor's intricate updo. When it was secured, she stood back to admire the bride. The beaded bodice sparkled under the lights but not as brightly as Honor's eyes.

"You're breathtaking," Violet said.

"Do you think?" Honor asked. "Because suddenly I feel like I'm going to be sick."

"You're just nervous."

"Thank God we didn't do anything too elaborate. You look beautiful too, by the way," Honor said. "Kyle's going to want to eat you instead of the wedding cake."

Violet looked at herself in the full-length mirror. The dress was the color of cranberries and cut low in the back. The halter top displayed her shapely shoulders. She'd had the hair and makeup girl give her bouncy, soft curls and a smoky eye. "I do look pretty good."

Honor laughed. "That's my girl."

Kara, Maggie and Sophie came into the room, carrying glasses of champagne. Maggie wore a long royal blue velvet dress that draped elegantly over her dancer body and contrasted beautifully with her fair skin. Her wavy hair had been coaxed straight and shone like a new copper penny. Kara had on a dark green taffeta with a short A-line skirt that showed off her muscular legs. Sophie, in contrast, was dressed in a simple pink sheath with spaghetti straps and a sweetheart neckline. She'd had the stylist pile her blond hair into a complicated updo. She reminded Violet of a young Grace Kelly.

"You ready to do this?" Kara asked.

All day long Kara had bustled around making sure every detail was taken care of while the other girls had their hair and makeup done. They'd finally had to force her to sit in the chair for makeup and hair. She'd opted to have her hair swept up into a slick bun, so she could show off the new diamond earrings her newly retired husband had gotten her for a birthday present.

"Is it time?" Honor asked, accepting the glass of champagne.

"Five minutes. Long enough for a toast," Kara said.

"I saw Jackson pouring shots for all the guys," Sophie said. "Zane's looking a little pale under his tan."

"He hates people looking at him," Honor said.

"It'll be over in a flash," Kara said.

"And then you'll wish you could do it all over again," Maggie said.

A knock on the door drew their attention. It was Flora and Janet. "You guys have room for two old ladies?" Janet asked.

Honor smiled and waved them inside. "Yes, yes, come in."

Flora's dark eyes flashed with approval. "My oh my, don't you look nice."

Janet nodded. "Like a doll."

"We won't keep you long," Flora said. "But we wanted to come say hello and give you a gift. Over the years, we've come to feel motherly toward you."

"You're part of our family," Janet said. "As are you girls." She nodded at Violet and the others.

"We weren't sure you had something old," Janet said. "I

thought you might like to carry this hanky. It was my mother's and I held it when I married Brody's dad. It can be your something old."

"How sweet," Honor said. "I would love to."

Janet brought a lace handkerchief from her pocketbook as well as a small box. "We also got you something. This is from Flora and Dax and Jon and me. We're sort of your parents de facto, whether you want us or not."

Honor took the box from Janet's outstretched hand and gasped as she lifted the lid. "Oh wow." She lifted a sparkly tennis bracelet from the box. "It's too much."

Flora shook her head. "No, we wanted you to have something special that would last a life time. Every time you look at it, please remember how loved you are by two women who would've been proud to be your mama."

Honor waved her hand in front of her eyes. "I cannot cry and ruin my makeup."

Janet fastened the bracelet around Honor's wrist.

"I couldn't love it or you two more. Thank you," Honor said. "It's not my mom I'm grieving today. I wish Hugh was here."

"Speaking of Hugh. We have something for you too." Violet grabbed the box from her bag. "This is from all of the girls."

"The Wags," Kara said.

"And me," Sophie said.

"You're a Wag," Maggie said. "A little sister Wag."

Sophie and Maggie linked arms as Honor opened the box.

The locket was adorned with gemstones the same color as Hugh and Zane's eyes. Violet had had it specially made from one of her former vendors. Photos of both Zane and Hugh were glued inside.

Honor lifted the necklace from the box. The gemstones caught the light and made a pattern on the ceiling. "Oh, ladies, it's so pretty."

"Open it so you can see the inside," Violet said.

"Violet thought of it," Maggie said. "She had it made just for you."

"This way Hugh is walking down the aisle with you," Violet said.

"And it's your something blue," Maggie said.

"For once, I don't know what to say," Honor said. They all embraced in a group hug, like a huddle before a football game.

"It's time to say *I do*," Kara said.

"Let's do this," Honor said. "Then we can party."

* * *

Kara and Brody's house had been transformed into a holiday wonderland. Lights were strung throughout the living room, everything in cranberry and silver, including the decorations on the thirty-foot Christmas tree. Silver snowflakes hung from the ceilings. Strings of berries and candles in glass containers wound around the mantel and shelving.

The ceremony was to take place in front of the large gas fireplace. Honor had decided against chairs. Instead they would form a semicircle around the couple as they exchanged vows. Regardless, Kara had insisted that Honor must have a grand entrance on Brody's arm. She would enter from the foyer and have her walk down an aisle defined by white rose petals.

Violet waited with Dakota, Jubie and Jackson in the foyer. Dakota held tightly to the pillow with the rings carefully tucked under a ribbon. Violet fanned her eyes to keep from crying. Jubie, eyes like saucers, gripped her flower basket with both hands. Jackson adjusted his tie. Behind them, Honor fidgeted beside Brody.

"Is it time yet?" Honor asked.

"Almost," Jackson said.

"Stop wriggling," Violet said to Honor. "We don't want your veil to fall off."

"What if I trip?" Honor asked.

"Don't worry. I'll hold you upright the whole way," Brody said.

"You're not that much bigger than a football."

From inside the living room, Maggie played the first notes of the Beatles' "Long and Winding Road". They'd had a piano brought in for the occasion. Violet didn't even want to know how much that cost.

"It's your cue," Violet said to Dakota.

"I remember, Mama." Dakota stepped into the room holding the pillow out in front of him. Kyle coached him from the front of the room, but he did fine, standing straight and walking slowly as he made his way toward Zane. When he arrived, he flashed his mother a jubilant grin, then moved close to Zane. Jubie's tiara sparkled under the lights as she tossed rose petals left and right. Violet took Jackson's arm and they entered the room. With her skirt swirling around her legs, it was like she floated down the aisle on Jackson's arm. Kyle smiled at her and blew her a kiss. Dressed in a dark blue suit and a cranberry hued tie that matched her dress, he took her breath away. Her man.

When they arrived in front of the fireplace, Jackson took his place next to Zane. As they embraced, Violet heard Jackson say, "Be in one another's pictures."

Zane smiled. "Yes."

Violet stood next to Jubie, who gazed up at her with a look of relief. She squeezed the little girl's shoulder.

Maggie paused in her playing and turned toward the entry to the living room.

It was time for the bride. Honor appeared just outside the double doors that led into the living room. She held a cascading bouquet of red and white roses that shook slightly in her hands.

A spot of sun broke through the clouds and shone down on her golden hair from the skylight above her head. Next to her, Brody looked even larger than usual, regal like a lion in his gray suit. He offered his arm and she took it.

Maggie played the first refrain of "Glasgow Love Theme" from the movie *Love Actually*. Just then, Honor's veil fluttered as if someone had opened a door. She removed her hand from Brody's arm and reached up to the locket that hung around her neck and brought it to her lips. *Hugh made it after all.*

Brody whispered to her and she nodded, then slipped her arm into his once more. They entered the long room and walked slowly toward them.

Violet stole a glance at Zane. His gaze never moved from his bride as his face contorted into a thousand shapes and tears streamed from his eyes. The notes from the piano continued as Honor made her way to him. When Honor arrived, she handed her bouquet of roses to Violet and turned to face Zane. The guests, as instructed, formed a semicircle around the couple. The music ended. Maggie came to stand next to Sophie. The sisters clasped hands.

Jackson handed Zane a tissue. He wiped his eyes and smiled down at Honor.

Doc glanced quickly down at his notes before beginning. "Friends, we're gathered here today to celebrate the union of Zane Shaw and Honor Sullivan. They've asked me to keep this simple. Apparently, the groom wants to get this over with as soon as possible."

Everyone laughed.

"Zane, your father told me more than once that you two belonged together. He wanted more than anything for you two to figure that out and make it official." Doc's voice shook with emotion. "How he wished for this day. I can't help but think he's here with us in spirit if not body."

Both the bride and groom nodded and dabbed their eyes.

"Now, without further ado, it's time for the couple to exchange vows."

Honor and Zane took each other's hands. Zane began. "I'm not much of a word guy but even if I was, there aren't any to describe the enormity of my admiration or love for you. You're the greatest thing that will ever happen to me. I promise to let you be yourself. I'll support your dreams and never make you compromise your ambition to satisfy my ego. I'll fight for us, for you, and for our family from this day forward, until death parts us. At which point, I'll wait for you to arrive in heaven, so we can start right back up."

Honor smiled up at Zane. She opened her mouth, then closed it again. For a moment, Violet thought she might not be able to talk, but she took a deep breath and started.

"Zane Shaw, the first person who loved me unconditionally was your father. If it were not for him, I would not be standing here today surrounded by all these people who love me. The first time I spotted you sweeping the floor at the bar, I felt something change in my heart. I had no hope of you ever loving me, or frankly, noticing me. But you did. And you do. I mean, seriously? You and me? I'm the luckiest girl ever. Who else on this earth would ever put up with me?"

From the circle, Kyle winked at Violet. Sophie openly wept as Maggie wrapped her arm around her sister's waist.

Zane wiped his cheeks. "It's my privilege to put up with you."

Honor continued, her voice husky. "I promise to be your best friend, to remind you how totally great you are, and to make sure you feel loved and supported every single day. I promise not to poison you with my cooking by ordering a lot of takeout from The Oar. I promise to try with all my might to bring Hugh's legacy of kindness and decency and integrity into our relationship and our family. I love you with all my bruised and damaged heart."

Doc spoke next. "Jubie, Zane and Honor would like you to come forward now and take their hands."

Jubie gave her basket to Violet and stepped forward. They all clasped hands, making a triangle.

Zane cleared his throat and glanced at Honor before turning back to the little girl. "Jubie, you're the most special gift anyone could ever ask for. Even though it's not official through the courts, it's official in our hearts. I promise to be the best father I can be. I'll be your biggest fan and love you with all my heart. I'll be there for it all. School plays and soccer games and tea parties or anything else you choose to do."

"Probably not soccer," Jubie said.

"Whatever it is, I'll be there." Zane said.

Honor's voice trembled. "Jubie, you know I lost my mother when I was young. Ever since then I've wanted a family of my own. Never in my wildest dreams could I have imagined having a wonderful girl like you to love. I'll never try to replace your mom. She will always be in your heart." Honor tapped her chest. "Just like Zane's dad is in mine. Someday you'll see her in heaven and you'll both be so happy to see each other again. But I promise to be your mom here on earth. I'll love you and look after you and make you eat your vegetables, even if I don't cook them."

Jubie grinned and threw her arms around Honor's waist, then did the same to Zane. "I promise to make you eat your vegetables too," Jubie said.

Laughter and a few sniffles echoed in the room.

Doc smiled down at Jubie. "Now you can go back to stand by Dakota."

"Okay, Doc."

Dakota beamed as Jubie took him by the hand.

"Zane Shaw, do you take Honor Sullivan to be your wife from day this forward?"

"I do."

"Honor Sullivan, do you take Zane Shaw to be your lawfully wedded husband from this day forward?"

"I do."

"With the authority vested in me by the great state of California, I pronounce you husband and wife."

* * *

The reception was held in a heated tent in the backyard. One long table was covered with a silver tablecloth etched with swirls. Shiny round canisters held votive candles. White roses and hydrangeas were displayed in tall glass vases. White lights hung from the rafters dangled over the table like tiny fairies.

Zane and Honor sat together on one end of the table with Jubie at the corner by Honor. Violet and Kyle sat together with Dakota. Mollie was asleep in her car seat at their feet.

After dining on salmon, baby potatoes, and grilled vegetables, the time for toasts arrived. Violet stood and swallowed nervously. Kyle squeezed her hand. "You got this. Just speak from the heart."

She clinked her knife against a glass to get everyone's attention. When everyone quieted, she began. "Hey. I guess it's my turn. Speeches aren't really my thing, but here goes. I don't know if I ever told you this, Honor, but when I moved back to town, you were the first real friend I'd had in a long time. Maybe ever. You didn't judge my baby bump or my lack of a husband. You were simply nice to me just because that's who you are. You're hilarious and clever and more fun to be around than anyone in the world. But when I first met you there was a sadness under the surface that I could relate to. That sadness disappeared when you and Zane fell in love. I know women aren't supposed to need a man these days. You certainly don't need anyone to take care of you. That said, the way Zane protects you and loves you—and the way you protect and love him—is more than I could ever wish for my best friend. And to Jubie, welcome to our extended family. We all love you and pledge to be your village from this day forward. Congratulations." She smiled and gratefully sank into her chair.

"You did great, honey," Kyle whispered in her ear.

Jackson stood next. "I've been practicing this speech for weeks. You know, always the over achiever. But as I stand here now, I can't remember one word of it. All I know is this. There were magical forces that brought you two together. Honor, a girl who had to fight to survive every day of her childhood, walks into Hugh Shaw's bar looking for a job. Instead, she finds the father she never had, and the man she'll eventually fall in love with." He wiped his eyes. "Sometimes great things happen to great people." He looked directly at Zane. "We've been friends...brothers...since before we could talk. You're one of the great ones. Always have been and always will be. I wanted this for you—to have a love like I have with my Maggie. That it's Honor seems so obvious now, but as all the women in this room know, the Dogs aren't always the brightest at recognizing the right woman when she appears. Except for me, of course." He exchanged a smile with Maggie. "Hugh told us when we graduated from high school to be in one another's photos. We're doing a good job of it." He raised his glass. "Here's to the Dogs and the women who love us. To our growing families. To our loving parents, whether here or in heaven. To this beautiful couple and their precious Jubie. May you always be as happy as you are on this day."

Everyone cheered and toasted.

Violet leaned against Kyle, exhausted. She'd been feeling off for the past few hours. The shrimp cocktail hadn't appealed to her, which was weird. Normally, she loved all seafood. Even the champagne tasted funny. Her breasts were tender. She'd felt more emotional than usual too. Her stomach flipped over, remembering the night she'd forgotten to take her pill. *No, please no. I can't be pregnant. Not now.*

My God, Mollie was only a couple months old. That would mean she and a new baby would be like eleven months apart. Irish twins. Dakota, thank God, would be almost five by then. But three children under five? Would that be the tipping point into insanity?

No, no. This couldn't be happening. She'd been on the pill for years to combat terrible menstrual cycles. How could she be pregnant? That night in San Francisco when she'd been so shaken up, she'd forgotten to take one. She'd taken it the next night when she remembered, but it must have thrown everything off.

Another baby? What would Kyle think? Would this scare him away, make him reevaluate her? She was a woman without a degree or any skills, basically a freeloader. Her father's words floated around in her head. *Loser. Failure. In love with failure. Whore.*

"Lettie, are you listening to me?" Kyle asked.

She apologized. "What did you say?"

"I asked if you wanted to dance."

Stifling a yawn, she nodded and pretended to be unworried. "I'd love to."

* * *

On Christmas Eve, Violet sat on the toilet with a pregnancy wand in her hand, waiting to learn her fate. The seconds moved like molasses. Finally, two minutes passed. She took in a deep breath and looked at the wand. Two pink lines. A silent scream echoed through her brain.

A knock on the bathroom door made her jump.

"Lettie, are you in there?"

"Yes." Her voice gave her away. He would know she was crying.

"What is it? Let me in."

She stood, still holding the wand in her hand, and unlocked and opened the door.

"Honey, what's wrong?"

She waved the wand in the air, unable to speak through the sobs.

He stared at it with a blank expression before his eyes widened. "Is that what I think it is?"

She nodded, crying harder.

"Are you? I mean, was it positive?"

She nodded again.

"For real?" Was that delight in his eyes? "Oh my God, Lettie, I can't believe our luck."

"Luck? What're you talking about? It's terrible. Awful timing. We're already so busy with the other two. And I wanted to wear a wedding dress."

He pulled her into his arms and kissed her forehead and each cheek. "We'll get married right away. Before you're showing. Next week if you want."

"I wanted a real wedding," she said. "Not one with a big fat stomach."

He laughed and lifted her chin to look at him. "Lettie, you're missing the big picture here. We're having another baby. Do you know what a gift this is? Heck, let's have a half dozen of them."

"You're crazy."

"Crazy in love with you." He kissed her on the mouth and lifted her onto the counter, and wrapped her legs around him. "Do you know how happy you make me? Giving me another baby— I'm thrilled."

She rested her cheek on his chest. "I'm embarrassed this happened again."

"Your dad's out of your life. You don't need to ever feel like that again."

"But what am I supposed to do with my life? Just be a mom? Is that enough for you?"

"There's no harder or greater job in the world. Later, when they're grown, you can do something else. Or whenever you want for that matter. There's no shame in wanting to be a full-time mom. I know it's not what your friends are doing, but that's okay. God gave you such a gift with children. You're a great mom, Lettie. I'm so proud of you."

More tears, but they were happy this time. "Thank you. Thank you for letting me be myself."

"Oh, baby, thank *you*. Tomorrow, we'll tell everyone. The Wags will help you plan a shotgun wedding."

She punched him. "Shotgun wedding? Oh my God."

"You're going to look so hot pregnant."

"You have a one-track mind."

He grinned. "I was going to wait until Christmas morning to give you one of your presents, but now seems like as good a time as any."

Kyle took her hand and they walked downstairs. Dakota was by the tree shaking one of his presents. Mollie was under her mobile gurgling and kicking her legs.

"I thought I told you to leave the presents alone," Violet said.

"Sorry, Mama."

"Dakota, I've decided to give your mom her big present now." He pointed to a small package under the tree and asked Dakota to give it to her.

"I know what it is, Mama." Dakota handed her the slim package.

"You do?"

Kyle put his finger to his lips. Dakota mimicked the gesture.

Violet peeled back the paper. It was a car key.

Dakota jumped up and down like a kid on a pogo stick. "It's outside, Mama."

"You got me a car?" she asked.

"It's not a car." He picked Mollie up and gestured toward the door. "Come see."

They stepped outside into the cold, damp air. A black Honda minivan was parked next to a silver Lexus SUV. "Where are our cars?"

"I traded my car in for that one." He pointed to the SUV. "It's big enough for all of us, but still nice enough to take clients around in. You, however, get this baby." Kyle took the key from her and pressed a button. The side door of the minivan slid open. "It even has a vacuum built inside."

"I know." Violet clapped her hands. "I saw it on television. You can suck crackers up as soon as they drop."

"You save that job for me," Kyle said. "I don't want you vacuuming in your condition."

"Very funny."

Dakota ran to the van. He jumped inside and crawled into the car seat Kyle had already installed. "See, Mama? I can get in and buckle myself."

Violet leaned inside to get a better look. The black interior smelled of new leather. She'd never had a car with leather seats. "It's enormous."

"We can put a half dozen kids in here. So, we're ready." Kyle laughed as she pretended to recoil in horror.

"It only seats seven, so we can't, in fact, have six children," she said.

"Five?"

"Three. We're already outnumbered."

"Maybe four?"

"You really have lost it." She smiled up at him as he wrapped his arm around her shoulder. "It's going to be fine. We'll get help if we need it. Remember what you said to me that first night with Mollie? Something about following my instincts."

"I was trying to calm you down."

"It worked," he said. "We'll be fine. I promise."

Just then, lights shone through the fog. "They're here." Dakota yelled from inside the van before toppling out to wait.

Stone and Autumn got out of the car. After hugs and holiday greetings, they all helped bring their bags and packages inside.

Once they were all settled around the fireplace, Violet brought out a cheese platter while Kyle opened wine. Autumn sat in the chair closest to the tree. Pink-cheeked from the cold and dressed in a white sweater dress that contrasted nicely with her auburn hair, she looked like an angel. *She's so beautiful.* Although she confessed to Violet that she was self-conscious about her scar, it was barely noticeable, especially given Autumn's flawless makeup.

Stone unloaded packages from several shopping bags and deposited them under the tree. He seemed enormous even next to the ten-foot tree. Today he wore a sweater and nice jeans over his bulky frame. No matter what he wore, he always had the look of a marine.

Violet joined Kyle on the loveseat and tried not to yawn.

"Are those for me?" Dakota asked.

"A few are for you and a few for Mollie," Autumn said. "And one for your mom and dad too."

"You mean Kale?" Dakota sat next to Mollie on the wide chair. "Kale's not my dad." He stared up at her with his big blue eyes.

Next to her, Kyle shifted slightly. "What if I could be? What if I was?"

"We have something exciting to share with you all," Violet said.

"Kale and my mom are getting married," Dakota shouted.

"End of January," Kyle said. "And we want you guys to come."

Autumn clapped her hands together. "How wonderful."

Stone, still standing by the tree, raised his glass. "Awesome news."

Violet caught Autumn wiping the corners of her eyes.

"Wait a minute," Stone said to Dakota. "Does this mean I'm your uncle?"

"Does it?" Dakota asked.

"Sure it does. Uncle Stone," Kyle said. "Has a good ring to it."

"We have some news too," Autumn said. "Given your announcement, I'm even happier we decided to do it." She looked over at Stone. "You want to tell them or shall I?"

"You go ahead," Stone said.

"I met with Nora at her office when I was here at Thanksgiving. She called a few weeks ago with an opportunity for a pharmacist position at the local drug store. I interviewed and got the job. I'm moving here at the end of January," Autumn said.

"And I'm taking you up on your offer, big brother, and letting you help me get my general contractor business started by taking the lead on your house."

Violet looked over to gauge Kyle's reaction.

"You're kidding me," Kyle said. "That's great news."

"You can stay with us," Violet said.

"I may need to short term. But thanks to Nora, I found a house already," Autumn said.

"You did?" Violet asked. "That's nearly impossible here."

"Nora told me that as well, but she had a lead on a little cottage on the left slope of town. A friend of hers recently passed away and her kids wanted to sell. It didn't even go on the market, so I got a great price. Her children didn't want to mess with it because the interior is awful—hasn't been touched for sixty years. I'll need to gut the whole thing and start fresh. She already hooked me up with a local designer. Trey Mattson, I think is his name. I'm meeting with him after the holidays."

"Trey is great. He did Maggie and Jackson's interiors," Violet said.

Autumn smiled. "That Nora knows everything. Jobs, homes,

eligible bachelors."

"Local lore says she has magical powers," Violet said. "Match-making powers."

"Maybe she'll find a boyfriend for me next," Autumn said.

An image of tall, dark, and handsome Trey Mattson played before Violet's eyes. He should be careful. Nora might put some magic love potion in his coffee.

"What about you?" Kyle asked Stone. "What's your plan?"

"Find a sugar mama?" Stone asked.

"You probably could in this town," Kyle said, laughing. "There are some widows with some serious money."

"I'm just kidding," Stone said. "I have a truck and a camper. That's all I need for now. I'll get your house built and then figure out what to do next."

"It's a big piece of property," Kyle said. "Room for another house."

"We'll see, big brother," Stone said. "I'm not really the settling down type. My camper suits me just fine."

"Pack-and play-life, huh?" Kyle asked.

Stone looked confused, so Violet explained their inside joke.

"Pack-and-play sounds good," Stone said. "I'm not ready to settle down anytime soon. Maybe get rid of some demons first."

"Nothing chases them away faster than the love of a good woman," Kyle said.

Violet looked up at him, teasing. "That sounds like a lyric to one of your country songs."

"You hear that, little man?" Kyle asked. "Everything you ever need to know can be learned in a country song."

* * *

Autumn and Violet worked together in the kitchen putting together the final dishes for dinner. More precisely, Autumn gave her specific directions and she followed them.

"I always wanted a sister," Autumn said.

"Me too." Violet mashed butter and cream into the potatoes. "Are you sure we should have left the skins on these?"

"Yeah, my brothers love them that way." Autumn sat on a stool at the counter, her cane propped on the wall for now. She whipped homemade salad dressing together in a bowl, hands flying as she added spices she'd found in the cupboards, mustard, balsamic vinegar, and olive oil.

"I'm not much of a cook," Violet said. "It's a joke in our friend group. Out of four of us, Kara's the only one who can cook. My mother made everything from a box, so I never learned."

"When you're poor it's always a quest to make something good from nothing. Stone soup, so to speak. Not our Stone, but a real one." Autumn giggled. "That wine's gone to my head. Speaking of which, I noticed you were having mineral water. Anything you want to fess up to?"

Violet laughed. "Very observant."

"Am I right? Is this family about to grow by one more?"

"God, I hope it's only one. Can you imagine if it's twins?"

Autumn grinned. "I haven't heard of any from our side, so I think you're safe."

"I'm still in shock. We just took the test this afternoon. I started crying immediately. Kyle's excited, which is so weird. Given the man he was when I first met him, I can't believe he so easily gave up his pack-and-play life."

"Maybe there's hope for Stone after all."

"It just takes the right person," Violet said.

"I hope so."

"What kind of man are you looking for? Not to act like Nora or anything."

Autumn screwed the top back onto the Dijon mustard. "One who doesn't mind a woman with a scar and a cane."

"Everyone's damaged. The only difference is yours is visible. The secret to love is finding someone who's baggage matches up with yours."

"So, I need a man with a scar and a cane?" Autumn waved the

whip at her. "He'd better not be eighty."

"I have a feeling it'll be the internal scar, not visible to the naked eye. Like me. Or Kyle. It just takes some peeling to figure out what it is."

"We'll see. I'm not sure there's anyone out there for me. I don't seem to have good luck with men."

"That's what I always thought and then, bam, there he was. Did I ever tell you we hated each other?"

"Really? How come?"

"It started with me picketing in the parking lot of his resort."

* * *

Christmas morning, Violet woke to Dakota jumping onto the bed and shouting something about Santa and reindeer. She opened one eye. "What time is it?"

"Don't know," Dakota said. "But Santa came."

"How do you know?"

"Because I heard him last night on the roof."

"You did?"

Dakota nodded. "Do you think he brought me a horse?"

"A horse? I thought you wanted a bike?"

"I do. But a horse would be good too."

Kyle stirred and opened his eyes. "Please tell me it's after five." She picked up his phone to look. "Just after six."

"Kale, it's Christmas. You've got to get up. Santa came."

"He heard him on the roof," Violet said.

"I totally did too," Kyle said. "They were really loud."

"So loud." Dakota nodded solemnly. From the baby monitor, Mollie's cries let them know she was awake too. Violet dragged her weary body out of bed. Could her breasts hurt more than they did right now? She didn't remember this with Dakota. She asked Kyle to get the baby up and changed. "I'll make the coffee. And you, little man, need to stay here with Kyle until I call you down."

"Hurry, Mama."

Violet slid her feet into slippers and covered up in her furry robe and headed downstairs. They'd stored the new bicycle in the garage in case Dakota had decided to investigate during the night. She wheeled it across the floor and placed it in front of the tree. The bike looked good with its red bow. Tree lights were already on, thanks to Kyle's timer. The man really did think of everything. Stockings were stuffed, including the ones they'd hung for Stone and Autumn. She turned the Christmas train on and left for the kitchen.

While she was in the kitchen making coffee, Stone appeared. A pillow crease dented his cheek and his hair stuck up in four directions. His pajamas were an old pair of sweats and a ratty t-shirt. But he had that same goofy, sweet grin even at the crack of dawn.

"Good morning. Did you sleep well?" he asked.

"Like a log."

"Pregnancy will do that to you," he said.

She flushed. "How did you know?"

"Kyle told me. He's so excited it's almost cute."

Autumn appeared next, looking like she'd just rolled off a movie set. Her hair was brushed and shiny. She even had makeup on. *She always covers her scar. Even at the crack of dawn.*

"I'll put in the breakfast casserole," Autumn said.

When had she made a breakfast casserole? "We have a breakfast casserole?" Violet asked.

"I made it after you all went to bed," she said. "Old habit from when we were kids."

Violet spontaneously threw her arms around her new sister. "I couldn't love you more than I do right now."

"We'll make new traditions too," Autumn said.

"As long as you're making casseroles, I'm all good," Violet said.

She called up to the boys that it was time to come down. Dakota bounded down the stairs. Kyle followed closely behind holding Mollie in one arm and taking video from his phone with the other.

Dakota screamed when he saw the bicycle. "I knew it. I knew it." He ran to it but stopped before he touched it. He stood and stared, almost like he was scared to touch the shiny paint.

"It's all yours, buddy," Kyle said.

"I don't know how to ride it."

"I'll teach you after we open presents."

"Is it hard?" Her little boy scrunched up his forehead and clasped his hands together.

Obviously, Dakota hadn't thought that through when he asked Santa for a bike.

"Not for someone as strong and brave as you." Kyle kept the phone focused on Dakota, still recording. "For you it'll be a piece of cake."

This way he had of complimenting and building up Dakota's ego was so foreign to her, given her own father. It touched her in a way she would never be able to express. Fighting tears, she reached out and took Mollie into her arms. She was rewarded with a slobbery grin. *Oh, my Mollie girl, how I love you.*

"Plus, I'll be right beside you until you're ready to go solo," Kyle said to Dakota.

With that, Dakota ripped the bow from his new bike and ran his fingers over the shiny metal.

"Would you like to open some wrapped presents?" Violet asked.

"Sure, Mama."

Stone had plopped into a chair, his long legs spread out in front of him, holding a steaming mug of coffee. "Man, what we would've given for a present like that. Did Kyle ever tell you, Violet? He asked for a train every single year from Santa. Never came."

From the couch, Autumn gave her brother a stern look. "Dakota doesn't need to hear all that."

Kyle put the phone aside. "It's fine. He should know that not everyone has it as good as we do now."

Dakota rummaged through the packages, looking for his name.

"Kyle did tell me that," Violet said. She handed Mollie to Autumn. "This could be the year Santa comes through."

She told Kyle to open the large package at the back of the tree.

He ripped open the paper like a kid. His mouth dropped open. "You got me another train?"

"*Santa* brought it," Violet said. "This is an *everyday* train, not a *Christmas* train. You and Dakota can play with this one all year."

Kyle grinned as he ran his hands over the package. "It's so pretty."

"I mean, it's no minivan," Violet said.

"It's absolutely perfect," Kyle said, taking her into his arms and kissing her on the mouth in front of everyone. "Like you."

They all sat down to open gifts. When the room was covered with wrapping paper and smelled of coffee and the spicy sausage from Autumn's casserole, Kyle called Dakota over to him. "I have one more present."

"For me?" Dakota asked, dutifully standing by Kyle's knees.

"No, it's a present for me." Kyle choked up and stopped for a moment with his fist pressed against his mouth. "It's a big present and only you can give it to me."

"Don't cry, Kale. I'll do it. Whatever it is."

"I was wondering if you would call me Dad or Daddy from now on."

Dakota's blue eyes widened. His long eyelashes fluttered. "Not Kale anymore?"

"Right. Because now that your mom and I are getting married, I'd like to adopt you and be your forever dad."

"Oh, okay."

"If you want, that is." Kyle looked over at Violet as if for help.

"I want that." Dakota studied his hands. "But I can't say it right now because I'm embarrassed."

Kyle released a long breath. "Not a problem. Just whenever it comes to you."

Dakota smiled. "Can I ride my bike now?"

CHAPTER NINETEEN

KYLE

ON NEW YEAR'S Eve, Kyle and his family arrived fifteen minutes late to Zane and Honor's for dinner. They were the last to show and came in like a rock band, only with baby equipment rather than instruments. He no longer traveled light and given that another baby was coming, he wouldn't any time soon. All the Dogs were there with their spouses, plus Lance, Zane's sister Sophie, and surprisingly, Mary. He wondered if there was anything going on between them. He'd caught Lance staring at her earlier.

Honor had decorated her long farmhouse table for a formal sit-down dinner. The food, she informed everyone, was from The Oar. Several salads, a giant pasta dish, and roasted chicken smelled delicious.

Honor shrugged when Kyle teased her about ordering take-out. "I'm not much for cooking."

"Which makes it handy that your husband owns a restaurant," Zane said.

"Husband. I love the sound of that." She beamed up at him.

"I'm also grateful my husband doesn't mind my lack of domesticity."

"You have other talents, baby," Zane said.

Honor laughed and tossed her blond hair behind her shoulders. "That sounded dirty, but he meant my head for business."

"Sure, that's exactly what I meant." Zane winked at Violet and made her blush.

"Stop embarrassing Violet," Honor said to Zane. "Let's eat."

Honor ushered everyone to the table. Kyle put Mollie on the floor with her mat and blanket. Dakota and Jubie were at a small table of their own looking quite pleased with themselves. The last to sit, Kyle found himself between Mary and Violet. Lance was on the other side of Mary with Sophie next to him. Jackson, Maggie, Kara, and Brody sat across from them. Zane and Honor sat at the heads of the table.

Zane said a prayer before they started passing dishes around the table. When everyone's plate was full, and Jackson had finished pouring everyone a glass of wine, Kyle tapped his glass.

"I have something to share. As you know, Violet has agreed to marry me."

Violet waved her hand. Her ring caught the light.

"I do love that ring," Honor said. "Well done, Kyle."

Kyle caught Brody's eye from across the table. "Brody helped me."

Brody shrugged. "I knew a guy."

"Is it from the Edwardian era?" Mary asked.

"How did you know that?" Kyle asked.

"I read a lot of books from that era," she said.

"But that's not my announcement," Kyle said. "There's more. We talked about it and although it's technically too soon to share we wanted you guys to know anyway. Violet's pregnant. According to our calculations, she's due sometime in mid-August."

Everyone stared at him for a moment before a chorus of congratulations echoed around the table.

"Obviously, it was an accident." Violet's cheeks flamed pink.

"A happy one," he said.

"These things happen, even on the pill," Kara said.

"Honey, doctor-patient privacy," Brody said.

Next, to him, Violet radiated heat. *Embarrassed*. She was so damn cute.

"Anyway, given everything, we want to get married as soon as possible," Kyle said. "Violet wants a wedding and I intend to give her one."

"Of course," Honor said. "Whatever you want, we'll make it happen."

"Well, we'll need to shop immediately for a dress," Kara said. "We don't want a repeat of Honor's dress."

"We're going to," Honor said. "If we're going to get them hitched before a baby bump." She looked over at Violet.

Violet nodded. "I know it's fast, but I've been dreaming of it since I was a little girl."

"We're on it," Honor said.

Maggie and Jackson hadn't said a word. Kyle looked over at them. Maggie was staring at her plate with a slight smile on her face. Kyle caught Jackson's eye and he knew. They were pregnant too. Would he say anything? But it was Maggie who spilled their secret.

She looked up from her plate. "We might as well fess up too. I'm pregnant and due right around the same time as you."

"What in the heck was in the water at Thanksgiving?" Honor asked. Only Honor would have figured the math in her head to come up with that fact.

Maggie had started crying. Jackson put his arm around her. "She's worried about what it will do to her career."

"I finally got my break," Maggie said, wiping her eyes with a napkin. "I'm happy about the baby, but honestly, it couldn't come at a worse time."

"My mom always said there was never a good time," Lance said. "You just take it when it comes."

Mary looked small and pale. Maybe she suffered from social anxiety. Was she bullied as a kid?

"Anyway, it won't matter," Sophie said. "The album's ready. Dad said they're going to release the first single in late January. You're on your way, baby or not." It took Kyle a moment to remember that Sophie's adopted father was Maggie's music producer.

"You'll be fine up until the end when you can't see your shoes," Violet said. "You can still do your concerts."

Honor's eyes shone from the other end of the table. "And you'll have the babies almost at the same time. How sweet is that?"

Was it? Did Honor mean what she said or did her infertility eat away at her? Kyle glanced at Zane. From his expression, some-where between protective and worried, Kyle knew he was wondering the same thing.

Honor picked up her glass of wine. "Why is everyone staring at me? I'm fine. I keep telling you all that. We'll figure out a way to have a baby. Don't worry about me. I'm too busy taking care of the biggest baby ever anyway." She pointed at Brody who grinned sheepishly.

"I do need a lot of help lately," Brody said. "This retirement thing is a lot of work."

"He has more requests for television interviews, endorsements, and offers from networks than we know what to do with," Honor said.

"Nothing finalized, but I might have an announcer position by next fall," Brody said. "Honor's been doing her magic and spreading rumors that I already have offers, so now they're fighting over me."

"See? I don't have time for a baby," Honor said. "Not to mention you know who." She gestured toward Jubie. Too busy giggling with Dakota, she didn't notice the adults looking at her.

Kyle wasn't convinced. A hitch in her throat made him suspect the news of two of her best friends being pregnant was harder than she pretended.

"I have a solution for them, but they're too stubborn to agree to it," Sophie said.

"Sophie, don't," Zane said.

Sophie smiled her twenty-one-year-old smile, so innocent and hopeful. "You guys all tell one another everything. Maybe we should run it by your friends and see what they think."

"It's not a good time," Zane said. "This is not a subject for dinner conversation."

"Why?" Sophie asked, somewhat petulantly. "I want so desperately to help. Now is the perfect time in my life to do so."

Tense silence was as pregnant as Maggie and Violet.

It was Zane's turn to stare down at his plate. Honor opened her mouth to speak but seemed to decide against it and drank from her wineglass instead.

"I want to be their surrogate," Sophie said. "A donor egg from a stranger, of course, with Zane's sperm, implanted in me."

More awkward silence.

"Sophie, I asked you not to say anything," Zane said.

"Well, she did, so we may as well talk about it," Honor said with a wink at Sophie.

"You want to be their surrogate?" Brody asked.

"Yes, it's the perfect solution. I'll present my case," Sophie said. "I'm just the incubator, so it's not weird when you really think about it. The egg and sperm will have already been merged into an embryo by the time it's implanted into my uterus. Furthermore, they can trust me. I'm family. I'm not going to decide I want to keep it or something weird like that. And, it's my way to pay homage to Hugh, who sacrificed so much for me to have a good life."

Honor teared up at the mention of Hugh. "Zane and I initially reacted with a strong no."

"Not to sound like a prude, but it's weird, right?" Zane asked.

"Anyone want to weigh in?" Sophie asked.

"I think it's lovely," Mary said.

Mary thought it was lovely. He hadn't seen that coming.

"What greater gift can you give someone than a child?" Mary continued. "And I agree, it's the least risky solution if you're considering going the surrogate route."

"As a medical professional, I have to agree that Sophie is only the vessel in which the baby grows. It's not a matter of anything incestual," Jackson said. "As a friend, I can't imagine anything better for you guys. And Sophie, wow, I'm amazed at your generosity. It's incredibly sweet."

"I agree," Maggie said. "I'm all for it. Sophie, what a gift you would give them."

Sophie ducked her head before speaking, sounding less matter of fact and more emotional. "If you guys could read Hugh's journal—the one he kept for me—you'd be inspired to do something for someone else too. He was such a remarkably generous man. It's changed my whole life to read his words, to be a witness to someone doing the unimaginable and letting his child grow up without him to make sure she was safe. I don't know how to describe it, but it's made me want to be a better person."

"He would be bowled over by you," Honor said.

"Yes, he would," Maggie said.

"I agree about the medical assessment," Kara said. "As the practical one in the group, it's a practical solution."

"But you think it's weird?" Honor asked.

"A little. But not enough that I would advocate against doing it," Kara said. "We're in the twenty-first century. Science allows us to do things we couldn't even imagine a hundred years ago."

Brody looked over at Honor, his usually stoic expression—or what the Dogs called his resting douche face—was replaced by one of sympathy. "You should think about it, seriously. You both want to grow your family." He glanced at Zane. "You hate to ask for help and I understand that, but this is different."

"I'm not ready to decide," Zane said. "We've had a lot of changes already. To add this on top might be enough to break us."

"I get that," Violet said.

"What about you, Violet?" Sophie asked. "You've been quiet."

Violet tilted her head as she looked over at Honor. "I want my best friend to have whatever she wants. She deserves to be happy. But it has to feel right, both the timing and the mechanism. For both of you."

"Well, we don't have to figure it out tonight," Honor said. "For now, I'll revel in the fact that I can still have wine. So, you two pregnant ladies can stop pretending like you're drinking yours and pass it on down."

Good old Honor. Tough as nails no matter what the situation.

CHAPTER TWENTY

WITH MOLLIE ON her lap, Violet sat in a chair on the front patio watching Kyle teach Dakota how to ride his new bicycle. The sky had cleared, and the subdued winter sun shone down on the yard. They'd chosen a spot on the grass. If he fell a forgiving cushion would save him from harm. They'd been at it for fifteen minutes. Each time Kyle had let go, Dakota had fallen shortly thereafter. But her little man didn't care. He was right back up trying again. Now, Kyle held onto the back as Dakota's legs pumped. After he was going, Kyle let go. This time he stayed up, riding across the grass yelling.

"Dad, Dad, I'm doing it."

Dad.

Kyle's gift had arrived.

Did you hear that, he mouthed?

She nodded and placed her hand over her heart. She looked down at Mollie who was burbling and kicking her arms and legs. Dressed in a fuzzy bunny suit, only her precious face showed. Her blue eyes that were so like Kyle's investigated Violet's. "I love you, sweet Mollie."

Mollie smiled and touched Violet's cheek with her chubby fingers.

Dakota continued to ride back and forth across the lawn. He didn't know how to turn yet, so he would leap off the bike and face it the other direction when he wanted to ride to the other side. Kyle joined her on the patio. He sat back and closed his eyes with his face turned toward the sun.

"How did I get this lucky, Lettie?"

"It started with a dance."

"A super-hot dance with the world's sexiest woman." His eyes were still closed as a sleepy smile settled on his face.

"Then a picket sign."

"Then a baby," Kyle said.

"And an Edwardian ring."

"And a pregnancy test."

"And soon a house of our own with a white picket fence."

Violet touched her flat stomach. A baby grew inside her at this very moment. Kyle's baby. Their baby.

He opened his eyes and turned his head to look at her. "You and me. Forever and ever."

She kissed him on the mouth, lingering for a second or two.

"You've made me so happy, Lettie."

Holding hands, they turned to watch Dakota. He shouted with glee every time he crossed the lawn. Mollie cooed, focused on the sparkle of Violet's earring. Sunlight filtered through the tall pines and fat sycamores. Out on the ocean, the sun paired with the sea to paint the horizon blue. The slight breeze brought the scent of salt water and marine life and the winter soil.

Are you happy? This was always the question people asked when they hadn't seen you for a while. Violet had always thought it impossible to answer correctly. What did it even mean to be happy? Surely it was impossible to answer. Life was too complicated to describe in such a generic way. But here, right now, she knew. Happy was the sun and the sea and her son's jubilant shouts and the cooing of the baby and the little peanut that grew inside her and the bulk of the man that held her hand in his. This was happy.

"Kyle, this is it. This is everything I've ever wanted. You've made every dream come true."

"I didn't even know what my dreams were until you arrived. But this, this is it. Family."

She leaned her head against his shoulder and memorized every detail of this moment. One day it would be one of many memories she shared with her children about how their family came to be.

It started when an angel named Mollie Blue arrived in the lobby of your daddy's hotel.

The End.

CLIFFSIDE BAY CONTINUES

If you enjoyed Kyle and Violet's story, the Cliffside Bay saga continues with Tainted: Lance and Mary. Have the Dogs and Wags misjudged Mary? Will Lance ever break through her shell to win her heart? What happens after a night of margaritas and two lonely people destined for each other?

Click here to download your copy of Tainted from your favorite retailer.

ABOUT THE AUTHOR

HOMETOWNS
and HEARTSTRINGS

Tess Thompson Romance...hometowns and heartstrings.

USA Today Bestselling author Tess Thompson writes small-town romances and historical romance. She started her writing career in fourth grade when she wrote a story about an orphan who opened a pizza restaurant. Oddly enough, her first novel, "Riversong" is about an adult orphan who opens a restaurant. Clearly, she's been obsessed with food and words for a long time now.

With a degree from the University of Southern California in theatre, she's spent her adult life studying story, word craft, and character. Since 2011, she's published 25 novels and 6 novellas. Most days she spends at her desk chasing her daily word count or rewriting a terrible first draft.

She currently lives in a suburb of Seattle, Washington with her husband, the hero of her own love story, and their Brady Bunch clan of two sons, two daughters and five cats. Yes, that's four kids and five cats.

Tess loves to hear from you. Drop her a line at tess@tthompson-writes.com or visit her website at https://tesswrites.com/

:bf: :tw: :g: :p: :BB:

Lightning Source UK Ltd.
Milton Keynes UK
UKHW010648221122
412637UK00007B/292

9 780998 583594